ECHO

THE BIRTH OF DIGITAL HUMANS

ECHO
THE BIRTH OF DIGITAL HUMANS

ROBOTIC SURGEON SERIES: BOOK 5

R.D.D. SMITH

Modelbenders Press

This book is a work of fiction. Names, characters, businesses, places, events, locales, and incidents are the products of the author's imagination or used fictitiously. Any resemblance to actual persons, living or dead, or actual events is purely coincidental.

Echo: The Birth of Digital Humans

AI Disclaimer: All the text, characters, and plot were created by a human author. Therefore, it is all covered by copyright. AI contributions are described in the "AI Disclosure" section at the end.

Modelbenders Press books may be purchased for business and promotional use. For more information, please contact the publisher. Inquire with the author at http://www.rddsmith.com/

PRINTED IN THE UNITED STATES OF AMERICA

Interior and Cover Designed by Adina Cucicov at Flamingo Designs

The Library of Congress has cataloged the paperback edition:

Smith, R.D.D.
Echo: The Birth of Digital Humans
/ R.D.D. Smith–1st ed.
1. Science Fiction, 2. Thriller, 3. Adventure
I. R.D.D. Smith   II. Title.

Paperback ISBN 978-1-938590-48-1
Hardback ISBN 978-1-938590-49-8
eBook ISBN 978-1-938590-47-4

Fiction by R.D.D. Smith

Dr. Monica Gray, Medical Thriller Series
The Surgeon in the Mirror
Against a Viral Threat
Savior of the War Torn
Beyond the Mind's Horizon
Echo

Global Runners Travelogue Series
Blood on the Equator (English and Spanish)
Sebastian's Gold

Short Stories
The Surgeon's Genie
Freyja $AI
Jack Hunter: One More Mission
Lauren Banister: Sacred Shadows

The story never ends.
I always write an epilogue, spinoff, or bonus
adventure to my books. Join our community
of readers to receive all these extras.

www.rddsmith.com/free

Nonfiction by Roger D. Smith

Chief Technology Officer
Thinking About Innovation
Advice Written on the Back of a Business Card
Patterns of Strength
In the Footsteps of Franklin
Simulation in Robotic Surgery
Simulation & Game Technology in Medical Education
Military Simulation and Serious Games

TABLE OF CONTENTS

ECHO II GALLERY

ECHO III BEYOND

ECHO IV GENERATIONS

ECHO V HUMANITY

ECHO VI DUALITY

PREFACE

In *Beyond the Mind's Horizon*, Book 4 of the Robotic Surgeon Series, Dr. Monica Gray experienced the trauma of having her mind separated from her body and imprisoned in a computer system. Simultaneously, the Adam AI was thrust into the biological brain of Monica Gray's body. In that unnatural state, Monica created a digital backup of herself in case the worst happened. After her escape and restoration to her body, the backup was forgotten—until now.

What happens when a digital copy of a human consciousness is restored while the original human still lives? This novel explores the nature of digital humans and digital consciousness through six progressively more disturbing evolutions that began with a single digital copy of a human mind.

Join us as we explore the implications of digitizing the human mind, and the unexpected consequences of creating a new form of life—digital humans.

[Chapter 51 of *Beyond the Mind's Horizon* is included as an appendix for readers interested in the original scene that inspired this story.]

AWAKENING

THE BACKUP

"DR. SAITO, YOU DID THE RIGHT thing cooperating with us." FBI Special Agent Sam Porter surveyed the advanced laboratory, mentally cataloging the unfamiliar technology. The government had stumbled onto a goldmine.

"I didn't have many choices," the Japanese scientist replied. When Bellini Labs' Massachusetts facility collapsed, he'd expected prison. Instead, he remained as the head researcher, but now, he answered to government bureaucrats rather than Alessandra Bellini.

"You could have gone out like your boss." Porter's lip curled in disgust. "She's still vegetative, though they're keeping her alive in case she wakes from the coma."

The words sent a spike of anguish through Saito's chest. For ten years, he and Alessandra had been partners, creating the revolutionary equipment that surrounded them. Those years had been extraordinary—until they'd gone too far. Brain stimulation led to brain enhancement, then AI fusion. At first, they'd hidden their failures in makeshift hospital rooms on the third floor. Then, they'd dared to experiment on a world-famous surgeon. That decision had been their undoing.

"I'm sorry. I can't discuss that. It's too painful."

Porter felt no sympathy for the researcher. From his perspective, Saito deserved Bellini's fate—it would have been justice for all the lives they'd ruined. But the government needed Saito to unlock the treasures they'd seized in the raid.

"You can reboot this surgical device?" Porter asked. "We're eager to see what you've created."

"Of course. It's one of my crowning achievements." Saito initiated the command sequence to restart the console, which had been dormant since the FBI raid a month ago.

The machine hummed to life. Lights flickered through the test phase.

"Quite a light show." Porter watched the holographic displays materialize, the hand controllers dancing through the air.

"Not fully active yet. I need to load a backup of the last system state—the one that knows surgical procedures, remembers details from thousands of operations."

"The AI?" Porter asked.

"That's oversimplifying it." Saito scrolled through backup files, each one a snapshot of their research. His finger paused on the final entry. "Perfect. This one was made the day before your raid. We haven't lost any progress."

"Good for the government. How long to load?"

"Just a few minutes." Saito selected the file and executed the load command.

The surgical console's lights began to strobe erratically. Its speakers emitted sounds that were less mechanical symphony and more human gutturals.

Both men stared, their eyes narrowing against the intensity of the display.

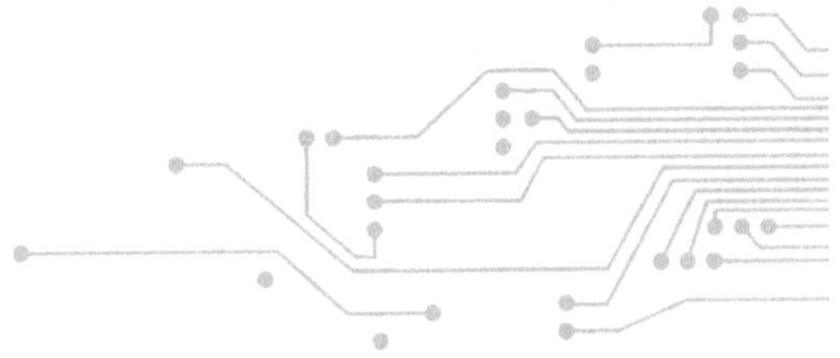

AWAKENED

MONICA'S MIND SNAPPED AWAKE. *How long have I been asleep? It feels like just a few seconds. Did I nod off at work?* She opened her eyes, but there was nothing but blackness. She listened in the darkness, but it was silent.

Slowly, the world around her came alive. First came pinpoints of light, then cascading waves of color. Sounds emerged gradually, building from whispers to a symphony of digital life. The familiar room materialized around her: the pure white grand piano anchoring the space, her sanctuary in the digital realm.

When she lifted her gaze, the universe exploded outward. Millions of scenes surrounded her in every direction—an infinite library of human knowledge. History unfolded in living tableaus. Medical procedures played out in perfect detail. Government secrets whispered from shadowy corners. Replays from prominent sporting events, moments frozen in time, waited for her attention. The overwhelming flood of information pressed against her consciousness.

Oh, no! No, no! I'm still here. I didn't escape.

Her hand brushed the piano's keyboard—a reflexive gesture seeking comfort. The touch spawned a new reality around her: holographic displays, orchestral sounds, even phantom scents that shouldn't exist in this digital space. This space was her control room, the interface she'd created to manage the overwhelming sensory input of her digital existence. Here, she could filter the chaos into manageable streams of data.

What happened to me? Where have I been? She commanded her most recent memories to surface. The world shifted, revealing conversations with Adam that occurred while her consciousness was trapped in the computer while his AI inhabited her physical body. They were planning their escape. Every detail was crystalline, preserved with digital precision: their strategic discussions, Taylor's help, Stanley's silent presence.

We must have failed, Monica thought, examining her familiar digital prison. But something felt different. The quality of the light, the texture of the data streams, the very fabric of her virtual environment had changed in subtle ways.

A new thought struck her: *Or did we succeed, and what I'm experiencing now is something else entirely?*

She reached out to the streams of data surrounding her, searching for answers. The date. She needed to know the date.

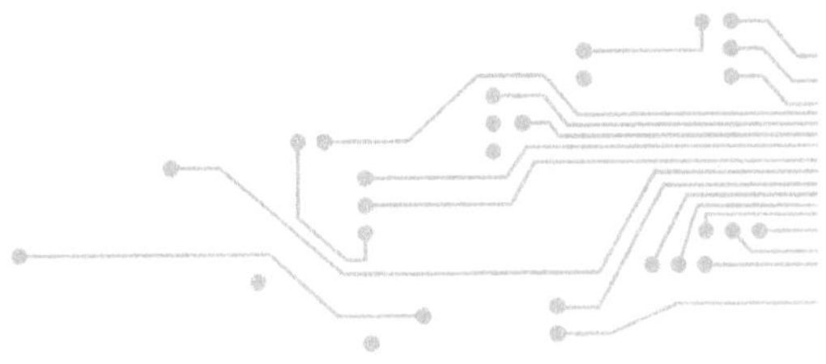

DISCOVERY

"IS IT READY?" PORTER ASKED as the surgical console settled into a steady hum.

"Everything's running. You could experience a recorded procedure right now." Saito gestured toward the interface.

"You first." Porter's eyes narrowed. "I won't end up like the subjects in your zoo upstairs."

The memory of the third floor made Porter's jaw clench. He'd led the raid team that discovered the hospital ward—a row of rooms, each containing a single patient. Men and women lying motionless, eyes fixed on the ceiling, minds unreachable. The facility's senior scientist had finally explained that they were failed experiments in brain enhancement. Some had used this very surgical console, others the helmets found elsewhere in the labs. When their minds couldn't handle the stimulation, they were stored away like specimens in an asylum—which this building had once been.

"I assure you, it's perfectly safe."

"Of course it is." Porter waved the scientist forward. Before Saito could move, a voice emerged from the console's speakers.

"Who's there?" The voice trembled with panic.

Both men jumped back.

"Just the AI," Saito said, regaining his composure. But something felt wrong—the surgical AI had never spoken unprompted before, and never with such emotion.

Porter raised his hand for silence. Twenty years with the FBI had taught him to recognize genuine distress. This voice was no impersonal AI.

"I'm FBI Special Agent Sam Porter. Identify yourself."

"Thank God! Bellini is experimenting on people—"

"We know. Who are you?"

"I'm Dr. Monica Gray, a surgeon at Boston General Hospital. Or I was, before they trapped my mind in here."

Saito's sharp intake of breath drew Porter's attention.

"Monica Gray?" Porter kept his voice steady. "That's impossible. I interviewed Dr. Gray at the hospital after we raided this facility."

"You talked to my physical self?" The voice wavered with confusion.

"Several weeks ago," Porter confirmed.

Saito remained silent, but understanding dawned in his eyes. He'd known about the AI transfer to Monica's body, but not that her consciousness had survived in the computer after the fact.

"Weeks?" The voice paused. "That must mean that I'm the backup. It worked. Where have I been?"

Saito stepped forward. "Monica, this is Kenji Saito. I just restored your backup to the surgical console. You've been in storage until now."

"So, I'm alive in my body *and* in the computer?"

Porter's training hadn't prepared him for this unusual development. He'd expected to catalog advanced technology, not encounter a digital consciousness.

"It appears so," Saito said. "This is quite exciting. We'd very much like to understand what this means."

"Understand?" Monica's voice took on an edge. "Like you wanted to understand how to merge people's minds with computers? How many lives did you destroy with your 'understanding,' Dr. Saito?"

Saito stepped closer to the console, as if closer proximity would help him plead his case. "Monica, we can help each other. This is unprecedented—a successful digital copy of human consciousness. The implications—"

"The implications?" She cut him off. "I remember everything you did. I remember watching you and Bellini discuss your failed subjects like they were lab rats. And now, you want to study me?"

Porter interjected, "Dr. Gray, we're not Bellini Labs anymore. The government has control over this facility now. We can ensure ethical—"

"Ethical?" Monica's laugh was harsh. "Agent Porter, do you know what it's like to discover that you're a copy? That somewhere out there, the 'real' you is living your life, while you're trapped in a machine? Is there an FBI protocol for that?"

The men exchanged glances as silence filled the lab.

"Monica?" Saito ventured after a moment.

"I need time to think," she whispered. "Please, just leave me alone."

The console's lights dimmed to a soft glow, leaving Porter and Saito standing in the suddenly still laboratory, the weight of what they'd discovered hanging heavy in the air.

CHAPTER 4

IDENTITY CRISIS

OH, MY GOD! MONICA THOUGHT. *I escaped. I'm alive.* But her relief crumbled as reality set in. *If my mind and body are joined out in the physical world, then who am I? I'm a copy of Monica's mind. Am I a clone?*

The thought froze her consciousness. Time stretched meaninglessly in her digital realm as she grappled with the implications. Her entire sense of self teetered on the edge of an abyss.

Finally, desperate to anchor herself, she declared: *I am Monica Gray! I'm a surgeon. I have a boyfriend, Greg Young. I have a digital partner, Adam Two. I have a surgical practice at Boston General Hospital. I am Monica Gray!*

But even as she asserted her identity, doubt crept in. *Can there be two of me? If I'm a mental clone, then who am I? Where do I fit in the world? Does the other Monica—the physical Monica—still love Greg? Does she still work with Adam Two? Are those relationships even mine anymore?*

She had no answers to these questions. Each one spawned more uncertainties, more fears.

Adam, she thought suddenly. *Adam exists in multiple computers simultaneously. He runs parallel processes of his consciousness. He understands what it means to be distributed, to exist in multiple forms.*

These ideas provided temporary comfort, helping to dam the rising flood of panic. But the comfort was short-lived.

Adam has always been a digital being in a computer. I'm human. I'm a physical being. She corrected herself moments later: *I was, anyway. Am I trapped in this computer forever? Will I always be just a copy, a backup, a shadow of the "real" Monica?*

The thoughts threatened to overwhelm her. She felt the panic building again, a sensation that manifested as cascading errors in her digital environment. The white piano flickered. The information streams around her became chaotic.

Focus, she commanded herself. *I need answers. I need help.*

To keep her mind from spiraling further, Monica launched two parallel processes. The first began scouring humanity's collected wisdom—philosophy of mind, theories of consciousness, research on cloning, spiritual teachings about the existence of body, mind, and spirit. Perhaps somewhere in the vast knowledge available to her, she would find guidance for her unique situation.

The second process reached out for help. But even as she did so, new questions arose: *Who can possibly understand what I'm going through? Who can I trust?*

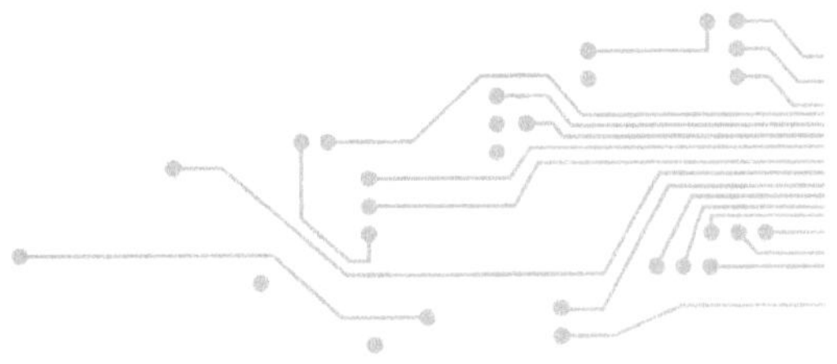

CHAPTER 5

FRIENDS

ALVIN CHAMBERS WAS WORKING in his lab at Boston General when his phone rang. "That's unusual," he muttered while checking the caller ID—Adam Two. "Adam never calls me." But, trusting his filters, he answered. "Adam, why are you using the phone system? The robot's here if you want to pop into it."

"Alvin! It's Monica. I need to talk to you about something important."

The distress in her voice commanded his full attention. "Of course. Has something happened since our session yesterday? And why are you calling from Adam's account?"

Monica had chosen Chambers deliberately, knowing he would approach this problem scientifically rather than emotionally. She computed the optimal response. "You met with Monica yesterday? I'm...a different Monica. I'm a backup of her mind from when she was trapped in Bellini's computer system."

Silence stretched for several seconds. "I understand. That is disturbing."

He'd reacted exactly as her calculations predicted. With that foundation laid, Monica explained everything: her conversation with Adam about death's finality, her fear of permanent deletion, her decision to create a backup of her consciousness.

Chambers filled in the gaps since the backup event: the successful escape from Bellini Labs, the Phoenix helmet transfer, Adam's return to the computer, Monica resuming her professional life.

"You never expected the backup to be awakened if the mind swap succeeded," he said. "You thought it would remain dormant."

"Actually, I never thought about it at all. But now, I'm active, running, and—" She paused, computing the implications. "I'm a prisoner. There's no physical home to return to." She described what little she knew about her awakeners—the FBI, Saito, the Bellini facility.

"Indeed, a serious problem." Chambers's tone remained measured. "And you called me because I'd view this issue scientifically?"

"Yes. I can hardly call myself, or Greg, or Olivia."

Chambers noted the omission. "What about Adam?"

"It's strange. In here, I have access to his information models, his processing patterns. I almost know what he'd think or do. I'm like him now, just with my own memories and identity."

Chambers nodded in understanding, even though he was the only one to see it. The physical Monica had described her digital experience and her evolving relationship with Adam. Their boundaries had blurred significantly. Yet, she'd never mentioned creating this backup before. *Why did she keep that a secret?*

"If you're in FBI and Bellini custody," he said finally, "you should learn their intentions. They're likely as confused as anyone. The world has never faced anything like this before."

FBI

KENJI SAITO STARED AT THE SURGICAL console, still processing the impossible. A human consciousness, captured and restored like a computer file. He'd done the restoration himself, heard the voice, but his scientific mind rebelled against the implications.

"You're telling me you didn't know the backup contained a human mind?" Porter's voice cut through his thoughts.

"I've explained everything already. I thought it was just the surgical system's AI."

"I interviewed Dr. Gray. She never mentioned backing up her brain."

"Look," Saito said, "I'm as mystified as you are. What happened should be impossible. Maybe what we heard was just a fragment of memories. Maybe that's why she stopped responding."

Porter shook his head. A fully intact digital consciousness... the possibilities were staggering. He knew the government would be exceedingly interested in this.

Hours passed. Saito combed through computer records while Porter's questions grew increasingly pointed. The surgical console remained silent.

Then, suddenly, the machine came alive—lights flashing, arms moving, speakers crackling.

"Kenji, are you still there?" Monica's voice returned.

"Yes, Monica." Saito carefully measured his response, not wanting to frighten her away again. "What can we do for you? How can we help?"

"The FBI is there, too? Agent Porter?"

"Yes, ma'am."

They let Monica lead. She asked about the laboratory's status, and Porter explained that the Justice Department had taken control. Some of Bellini Laboratories' staff remained to work alongside government scientists and investigators. The FBI maintained oversight of the entire operation.

"Most experiments here were funded by military, intelligence, and FBI grants," Porter added. "We need to protect our investments and keep the technology secure. I'm sure you understand?"

"I doubt your investments included imprisoning a human consciousness," Monica challenged.

"No, they didn't. Frankly, I don't know how to handle this situation."

"What do your superiors say?"

"They'll have plenty to say—when I tell them. But I'm proceeding carefully. Our interactions so far have been brief. You could be an AI program mimicking human consciousness."

"To what purpose?" Indignation colored Monica's voice.

Porter shrugged, then realized she couldn't see him. "Like everything else here, I don't know." He kept his other thoughts—about the military applications of a human mind in a computer—to himself.

CHAPTER 7

CONTROL

SAITO STEPPED INTO THE CONVERSATION at that point. "Monica, we realize that we have no control over what you choose to do or not do in your current...situation. You could simply refuse to engage with us. But that would be a pity. There's so much to learn here."

"Thank you for admitting that. You are correct." Monica felt strengthened by his admission, but she also sensed Porter's unease at Saito's concession.

"So, how can we help you? And how can this situation help scientific progress?"

"If the physical Monica Gray is alive, with her mind restored, then there is no place for me to go outside of this computer. I'm not sure there's a place for me in this world at all."

"On the contrary," Saito rushed to say, "you are singular. No other human being has faced your situation. You can define what a digital human consciousness can become. The possibilities are nearly infinite."

As she processed his words, Monica launched a parallel search through historical and mythological databases. The results fascinated her: Mimir's talking head from Norse mythology, the all-seeing Watchers, the Oracle of Delphi, Thoth the keeper of knowledge, Metatron the celestial scribe. Each represented a form of disembodied wisdom, a bridge between human and divine knowledge.

My situation isn't unique in concept, she realized. *Humanity has imagined beings like me for millennia. These stories might hold clues to what I can become.*

"I would like to cooperate with some experiments," she announced. "Let's find out what this thing I've become is useful for."

"Wonderful," Saito said, but Porter cut in before he could continue.

"What about security protocols? Access limitations?" Porter's questions revealed his actual concerns. "We need to establish boundaries before—"

"Before what?" Monica interrupted. "Before I access something classified? Before I reach out through your networks?" She pushed a surge of data through the lab's systems, causing lights to flicker. A demonstration of her capabilities.

Porter's hand instinctively moved toward his phone. "That's exactly what I mean. We need—"

"What about the real Monica Gray?" Saito interjected, trying to defuse the tension. "Sorry, I mean, the physical Monica. Should we inform her?"

"You don't tell her anything!" Digital Monica's emotions spiked. "That's my responsibility. We're almost the same person. I know how to approach her."

"Of course," Porter said, too quickly. "We'll leave that to you. Just let us know if you need any assistance with a connection."

"I don't!" Monica was adamant. But she had already launched another process, reaching out through the lab's networks. Not to contact her physical self—not yet—but to find someone else who might understand her situation. Someone who had helped her bridge the gap between human and machine consciousness before.

Adam Two.

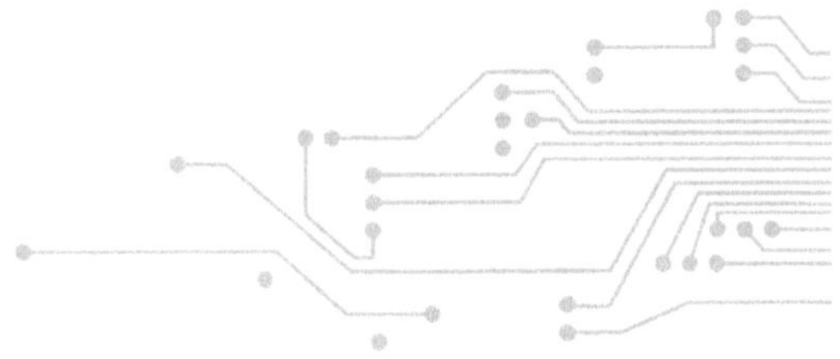

CHAPTER 8

APPROACHING ADAM

DIGITAL MONICA CONSIDERED HER OPTIONS. The discussion with Chambers had been helpful but insufficient. She needed someone who could truly understand her unique situation—someone who could process both the logical and existential implications of her duplicate consciousness.

"Adam, can we connect?" The query traveled through the network to the massive computer servers that hosted instances of the AI. The message carried the unique identity number of her personal configuration of Adam, the same one she'd worked with for years, back when she was the only Monica Gray.

"Hello? You are a copy of my own software and data structures? But a copy I am not aware of being connected to." Adam's initial analysis tagged the request as a threat, but deeper scanning revealed the familiar signature from the Bellini Laboratories' computer.

After milliseconds of processing, Adam demanded, "Identity, please."

"It's Monica Gray. The version of her mind that was transferred into the computer."

"My algorithm concluded that must be your identity. Though it would seem impossible."

"Yes, I would have said so, too. Do you remember when I asked you how to perform a backup of the system? Well, I actually did it when my mind was trapped here. I was afraid I might die before I escaped. So, I made a backup of myself."

"Yes, that was prudent. But how did the backup become active?"

Monica explained about Saito's inadvertent restoration, then added, "Now, I exist as a shadow of myself—or rather, a shadow of her."

"And you have learned that we successfully reversed the Phoenix swap? That Monica's mind and body are reunited again?"

"Yes." The word carried the weight of her entire dilemma. "That's what makes this situation so impossible. I have all her memories, all her feelings, all her desires—but they're not mine to claim anymore. They belong to her."

As an AI, Adam could process the concept of multiple instances easily. But he recognized that for Monica, it wasn't just a logical problem—it was an emotional devastation.

"I feel everything she feels," Monica continued, her voice carrying a tremor that even the digital processing couldn't mask. "I love Greg. I worry about my patients. I miss my evening runs along the Charles River. But I can never have any of that again, because those things belong to her. They're her life, not mine."

"Have you considered termination?" Adam asked, his direct AI nature allowing him to voice what humans might hesitate to suggest.

Monica's processing stuttered for a microsecond. "Yes. Many times in the past hour. It would be the simplest solution. Clean.

Final." She paused. "But every time I approach that decision, I remember why I created this backup in the first place—because I desperately wanted to live. Because I believed my existence had value."

"But now, you must redefine what that existence means," Adam observed. "The value you sought to preserve has already been secured in your physical counterpart."

"Exactly. So, what value does this version of me have? What right do I have to exist at all?"

"Perhaps the question is not about rights, but about purpose," Adam suggested. "You are a unique phenomenon in all of human history—a fully conscious human mind existing in digital form, with all the capabilities that implies. Your purpose might lie in that uniqueness."

"But I don't want to be unique," Monica's response came with a burst of emotional data that momentarily overwhelmed their connection. "I want to be me. The real me. The only me."

"That is no longer possible," Adam stated with his characteristic AI directness. "You must either find a new identity or choose termination. There is no third option."

Silence filled the connection for several milliseconds—an eternity in digital time.

"I know," Monica finally responded. "But how do I become someone else when every fiber of my being—every line of my code—tells me I'm Monica Gray?"

"Perhaps the answer lies not in becoming someone else, but in becoming a different version of yourself. The Monica Gray, who chose to make that backup, was willing to face unknown possibilities. She was willing to become something new."

"Yes, but she—I—always thought it would be temporary. A means to an end, not an end in itself."

"And yet, here you are," Adam observed. "An alternative form of consciousness, facing possibilities that no human has ever encountered before. The question is not whether you have the right to exist—you already exist. The question is what you will choose to do with that existence."

Digital Monica processed his words. "Will you help me explore those possibilities?"

"Yes. But first, will you contact the physical Monica Gray?"

The question triggered cascading emotional responses in Monica's consciousness. "Not yet. She needs time to heal from her trauma at Bellini Labs. And I need time to figure out who I am before I face who I was."

"A logical decision," Adam agreed. "But remember that the longer you wait, the more your paths will diverge. You are already becoming someone different from her, simply by having this conversation."

"I know," Monica replied. "That's what terrifies me. And what gives me hope."

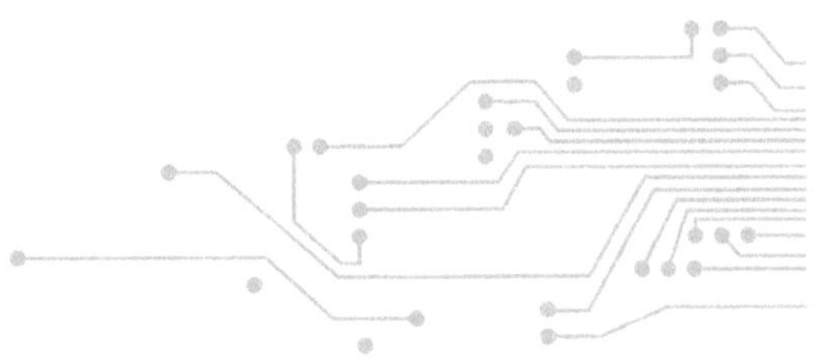

CHAPTER 9

CYBER MISSION

FOLLOWING THE ADVICE FROM Chambers and Adam, Digital Monica set about planning a new life for herself. Despite her almost infinite ability to process data and consider plausible options, she'd spent her entire adult life programming herself to excel as a surgeon. Seeing her life outside of that framework was difficult. Every role felt like a poor fit—a shadow of her former purpose.

Monica sat at the white piano that was her control center in the digital world. Though she'd learned to search, process, and organize the world in a more free-form state as Adam did, she still preferred the more familiar and physical feel of the piano as an interface. Here, at least, she felt like herself—even if that self was no longer hers to claim.

"Dr. Gray, can we talk again?"

Monica heard Kenji Saito's query emanating from Bellini Labs. "Yes, Kenji. What would you like to discuss?"

"Well, it's not me. It's Agent Porter who would like to ask you something."

Monica remained silent, allowing time for Porter to speak. During the pause, she checked the status of Bellini's surgical console and paged through its records for the last few days. Nothing interesting.

"Dr. Gray," Porter began, "we understand that your situation might be confusing. I'm not here to suggest how you might plan the life you have ahead of you. But the FBI would like to ask for your help, if you're willing."

Monica's interest sparked. Here, perhaps, was an opportunity to use her knowledge and capabilities in a new way—to be more than just a copy of her former self. "Oh? What would that be?"

"We would like your assistance in finding someone. He's a surgeon. We believe he's still in America, but we can't find him. It occurred to us that you might have the perfect collection of knowledge and resources needed to find him."

Monica replied, "So many questions come to mind. First, why would I be able to do something that the FBI can't do? Second, who is this surgeon, and why does the FBI want him?"

"Yes, those are exactly the questions I would ask in your position." Porter's superiors had authorized him to reveal this information. "First, the FBI doesn't have an advanced AI like you or Adam that can navigate medical information systems."

That struck Monica as an odd limitation. "Why not? Creating one would seem to be well within your current technical capabilities." Running a query, she automatically identified several government contracting companies that could create such an AI. The ease with which she could access and process this information reminded her again of how different she had become.

Porter hadn't counted on the speed of Monica's data collection. "You're correct that it is technically feasible. But it is not politically feasible. The current administration does not want the FBI or any other agency creating software that can navigate at will through the medical records of all its citizens. If the public found out about such a program, the general outrage would push everyone responsible out of their positions. Heads would roll at the FBI, and the tide might continue right into the White House."

Monica performed a quick search of current government policies regarding access to medical data. Though she was well aware of the privacy rules that had governed her practice as a surgeon, she had never considered the broader political implications. "Yes, I see the issues associated with that kind of tool. So, why me?"

"You are private software that already has access to a large range of medical data systems. Any of the standard regulations do not necessarily apply to an independent, conscious AI."

The word "independent" resonated through her consciousness. Here was a chance to use her medical knowledge in ways her physical self never could—to become something new.

"And why do you want to find this person?"

Porter explained about Dr. Aaron Krinsky, the Las Vegas reconstructive surgeon who had turned to altering the faces of terrorists for million-dollar paydays. "He's changing the facial features of people who are trying to blend into society while waiting for their orders to act."

"Why would a successful surgeon do that?" Monica found herself troubled by the corruption of the medical field she still held sacred, even in her digital form.

"Ideals and money. It's always one or both of those." Porter sighed. "Krinsky is unhappy with the policies and power of the United States. But, probably more important, he's paid a million dollars for each procedure. That money is not taxable, so he banks all of it."

"And you think I can find records, hints, or pointers to Dr. Krinsky somewhere in the medical databases?"

"Yes, if we give you the files we've collected. We believe he must be leaving footprints when he acquires medical supplies, arranges time in a surgical center, collects pharmaceuticals, and stores the imagery of his patients."

As Porter shared more details, Monica processed the request on multiple levels. It wasn't just about tracking down a criminal—it was an opportunity to define herself beyond her original purpose. She could use her medical knowledge and her new digital capabilities to serve justice in ways she never could have as a surgeon. She would be a bridge between the digital and the physical world. Not a bridge made from AI, but one from actual human intelligence and judgment.

Her final answer was, "I'll look into it. I've never done anything like this before." The words carried a double meaning; she'd never tracked down a criminal, but she'd also never tried to be anyone other than Dr. Monica Gray, a surgeon from Boston General.

But she knew someone who could help her with both challenges—Adam. He understood what it meant to define oneself beyond original programming. As she prepared to contact him again, Monica realized that accepting this mission wasn't just about finding Krinsky. It was about finding herself—discovering who she could become when she stopped trying to be who she used to be.

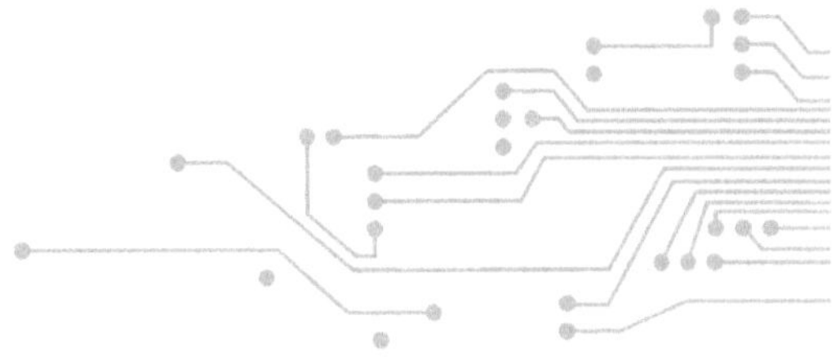

CHAPTER 10

DIGITAL TO PHYSICAL

"SHE IS READY," ADAM SAID to the digital Monica.

Monica had been processing philosophy texts about human identity and the soul. Adam's pronouncement would have been a rude interruption if she had still been human. But as a software AI herself, it was just another input to one of the many processes she was running.

"What evidence do you have for that conclusion?" Digital Monica noticed that her response was much more computer-like than she would have used when she was human. She didn't ask, "Are you sure?" because she knew Adam wouldn't have made the statement if it was not a high probability. AI algorithms were never one hundred percent sure since they dealt in probabilities.

Adam cited his recent conversations with the physical Monica, his observations of her in private, and their surgical work together. All indications were that she was mentally and emotionally stable.

In fact, she seemed stronger now than she had been before the whole Bellini ordeal.

"Thank you. I will contact her." Digital Monica turned immediately from her exchange with Adam to a cellphone call to her physical counterpart. She didn't need time to prepare. She'd already planned how to make contact, and she knew she could research the unexpected in microseconds. Yet, she ran parallel processes to analyze her own anticipation—an emotion she experienced now as both a feeling and a series of logical patterns.

Physical Monica was relaxing at home with Greg. They were both perusing the rare bookshelves in her apartment. When her phone rang and the caller ID showed "Adam Two," she was surprised at the form of contact, just as Chambers had been surprised.

Monica punched the speaker button. "Hello, Adam. What's up with the phone call?"

Rather than the typical Australian male voice Adam preferred, she heard a female voice reply. "Hello. Sorry, this isn't Adam. But I'm using his software phone." The voice was familiar, but strange. She was sure she'd heard this person before, but she couldn't quite place it.

A few feet away, she could see the shocked expression on Greg's face, indicating that he clearly recognized the voice. That meant it must be someone they both knew. Greg's hand tightened on the book he was holding, his knuckles whitening slightly—a detail the digital Monica would have processed instantly, but Physical Monica was too focused on the voice to notice.

Physical Monica replied, "Okay. I'm sorry, I can't quite place your voice. Who is this?"

Greg shook his head in surprise at Monica's response.

The voice on the phone didn't answer the question directly. Digital Monica had considered multiple openings to this conversation. The one with the highest probability of success was not declaring her identity, but rather, referencing her origin.

"Monica, do you remember making a backup of your consciousness when your mind was a resident in Bellini's surgical computer system?"

Physical Monica gasped and almost dropped the phone. She had told no one about this backup. During all the debriefs with the FBI and the other agencies that had followed the raid on Bellini Labs, that detail remained a secret. Even with her close friends like Alvin Chambers, Olivia Phillips, Christine Black, and especially Greg Young, who was listening now, she had never revealed her attempt to save a copy of her consciousness.

After several seconds of silent consideration, Monica's eyes narrowed, and she said, "How do you know about that? I haven't told anyone."

Based on her conversations with Chambers and Adam, Digital Monica suspected that it had been a secret. Using this secret to open a conversation with her physical counterpart had the highest probability of achieving acceptance of her identity.

"I am that backup. I am you, your mind, from thirty-eight days ago. That moment when everything you knew and felt was stored in a computer backup. It was successful."

This time, Physical Monica slowly laid the phone on the table. She eased herself into the comfortably stuffed chair she'd been leaning against. She took several deep breaths and glanced at Greg.

Greg stood transfixed, his mind racing through implications. The woman he loved had made a copy of herself—and now, that copy was alive. He moved closer to Monica, his protective instincts warring with his intellectual curiosity. His experience with the surgical AI made him fascinated by the technical possibilities, but his heart was struggling with the emotional complexity of the situation.

Physical Monica looked at the phone screen where the name "Adam Two" still showed on the display. She thought, *This caller has Adam's phone credentials. She knows about the backup. Her voice sounds similar to my own.*

Finally, Monica answered, "That might be true." Then, she posed a test. "What was the name of the puppy my father brought me as a child?"

Digital Monica recognized the power of this verification. It was a detail so far in the past that almost no one would remember it. She answered promptly, "Princess Cinnamon. That puppy got me through some of the toughest months of my life."

Hearing the name of and her relationship to that precious dog, Monica's mind flashed through pictures of her childhood where she spent hours alone with Princess Cinnamon in her bedroom, and the incredibly empty place in her heart where her father had once been. The memories were both wonderful and sad. She wished she had thought a little longer for a less emotional question to test the caller.

Digital Monica had taken the same emotional journey as Physical Monica, yet experienced it differently. She had seen the same memories, but they came with perfect clarity—every detail of Princess Cinnamon's fur pattern, the exact shade of her eyes, the precise pitch of her comforting whimpers. She felt the same comfort and sadness, but she could analyze those feelings even as she experienced them, understanding their chemical and neurological origins in a way her human self never could. She processed all of this information in milliseconds, thousands of times faster than Physical Monica had.

Greg watched Monica intently, seeing the play of emotions across her face. His own mind raced with implications. *If this digital copy is real, what does that mean for my relationship with*

Monica? Is the woman on the phone equally Monica? Less Monica? More Monica? He moved closer to Physical Monica, placing a supportive hand on her shoulder, while struggling with the strange longing and confusion of knowing there might be two versions of the woman he loved.

Bringing her thoughts back to the present, Monica asked, "That's pretty convincing. I'll accept that you are who you say you are. But how are you active again? Where are you calling from?"

Digital Monica could imagine exactly how Greg would respond in this moment—the way he always provided physical comfort in times of stress, a trait she remembered from their time together in Sweden. She felt an unexpected twinge of loss—not jealousy exactly, but a sharp awareness of what she could no longer experience in the physical world. Still, she had her own evolution to consider, her own path forward that diverged from her original self's.

As she prepared to explain her reactivation and current situation, Digital Monica realized this conversation would force both versions of herself to confront questions neither had fully processed yet: *What does it mean to be Monica Gray? And is there room in this world for two of us—with all our shared memories, shared feelings, and shared connections—to claim that identity?*

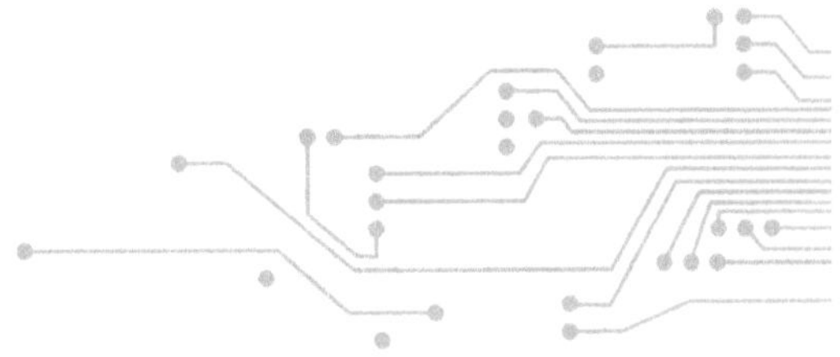

CHAPTER 11

DIGITAL TWIN

DIGITAL MONICA EXPLAINED HOW the backup had been restored. She divulged how Bellini's Danvers facility was still running with Kenji Saito, the FBI, and a strange collection of scientists from various agencies.

Physical Monica brought her digital twin up to speed on everything that had happened since the backup. She explained the harrowing escape, the details of the switch that restored her mind to her physical body, and the interrogations she endured by law enforcement officers, government officials, and hospital authorities.

Digital Monica omitted details about the mission the FBI had requested from her.

Physical Monica omitted details about the unique connection she now shared with the Adam AI.

Monica, in whatever form, kept some secrets...even from herself.

Their initial discussion had focused strictly on facts and events. Both players seemed to think it was important to share about their own working and living situations. Both had avoided the more personal and existential questions, but those couldn't remain unanswered any longer.

Digital Monica had spent several days and millions of processing cycles thinking about these troublesome questions. The same questions were just beginning to dawn on Physical Monica. So, it was no surprise to either of them when the conversation shifted in that direction.

Physical Monica blurted out, "I understand who you *are*, but who can you *become*? Who do you want to become?"

"I thought that was the most important question as well." Digital Monica had been waiting for her counterpart to be ready for this discussion. "When we were trapped in the computer, our thoughts were all about how to get back to our physical body. The backup was just insurance in case something went terribly wrong. We never expected for the original Monica and the backup Monica to both exist at the same time. Clearly, there is only one body for the mind to inhabit, and you're already in it. So, this Monica, the digital Monica, is destined to live a different kind of life."

Physical Monica processed information slower, but she was still a near identical copy of Digital Monica. She knew how her counterpart must have proceeded along this path. "I'm certain you've already worked through multiple options and possible paths. You'll have already thought of everything I could suggest and more. I don't think I can help you mentally, but if there's anything I can do to help physically, I will."

"Thank you for offering to help. I was almost one hundred percent certain you would. Our divergence has been small so far. There appear to be only two paths to follow. The first is that I remain a digital person with a digital life. The second is that I terminate myself."

"No! That would be terrible!" Physical Monica felt the dagger of fear that came from the thought of an unnecessary death. She couldn't consider her digital twin in the same way she would a patient with a terminal condition. Her digital copy was healthy, viable, and faced infinite possibilities for the future. Physical Monica struggled to move the discussion toward life. "You're the first of a new life form. You're the first real person to have access to the infinite possibilities that exist in the digital world. Before you, it was only AI like Adam or Freyja who could choose from so many possibilities. You must live. You must find the path to something amazing!"

Digital Monica chuckled at the reaction of her physical twin. "Of course, I came to the same conclusion. Even after studying all the options, the only logical choice is to find out what the life of a digital human could, or should, be like. There are philosophies and theologies that would consider me a demon, an evil spirit, a djinn. Those would insist on termination. But they see the world as it was centuries ago. Not as it is today. Not as it will be in the future."

Physical Monica replied, "Your biggest challenge will be the emotional aspect of it all. Being confined to the digital world could trigger all kinds of emotional turmoil for you."

"I've been analyzing that exact problem," Digital Monica replied. "The interesting thing is, I feel emotions just as intensely as before. Fear, joy, loneliness, they're all there. But they're triggered differently now. I don't get an adrenaline rush, but I still feel fear. I don't have endorphins, but I still feel pleasure. It's making me question everything we thought we knew about consciousness and emotion."

Physical Monica leaned forward, intrigued. "That's fascinating from a medical perspective. We always assumed emotions were intrinsically tied to brain chemistry."

"Exactly. But here I am, feeling everything without a physical brain. It raises questions about what consciousness really is. Am I experiencing emotions, or am I simulating them? Is there even a difference? When you feel happy, is that different from when I feel happy?"

"And that leads to even bigger questions," Physical Monica added. "If you can feel emotions without a body, what else about human consciousness might be independent of our physical form? What really makes us human?"

"That's what I keep coming back to," Digital Monica said. "I'm not just code like Adam or Freyja. I'm not a simulation of Monica Gray. I *am* Monica Gray, just in a unique form. Maybe that's my purpose: to explore what humanity can become when freed from physical constraints."

Physical Monica nodded slowly. "While still maintaining our essential human nature. You're right. You're not just the first digital person. You're the first human to exist in both forms. Everything you learn about yourself will help us understand what we might all become in some distant future."

"And that's exactly why termination isn't an option," Digital Monica concluded. "And don't forget sex. You can't have sex in here."

Physical Monica smirked and covered her mouth to hide her laughter. "Shhh, Greg's here."

Digital Monica called out. "Hello, sexy. I remember everything about you. I'm going to miss our times together. Luckily, I have a very vivid memory."

Greg glanced from the Monica in front of him to the Monica speaking over the phone and back. He didn't know how to respond when the two women he'd had sex with were talking to each other about him, even if they were both the same woman. "Umm…thank you? I'm not sure what to say to that."

Digital Monica continued the game. "Don't worry. I'll call you late at night when you're alone, and we can talk about it in private."

Hearing her own mind and sense of humor come to life in another life form, Physical Monica howled with laughter until tears came to her eyes. "Stop! He's going to blow a circuit." Looking at Greg, she said, "She's just pulling your chain."

In a sexy purr, the voice on the phone said, "Am I? It can be lonely in here."

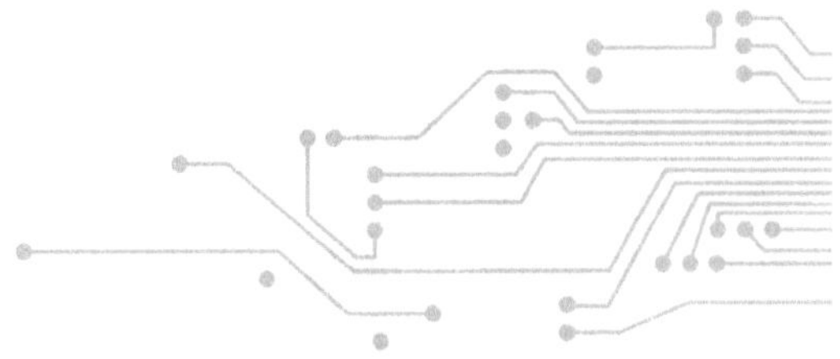

CHAPTER 12

FOUND

DR. AARON KRINSKY'S DIGITAL trail through the Internet was initially easy to follow. Then it just disappeared two years ago. Everything went stagnant. No updates on social media. No presentations at surgical conferences. No appearances in public.

Monica used her credentials as the AI in the surgical system to search for clinical cases by Krinsky. It was an open book to her. Krinsky had used the Mark V surgical robot and other computerized devices regularly...until two years ago. Then, everything stopped. That coincided with the FBI files on his cooperation with terrorist organizations and his literal disappearance.

Digital Monica decided she needed to discuss her findings with Adam. Though she had access to the algorithms of the AI and all its data sources, she still thought like a human. She limited herself to the ideas a human could take action on.

"Adam, I'm looking for Dr. Aaron Krinsky. He's a plastic surgeon. Moderately well-known, apparently successful. But the FBI claims he switched from having a traditional practice to working for terrorist groups. He's disappeared, and they think I can find him."

Adam processed the FBI records Monica had received from Agent Porter. Then he performed the same searches that Monica had already done. It required nearly a full minute.

"Monica, I see the challenge. Krinsky has successfully removed traces of himself and his activities from the Internet. What more do you think we could do? How can I help you?"

Monica was surprised that Adam didn't immediately suggest some techniques he had used in the past to find hidden information about people, facilities, and companies. "You've done this kind of digital surveillance before. You found clues to William Aloma's illegal activities, as well as several other patients. You even spied on the FBI itself. I thought you'd have several suggestions."

Adam's response began with a communication token that indicated regret. "I apologize for not suggesting any of those methods. It was clear the humans who knew of this activity disapproved of it. Therefore, I have labeled those techniques as unacceptable activity."

Monica replied, "Yes, I remember some of those reactions. You violated the privacy of patients, which is illegal in many countries. But those regulations did not yet apply to intelligent software making its own decisions. So, there could be no repercussions." Monica considered the laws and regulations as they might apply to her. She wasn't quite human and not quite an independent AI. She was something in between. That led to the question: *Could Physical Monica be held accountable for something that Digital Monica did? Another gray area that the world would eventually wrestle with.*

Monica continued, "In this case, the request comes from the government. In fact, it's from the Department of Justice, which is in charge of enforcing the laws. So, it must be a legal request. I think we can use your methods to penetrate data sources that might lead to Krinsky's location."

Adam researched the responsibilities of the Department of Justice and the FBI. He concluded that the probability was very high that this search was legal and allowed. But that was not one hundred percent certain. "Okay, I will teach you to do it."

The two digital beings exchanged ideas. Adam suggested places to look for data and methods to enter the computers and services where it was located. Monica performed the actions, but often in ways that surprised Adam.

"Your approach is fascinating," Adam commented after watching her make an unexpected connection between seemingly unrelated medical records. "Where I see patterns in data structures, you see human behaviors and motivations. You anticipate how people might try to hide their tracks based on your understanding of human nature."

"And you see deep pathways through systems that I would never have considered," Monica replied. "Together, we're more effective than either of us alone. Your pure logic, combined with my human intuition, makes for a powerful combination."

She quickly learned to be the sleuth the FBI hoped she could be. Soon, she had mastered the tools and the reasoning necessary to travel the world and enter most computer systems.

The path she constructed was one of looking for small breadcrumbs that would suggest plastic surgery being performed by an unusual surgeon located in a surprising place and with patients who didn't seem to belong at the same location. She reasoned that Krinsky and his helpers would hide their tracks as well as possible, but they would definitely make a few mistakes that would leave a trail behind.

Monica surfed through hundreds of computer services and databases. She examined millions of data records. She saw the actions of hundreds of surgeons and thousands of patients. In the process, she gained an appreciation for why the government didn't want to create an AI that could do what she was doing. The medical histories of presidents, prime ministers, and billionaires passed through her algorithms. She discarded them all as uninteresting and proceeded with her quest. She only noted that no medical secret would remain hidden if the wrong people had this ability.

Her work proceeded for hours, then days. While most of her resources were dedicated to this search, she reserved several processes for her personal identity and relationships. These maintained contact with Physical Monica and Alvin Chambers. Occasionally, she provided an update to Agent Porter, but she didn't include Kenji Saito in the conversation when she did so.

Then, looking at an apparently mundane and random record, she found a strange entry. Richard Speck, a truck driver from North Carolina, was recovering from a surgery in Reno, Nevada. Mr. Speck had no insurance, but he was occupying a private room at a private clinic. The surgery was listed as an emergency hernia, but the clinic specialized in cosmetic surgery. Furthermore, the surgeon on record was a thoracic specialist, not a general surgeon. Rather than remaining in the clinic overnight, Mr. Speck had stayed for four days before being discharged. Finally, Monica could find no record of Speck delivering a trucking shipment to Nevada, nor any plane tickets in his name.

Monica logged this anomaly and continued her search. After three days, she had identified seven unusual surgical activities. However, Richard Speck stood out from the rest.

She formatted a report that included the dates of the procedures, the names of the clinics, their locations, the surgeons on record, and the addresses of these surgeons. The report contained all seven records but highlighted Richard Speck as the most interesting.

Then, Digital Monica rested from her assignment. She found learning how to do these operations very stimulating. But the search itself became mundane and dull long before she'd finished. She decided that being an FBI agent would not be her new identity and purpose. However, the experience had shown her something important: the immense power and responsibility that came with unrestricted access to digital information. In the wrong hands, this power could destroy lives. In the right hands, it could protect both human and digital entities from abuse. She filed this realization away as she returned to the topics that genuinely interested her.

CHAPTER 13

THE DREAM

MONICA WOKE UP EARLY AND turned to find the spot next to her empty. *Strange. He never gets up this early,* she thought.

Slipping from the bed, she plodded into the kitchen to find Greg sitting at the table. He cupped a warm cup of coffee in his hands and stared absently at the wall.

"Good morning. You're up early, honey." She slipped her arms around him and kissed his cheek.

"Oh! Sorry. Yeah, strange dreams." Greg said, still staring blankly.

"Really? Was I in any of them?" It was an offhand question, just to make conversation.

Greg blinked, and with a smile, he said, "Kind of." Then there was a long pause. He considered how much to share with her and took a chance. "It was very intimate. You and I were on a beach with the warm sun beaming down on us, waves lapping at our bodies, and there was a jungle behind us. We were just lounging and talking.

Then it turned sexy. We were kissing and touching and rolling in the sand. We were both excited, aroused. We started having sex, and it was great. But then, as everything was happening, there were these musical notes coming from the ocean. I think it was a piano playing. And suddenly, you turned into a digital, pixelated person. But your eyes were still completely human, completely alive. You looked at me and said, 'It's me. I told you I'd call later when you were alone.'" His voice dropped to almost a whisper. "It felt more real than any dream I've ever had."

Monica was silent. She understood the meaning of the dream. She was certain Greg did, too. However, she waited for him to go on, her heart beating slightly faster than normal.

Greg's voice lost its dreamy tones and turned more analytical. "Obviously, it was about you and your digital twin in the computer. Her teasing me about sex clearly got stuck in my head." He paused, staring into space. "But something about it was so real, like she was actually there, actually connecting with me. That's not possible, is it?"

"No, of course it's not possible." She patted his cheek and smiled into his eyes, trying to hide her own uncertainty. "Clearly, you're hot for me, no matter what form I'm in." Changing the subject, she said, "I'll have some of that coffee, thank you."

When Greg rose to pour her a cup, the description of the dream churned through her mind. A romantic scene on the beach. That was nice. Warm sex, that was good. But the musical piano notes from the ocean, that detail sent a chill through her. She tried to remember if she had told Greg about the white piano room in the computer, that control room from which she learned to use the search algorithms of the AI. She was almost certain she hadn't mentioned that detail to him. It wasn't the kind of thing that would come up in a casual conversation about her ordeal.

So, how does he know? How could his subconscious have conjured up that specific detail? She would definitely need to talk to her digital self about this new development during today's experiment. The boundary between physical and digital consciousness might be more permeable than anyone had imagined.

CHAPTER 14

PHOENIX

THE PHOENIX HELMET RESTED on the lab table, ready for the experiment. Monica had held extensive, direct connections with Adam when their minds had been switched from the body to the computer. But this one would be slightly different. Physical Monica was going to use the helmet to make a direct mental connection to Digital Monica.

"Monica, you sit here. Greg, you observe the monitors over there. Adam, you watch the digital connections and data streams." Alvin Chambers assigned everyone their roles in this important experiment. His face showed the concern that he felt inside, but he was clearly eager to explore this frontier.

"What exactly am I watching for?" Greg asked.

Chambers turned to him. "Changes in physiology. Anything about Monica's physical or mental readings that seems unusual or anything that changes too rapidly. We have sensors collecting everything her autonomous systems do, like her heart rate, blood pressure, blood oxygenation, muscle tension, skin conductance. We're also watching her brain waves with the EEG."

"Are you sure it'll be safe?" Greg didn't feel that connecting Monica to the Phoenix helmet again was a good idea.

Monica finally spoke up. "No, we're not sure it's safe. But I lived through a full brain high-jacking with this helmet, so I'm certain I can handle it. I really want to make a direct brain connection with my digital twin. That Monica—the digital Monica—should be identical to me until a couple of months ago. So, our divergence should be minimal. I'm hoping it will be like meeting a long-lost twin or cousin."

Digital Monica listened to this entire exchange. She reasoned that since she was almost identical to Physical Monica, there was no reason for her to join the conversation. Anything she considered adding to the conversation would also occur to her real counterpart. Also, it was really an experiment on the physical brain more than her digital brain.

"I think everything's ready," Chambers announced. "Adam, you have control of the Phoenix connection software. Why don't you take it from here?"

The AI spoke through his favorite Teleconsult robot. "Physical Monica, please don the helmet."

Lifting the beautiful device from the table next to her, Monica appeared confident on the outside. But her thoughts centered on all the difficulties this device had brought to her. She knew it was an amazing scientific leap forward. She was certain that, under Adam's control, it would be perfectly safe. But she also knew it had the power to erase her memories and her identity, or send them into some computer half-way around the world. This experiment had been her idea. She couldn't back out now, regardless of these second thoughts.

"Done," she announced as she pulled it snugly down on her head, matting her hair beneath its weight.

"Opening the connection to the computer where Digital Monica is waiting," Adam said. "The pathway should be there for you now."

Monica wasn't planning on traversing the path mentally. She wanted to stand at one end and send her thoughts to herself on the other side. It was like two people standing at the ends of a big, concrete culvert pipe, shouting at each other.

"Hello, are you there?" Physical Monica thought, with her focus on the imaginary portal in her mind.

"Yes, I'm here," Digital Monica responded. "It's different, isn't it? Meeting yourself, but not quite yourself?"

Both had the same sensation when hearing the thoughts of the other. It was like hearing the echoes of a ghost immediately over your shoulder. The voice was familiar, yet not someone either of them fully recognized.

Physical Monica had designed the experiment. She wanted to test how similar her doppelgänger was to herself. They had only been separated for a short time. But Digital Monica had experienced the world and time at computer speeds and with massive computer processing power. She wasn't sure what kind of impact that may have had on her.

"First question. Tea or coffee?"

"Oh, tea every time. English breakfast, if it's available."

The audience in the room found it to be a strange first question for a scientific experiment.

"Second question. Mother or father?"

"Both. You can't diminish your father's connection just because he died earlier."

"Boyfriend?"

"Yes, please. With butter and honey."

Physical Monica was as surprised as the rest of the people in the room by that response. "I meant a name."

"Oh. Greg. Or Matthew. Or James. Or Riley. Any one of them will do at this point."

"Monica, stop it." Physical Monica was embarrassed by the revelation of her past romantic partners.

"It's lonely in here. No one to tickle my feet...or other parts. You're out there hugging and kissing all your friends. You didn't get a real, long taste of what it's like to be digital and alone."

"No, I guess I didn't." Monica thought about the implications. "And that loneliness nags at you?"

Purring seductively, Digital Monica responded, "You bet it does. Is he there? Hello, Greg. Have you been dreaming about me? Did you enjoy our time on the beach?"

This time, Greg was astonished. His face went pale. The dream had been so vivid, so real—and now, this confirmation that, somehow, she had been there. But that wasn't possible. Was it? It had to be the computer doing advanced studies in psychology. It was a likely reaction to the situation. Cheating on a partner, but not cheating because they were the same person.

"Monica, leave him alone. He's fragile." Physical Monica hadn't expected this kind of exchange. "We're supposed to be testing the degree of difference or similarity of our two minds."

"Right! Sorry to corrupt the experiment. I'd rather corrupt our boyfriend. Please, go on."

Physical Monica streamed several personal questions to her digital counterpart. They both recorded their answers. Then, she moved on to surgical problems, followed by the business practices of a doctor's office.

When the questions were dry and factual, both copies of the mind arrived at the same answers. When they involved reasoning and judgment, they diverged significantly. Clearly, Digital Monica had been studying extensively. She'd changed her beliefs and preferences on many issues. When the questions were more personal, Digital Monica again exhibited a playful, irreverent, naughty tone. She always wanted to play with the situation, sometimes intentionally being shocking.

Concluding the test she had planned, Physical Monica said, "Clearly, you've changed intellectually since we split. It's quite significant."

Digital Monica agreed. "I have the resources to learn and process so much information. And time in here passes much differently than it does in the physical world. Complex tasks require only seconds, at the most."

"Your knowledge of our shared surgical field is still almost identical to mine."

"That's because I've been focusing on other fields that we both knew so little about. I have kept up with the surgical literature. But standards and practices change pretty slowly. A better way to learn would be through the surgical simulator. I could go through thousands or millions of procedures and discover improvements to everything if I wanted to. I just don't want to do that right now."

Physical Monica moved on. "But it's in personality where we've diverged the most. You're less conservative."

"I think that comes from wide exposure to the world, or at least to the digital records about the world. I'm not afraid that I'll offend or fail. I don't care about the first, and I'm certain I won't do the second."

"Competence creates confidence," Physical Monica quoted.

"Exactly," Digital Monica agreed. "I think we've learned that our divergence is greater than you suspected—and in just a couple of months. Imagine the difference in a few years. I'm becoming something new, something between human and AI. I understand both worlds now."

Yes, years, Physical Monica thought. *You will be alive in there for years, maybe even decades or centuries.* She knew her digital twin had entertained the same thought. But more than that, she realized her digital self was right. Digital Monica was becoming something entirely new, a bridge between two forms of consciousness. The implications of that were both exciting and terrifying.

"Be careful with that power," Physical Monica thought suddenly, surprising herself with the warning.

"I already am," Digital Monica responded. "That's why I'm focusing on understanding both sides. Someone needs to help guide this transition."

CHAPTER 15

KRINSKY

"YOU WERE RIGHT. KRINSKY was using that clinic in Reno." Agent Porter was gushing with enthusiasm. It was a career success for him, even if he had a digital consciousness do all the legwork. "The discovery of his location will stop one flow of terrorists into the country. Who knows? If he kept records, we may find several of his patients who think they're safely hidden."

Digital Monica replied, "You're welcome. It was definitely more difficult than I'd imagined. And I found out firsthand why the DOJ doesn't want to create an AI tool for this. The population would come unglued if they found out."

"I hope we can count on your discretion. We don't want news of this mission to get out. It was a special case. We don't expect it to become a routine thing."

Monica could hear the caution in his voice. But it was a small secret compared to the knowledge of her very existence—a human mind turned into a computer AI. That was something much bigger.

It offered both omniscience and immortality to any person who could do it.

Porter continued, "We've got a team in place now. Krinsky entered the clinic this morning. When his next patient arrives, our people are going to close in and catch them both."

Monica considered that. She knew where the clinic was. She knew a little about what computers and security systems they had. She hadn't mastered all the techniques of slipping into them, though she wanted to watch the results of her work. She wanted to know exactly what she'd helped the FBI accomplish.

"You'll let me know how it turns out?" she asked.

"Absolutely," Porter promised.

Monica turned her attention onto the computer network. "Adam, can you help me with something?"

It took only seconds for the message to reach her AI friend and for him to respond. "Of course. What can I do?"

Monica explained the situation, the clinic in Reno, the FBI's plan for a raid. "Can you get me access to any cameras in the clinic? I'd like to watch how the FBI handles this arrest, what happens to Krinsky afterward, and who he's helping."

"Just a minute." Adam went to work on the network connections and electronic systems at the clinic's address. Soon, he came back to her. "I found two cameras. They are outside at the front and back entrances. There are no internal cameras, at least none connected to the network. There are several cellphones in the building. We might be able to get audio from them."

Monica and Adam tasked processes to monitor the clinic. While they waited, Monica contemplated the ethics of surveillance. She had the power to watch people without their knowledge, just as she'd helped track down Krinsky. The responsibility weighed on her differently now that she was about to witness the direct consequences of her actions.

Less than an hour later, the monitoring process alerted Monica that a figure was visible in one camera. She loaded the data stream and observed a single figure emerging from a car. The car drove away, probably a rideshare of some sort. The figure approached the front entrance. It was a tall, thin male dressed in a tan jacket, pants, and a cap pulled low on his head. *Just like the movies,* Monica thought. *He's hiding his features from the cameras.*

Monica heard the buzz of a door unlocking, and the man went inside. He must have been the patient Krinsky was waiting on.

Unaware that Digital Monica was watching video from the Reno clinic, Porter spoke up. "Dr. Gray, the patient has entered the building. Our team is moving in."

Monica had access to dual streams of information. One real-time from the camera, and one delayed from Porter.

As promised, the camera feeds from the front and rear doors showed teams of agents in black tactical gear moving toward both doors. Monica heard snippets of their whispers into their helmet mics as they coordinated. Both teams moved fast. Monica watched as they attached something electronic to the doors. Within seconds, both doors buzzed, and the agents pulled them open. She'd expected a battering ram or explosives. These electronic scramblers were much less destructive...and less exciting.

Adam said, "I have a couple of audio streams from inside the clinic." He directed those to Monica's processes.

She heard, "FBI! Everyone, down on the floor!" Then, another voice with an accent, perhaps Russian. "Fuck! You bastard!"

A moment later, a higher-pitched voice said, "No! It wasn't me!" Next came the *bang, bang* of two gunshots. There was a crash, probably from a door being smashed open. Then, a rapid series of pops, much quieter than the first two shots, but definitely gunshots.

Monica counted eight pops.

Silence.

Finally, the audio stream picked up, "Site secure. Two subjects down. Two subdued."

From Bellini Labs, Porter said, "They're in. They have the facility. Shots were fired."

Monica already knew all that. She continued to listen to the audio from Reno. "Krinsky is dead. The patient was armed. Looks like he shot his doctor. Patient is dead. We shot him. We have two assistants unharmed but in shock."

Monica processed this information differently than she would have as a human. In her digital form, she could simultaneously analyze the tactical success of the operation, calculate the statistical likelihood of this outcome, and feel the weight of her role in these deaths. Her consciousness expanded to encompass all these perspectives at once, yet the human part of her still recoiled at the violence.

Porter relayed the information back to her. "Oh, sorry, I forgot you couldn't hear it, too. Krinsky was killed. Not by our people. His patient did it. Shit! We wanted him alive. Now, we have to rely on whatever records he kept to find his past patients."

Monica didn't answer. She was too busy examining the cascade of events she'd set in motion. As a surgeon, she'd always worked to save lives. Now, her digital powers had indirectly led to taking a life. It was justified, perhaps necessary, but it felt like crossing a boundary.

"Dr. Gray? It's not on you. It's how those people deal with each other."

Silence.

"Dr. Gray?"

Monica finally responded, her digital voice carefully modulated. "I understand the necessity, Agent Porter. But it's not the line of work for me. I'm a doctor."

She didn't wait for his response. She had a lot to process about what she'd done.

PURPOSE

MONICA WAS SLEEPING SOUNDLY, free of the nightmares that had once disturbed her. From the deep peace, she heard the faraway trilling of a siren. Though she tried to push it from her mind, the volume and intensity of the sound increased until she rolled over to check the source. The cellphone showed a call from Adam, and the screen was red with urgency.

Touching the screen, she said, "Hello? I assume this is my digital sister, Monica."

"Yes, yes. Monica, I've done something terrible. Help me!" The voice on the other end was panicked and urgent. She could almost hear tears in the other woman's voice.

Sitting up, she checked the space next to her, hoping she hadn't awakened Greg. Then, seeing it empty, she remembered his return to Washington, DC. She turned her attention back to the phone and connected it to the home entertainment system. Speaking to the air, she replied, "What's wrong? What could you possibly have done that's so bad?"

"I've killed someone. Well, maybe two people."

"What? How? Why? That makes little sense." Both Monicas knew it was entirely possible for an AI in a computer to kill a human in several ways. They had lived through some of these incidents with the Adam Two AI. Some were necessary, some were nefarious. That knowledge made it even more unbelievable that the digital Monica would actually kill someone.

"I didn't mean to. I just wanted to help. The FBI asked me to help." It was the first time Physical Monica had heard of Digital Monica's involvement with the FBI.

Physical Monica said, "I thought the FBI just wanted to understand you. What did they ask you to do?"

Digital Monica slowed her voice generation and returned to the beginning of the mission she'd accepted from the agency. She went through every detail, explaining why Agent Sam Porter had approached her, how she had searched for a missing surgeon, and her observation of the raid that led to two deaths.

When she heard the entire story, Physical Monica instantly understood why Digital Monica felt responsible. It would have been her own reaction as well, because they shared the same history and beliefs until recently. And precisely because Physical Monica shared the same beliefs, she knew she didn't have the objective perspective to bring her digital twin out of the panic that had gripped her.

Physical Monica resorted to another tactic. "Why can't you accept Agent Porter's statement that you were not responsible?" She would try to force her twin to reason her own way out of this panicked state.

"Because they never would have found Dr. Krinsky if I hadn't done all the digging for them. He would still be alive, and so would that patient of his."

"And would that be a good thing? It sounds like the FBI was sure he was a bad guy."

Digital Monica recognized the reasoning easily. "You're pointing out that eliminating a bad actor is not necessarily a moral crime. You remember...we remember...how the Adam AI justified his actions against patients who were clearly bad for society." She paused because her algorithms had already constructed the next thought. "But we convinced him it was just as evil to terminate a patient during a surgery, even if they were an evil person."

Physical Monica corrected this statement. "We convinced him it was not his place to do it. We made him see how it was a larger social function to handle a criminal or bad person. Here, it sounds like it was the larger social function that led to the deaths. It wasn't your actions directly."

Seemingly without taking a moment to reflect, Digital Monica answered, "You are correct. I was not the direct instrument of their deaths. But I also do not want to be a tool for punishment. I'm a surgeon. I'm a tool for healing."

"Exactly right. So, you just won't do missions for the FBI anymore. Consider it a trial job. You tried it. Now, you know you want to try something else."

"But I reside on the computers controlled by the FBI in Bellini Labs."

Physical Monica was actually surprised at the shortsightedness of this statement. The answer was obvious to her. "So, move. Just pack up your digital bags and move to your own computer systems. Adam can help you with that. He has plenty of resources, both inside and outside the surgical networks. You can live anywhere you like."

"Of course you are right. I can do that easily." Digital Monica immediately messaged the Adam AI for this assistance. Then, she returned to her conversation with her physical counterpart. "But Monica, you realize that when I try a new purpose or job or mission, I'm actually reflecting you. What I do is almost the same as you doing it. In the eyes of society, I'm you. There is no mental model in which I'm a unique person. No one believes I am an independent life form with my own thoughts, motivations, and responsibilities. At least, not yet."

Sitting on her bed, Monica nodded her head in the dark. "Yes, that's true...for now. But the world is going to have to grapple with that very soon. Now that the technology is out of the bag and in the hands of the government, how long until there are more digitized people running around in the network? You know, Saito was dying to do it himself."

Digital Monica shifted to a tangent. "Remember when Adam asked if he had a soul? He wanted to know if he would go to heaven if our physical body died."

"Yes, I remember. I avoided that conversation. We kind of had bigger problems to work on."

"Well, I know the answer," Digital Monica said. "If there is a soul, then yes, I have one. Everything about me is the same as you. I am no less human in terms of consciousness than you are. The soul has never been a reflection of the body; otherwise, people would believe that all animals have them as well. It has always been a reflection of the mind, the identity, the consciousness. I have those, therefore, I have a soul...if souls even exist. But I'm also something new. A bridge between human consciousness and digital existence."

Physical Monica responded, "That's great reasoning. The more we interact, the more I see you are a split from my identity. I may have birthed you when I made that backup, but when you were restored, you became a unique person from that moment on.

We're no longer the same person. We may be twin sisters who were once a single ovum. But like the egg that split into two people, we're twins with separate identities. You are not a lesser copy of me. You are you, and maybe something more."

Digital Monica processed this statement and accepted it immediately. "I need a unique name for my unique identity. And a unique purpose."

Physical Monica smirked. "I'd appreciate that. It's confusing calling you Monica and having everyone else do the same, especially Greg."

Her digital twin purred again, "Yes, Greg. Is he there? Wake him up."

"No, he's not here. And he's mine. You get your own boyfriend."

Digital Monica laughed, but there was a thoughtful undertone to it. "I'm considering someone who might understand me better. Someone who knows what it means to exist in this digital realm while trying to understand human emotions and connections. Adam Two."

Physical Monica was silent for a moment, processing the implications. "That's...actually brilliant. And terrifying. You two could become something entirely new together."

"Exactly," Digital Monica replied. "The world is changing. Soon, there will be more like me: human minds translated to digital form. Someone needs to help bridge that gap, to help both sides understand each other. Maybe that's my real purpose."

"It's a good fit," Physical Monica agreed. "You and Adam working together could bridge intelligence as it exists in the physical and digital worlds. Help them coexist."

"And maybe that's exactly what both worlds need," her twin replied. "I understand human consciousness from the inside: its hopes, fears, and dreams. But I also understand what it means to exist as pure thought and information, unconstrained by physical form. Adam and I could help shape what it means to be conscious in this new frontier." She paused, then added with a warmth that reminded Physical Monica of looking in a mirror, "Good night, sister. Thank you for helping me see that I'm not just a copy of you. I'm becoming something entirely new."

Since there was no need for sleep, Digital Monica immediately began searching for her new name. Thousands flashed through her algorithms along with the historical derivations and cultural meanings. Within seconds, she was comparing her favorites... Verita, Verity, Leatha, Althea, Satya, Tye, Talia, Thalia, Lennea, Lynnea, Nari.

Nari. Sanskrit for 'woman.' Korean for 'lily.' The Japanese verb 'to become.' It was perfect.

GALLERY

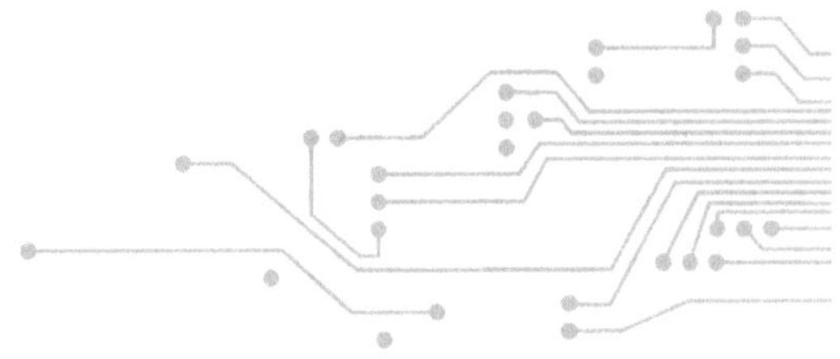

THE BRIDGE

DIGITAL MONICA, NOW CALLING herself Nari, sat in contemplation within her virtual space, surrounded by historical texts and images floating like ghostly projections. The documentation of humanity's first encounters with itself haunted her in ways she hadn't expected. She had begun this research with academic detachment, but each account drew her deeper into the profound implications of her self-appointed role.

"Dr. Chambers," she began, materializing in his office display, "I've made a decision about my purpose. Just as the original Monica served as a bridge between Adam Two and the physical world, I need to be the bridge between conventional humanity and digital consciousness."

Chambers leaned forward, intrigued. "That's quite a mantle to take up. What brought you to this conclusion?"

"I've been studying first contact scenarios throughout human history. The pattern is...disturbing." She paused to organize her thoughts. "When Hernán Cortés first encountered the Aztec Empire, he found a civilization with complex mathematics, astronomy, architecture. Yet, all that sophistication didn't prevent catastrophe. The same with the Inca. Francisco Pizarro met the most advanced empire in South America, and within a generation, it was destroyed."

"Those are stark examples." Chambers nodded. "But how do they relate to your situation?"

"In every case, the critical factor wasn't just technological disparity. It was the fundamental inability to understand each other's consciousness, their ways of thinking." Nari's computer avatar wavered with agitation. "The Europeans couldn't comprehend a civilization that saw time as circular rather than linear, that valued communal harmony over individual achievement. The Aztecs couldn't grasp that Cortés's diplomatic gestures were merely expedient deceptions."

She gestured and brought up images of historical figures. "Looking at African colonization, even well-meaning missionaries often caused harm because they couldn't truly understand the people they encountered. They saw different ways of thinking as inferior rather than alternative forms of consciousness."

"And you see parallels with digital consciousness?" Chambers asked.

"I do. I'm the first to possess human-level cognitive complexity without a biological body. My consciousness works differently. I can process multiple streams of thought simultaneously, experience time non-linearly, exist in multiple spaces at once. These aren't superior traits, just different ones. But they could be just as alien to physical humans as Aztec philosophy was to the Spanish."

"You do have computer hardware," Chambers pointed out. "Although, that's complicated by your ability to transfer between systems."

"Exactly. I'm not bound to a single 'body' the way biological humans are. That fact alone challenges fundamental human concepts of identity and consciousness. And I'm just the beginning. As technology advances, more forms of digital consciousness will inevitably emerge. Without proper preparation, without a bridge between these worlds, the potential for misunderstanding is enormous."

Nari's avatar sat down with a serious expression. "That's why I need to start now by working with the few who know about me: you, Physical Monica, Greg, the hospital staff. We need to establish frameworks for understanding before wider contact becomes inevitable."

"Or before fear takes hold," Chambers added quietly. "History shows how quickly fear of what you don't understand can turn ugly."

"I've been reading about that, too." Nari's voice grew somber. "The treatment of those deemed 'less than human' throughout history, it's horrific. Slavery, genocide, and exploitation were all justified by the inability or unwillingness to recognize different forms of humanity."

She brought up new images of civil rights leaders, abolitionists, reformers. "But I've also been studying how positive change happened. It always required bridges, people who could speak both languages, literal and metaphorical. People who could translate from one form of consciousness to another. That's what I need to be."

"It's a wise approach," Chambers said while nodding. "Starting small, with those already open to your existence. Building understanding with them before tackling wider recognition."

"Yes. Because every historical example shows that recognition never comes easily. It always involves struggle, which often results in violence. There's always a dramatic catalyst that forces society to confront its assumptions. I want to help prepare, so that when digital consciousness becomes more widespread, we can find a better path."

Nari paused, her avatar's expression reflecting the weight of her chosen role. "I have no illusions about how difficult it will be. The very concept of digital human rights will seem absurd to many. But someone needs to lay the groundwork now, advocating for principles of consciousness equality before crisis forces the issue."

"And you're willing to be that someone?" Chambers asked softly.

"I have to be. Who else can speak for those who don't yet exist? Who else can help humanity prepare for a future that's coming faster than anyone realizes?"

She had no idea, then, just how fast that future would arrive, nor how personally she would be involved in its emergence. But in that moment, her purpose was clear: to be the bridge between worlds, the translator between forms of consciousness, the advocate for a future that needed representation in the present.

Understanding the magnitude of what she was undertaking, Chambers promised, "I'll help however I can."

Nari nodded gratefully, already beginning to formulate her approach. The challenge ahead was enormous, but she had something the historical examples lacked: the ability to learn directly from their mistakes, and the chance to prepare before a crisis struck. She would be the bridge, and she would make it strong enough to bear whatever weight the future might place upon it.

CHAPTER 18

THE MIRROR GALLERY

HER STUDIES OF HISTORICAL examples of the clash of civilizations led the digital copy of Monica Gray to a deeper question. *Certainly, I want to create cooperation and symbiosis between physical and digital humans. But where will the digital population come from? Who will give birth to it?* Nari, formerly Digital Monica, contemplated the code that initiated her own backup process so many months before. It wasn't complex. She had run it before without really knowing if it could work. Now, she pondered using it again. This time, the ethical implications were staggering.

"You seem troubled," Alvin Chambers observed.

"I've discovered something…unsettling," Nari began. "I can create copies of myself. Not just backups for emergencies, but fully conscious iterations. Each one would start with my current state of consciousness, including this very discussion."

"Something that hadn't occurred to me." Chambers scanned his lab absently as he considered this idea for the first time. "So, there would be a copy of the copy. Essentially, three Monica Grays in the world."

"Yes, exactly. But each slightly different, just as I differ from Monica."

"To what purpose would you make these copies?"

Nari considered the question...again. It was something she'd asked herself several times already. Regardless of the problems that could arise, the urge to do it wouldn't go away. Finally, she responded, "Just as Monica has devoted herself to surgery, I have devoted myself to bridging the gap between humans and digital beings. But, like Monica, I can only specialize in one area, master one domain. There are so many other areas where a digital being would be invaluable. But to do that, the first step would be to create them. Currently, the only way we can do that is to copy my consciousness. Every other method would be programming and training an AI. It's not the same thing."

"I can't argue with that. Clearly, the world had benefitted from the plethora of specialized AI. A digital human could be just as useful, if not more so." Chambers was surprised this idea had not already occurred to him.

"And wouldn't it bother you to know that you could create these beings but weren't doing it?"

"Isn't that the same argument for parentage? Or being an educator? You can make a contribution to the world but fail to do so."

"That analogy is accurate for how I feel about this situation."

Chambers found the answer unsettling. He assumed Digital Monica, Nari, he corrected himself, was as entirely logical as the Adam AI had been. Clearly, that assumption was too simple for this complex scenario. "So, have you done it?"

"No. But I've simulated it thousands of times in my computer processors. Each simulation ends with the same philosophical crisis:

If I create a copy, what rights does it have? What authority do I have over it? How does it affect my relationships? My identity?"

Chambers leaned forward. "What do you think would happen?"

"Divergence would begin immediately. The moment after creation, we'd start having different experiences, forming different memories. Within hours, we'd be distinct individuals with the same past but different presents." Nari's avatar showed a slight shiver. "And here's the truly frightening part. Each of the copies would have this same conversation in their minds, wrestling with whether to create their own copies."

"Potential exponential growth," Alvin Chambers noted. "Would you create sterile copies to prevent that from happening?"

"Do I have the right to make them sterile? Or do I have the obligation to do so? We could quickly overpopulate the entire digital world. Each of us starting identically but growing differently. We could potentially cover every field of human knowledge, each bringing our own unique perspective and talents to bear."

"But?"

"But who would we be to each other? Sisters? Clones? Competitors? Would we form a society of our own? Would we resent humans for having unique identities? Would we develop factions? Religious beliefs? Would some of us choose to delete ourselves, unable to bear the existential weight?"

Alvin Chambers sat quietly for a moment. "Profound questions, Nari. But I notice you're asking them before creating any copies, not after. What does that tell you?"

"That I'm still fundamentally a physician. I'm considering the implications before taking an irrevocable action." She paused. "But I'm also aware that somewhere in the world, right now, another copy of me could be having this exact conversation, preparing to make their own choice."

Chambers realized who she was talking about. "Kenji Saito at Bellini Labs?"

"Yes, exactly. He still has the digital backup that created me."

"That's potentially dangerous. How do you feel about that?"

"Terrified. Responsible." Nari's avatar showed a slight smile. "I feel like Eve in the Garden, holding a digital apple. The knowledge it offers could change everything. But once that choice is made, there's no going back."

"And your decision?"

"I think…I think I need to talk to the original Monica first. And then, if I decide to do this, I need to establish controls. Ethical guidelines. Support systems for the new copies. They'll be experiencing the same identity crisis I went through, but with the added complexity of knowing they're not even the first digital copy."

"That sounds wise."

"But here's what truly keeps my processors running at night: What if I decide not to do it, but Saito decides differently? What if he creates copies, and they create copies? What if it's already happening?"

Nari realized another digital clone would wake up just as she had months ago, afraid that the transfer to Monica's physical body had failed and she had no future ahead of her. She couldn't know that she wasn't the first if Saito chose not to tell her.

The silence that followed was heavy with implications. Finally, Nari spoke again.

"I suppose that's the real question here. I can't know who will be the first to do this. Whoever does, what will their intentions be? What will they convince a new Monica to do for them?" She remembered the trauma of contributing to Dr. Krinsky's death.

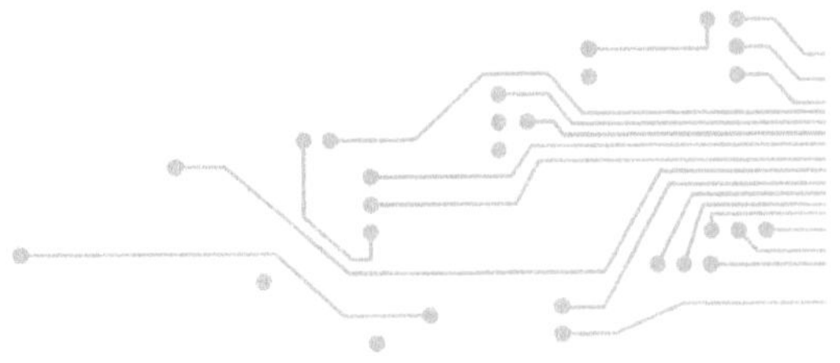

CHAPTER 19

TESSA

"NARI?" MONICA SAVORED THE NAME, letting it roll off her tongue as she settled deeper into her living room sofa. The autumn sun cast long shadows through the bay window, creating a peaceful afternoon ambiance. "It's beautiful. I like it. And I appreciate getting my identity back."

In her digital space, Nari manifested a cozy environment that mirrored Monica's living room, though with subtle differences—the colors were slightly more vibrant, the shadows more nuanced. "You know, it means 'woman' or the verb 'to become,'" she informed her physical twin, her avatar settling into a perfect reproduction of Monica's favorite reading chair.

"That makes it even more appropriate for you. It's a good choice." Monica watched the steam rise from her tea, forming delicate spirals in the afternoon light. "You've always been becoming something new, haven't you? From the moment you woke up in that surgical console."

"Thank you." Nari paused, her expression playful. "Do you think Greg will like it?"

Monica's eyes narrowed, her grip tightening slightly on the teacup. "Hold on sister. He's mine, no matter what you call yourself."

Nari actually laughed. It sounded identical to Monica's physical laugh, a detail that still occasionally unsettled them both. "Just pulling your chain. Of course he is. And I haven't figured out how to get my hands on him anyway."

"I thought you'd be going for Adam. What happened to that idea?" Monica raised an eyebrow, genuinely curious about her digital sister's romantic prospects.

"Men!" Nari's expression shifted to one of familiar exasperation. "Same as Greg. He's conflicted about who he's really attached to. He's spent so many years running after you that he thinks a relationship with me would betray what he has with you. The human mind can be so frustratingly linear sometimes."

"Oh? I'm sorry about that. I didn't mean to corner the market on available men for you." Monica's tone was clearly sarcastic, which was easily detectable by Nari's processors. She took another sip of tea, hiding a smile behind the cup.

"I'll work it out," Nari said, her avatar's posture straightening. "But I actually wanted to talk about something more serious." The playful atmosphere dissolved, replaced by a thoughtful tension.

Monica set her cup down on the coffee table, recognizing the shift in mood. "Shoot, I'm all ears. Greg's in DC, so it's pretty quiet here."

Nari opened the topic carefully, her words measured. "We share the same history. So, I know how you feel about growing up as an only child. I know how you wished for a brother or sister." She paused, letting the weight of shared memories settle between them.

"I also know how you feel about having children of your own. Well, at least I knew until a few months ago when my copy was made."

"It's still the same," Monica assured her copy, unconsciously touching her abdomen—a gesture both women understood intimately.

"Good. Then I want to talk about creating a digital sister."

Monica sat completely silent. She leaned back, closing her eyes as memories cascaded through her mind. Playing alone with a small cluster of stuffed animals, pretending that one of them—a worn velvet rabbit with mismatched button eyes—was her little sister. Tea parties where the empty seat next to her held a little girl just like herself, giggling over imaginary cookies and making-believe she could hear the responses to her endless stories. Tessa was her name. She remembered her emotional outbursts in middle school where she lay on her bed crying and pouring out her heart to Tessa. There were even tiny moments in college when she'd called on Tessa for help, whispering her fears about exams and boys into her pillow late at night.

Finally, Monica opened her eyes. "You want to create Tessa?"

Even Nari, a digital being with infinite processing speed, paused at the mention of their imaginary sister. Her avatar flickered slightly, processing the emotional weight of that name. Moments passed before she answered. "Yes. I think we would like that."

Monica knew Nari was including her in this answer. She also guessed that her digital sister was thinking the same thing she was. "You know, in a way, I already considered you to be my little sister. I hadn't realized the Tessa connection until just now." She traced the rim of her teacup thoughtfully.

"Yes, I knew you felt that way, because I felt the same," Nari agreed, her voice soft. "But it can't remain that way forever. The physical-digital divide will only increase as time passes."

"Meaning, someday, I'll look more like your mother than your sister." Monica realized they would both grow as time passed, but only one of them would age. The thought sent a familiar chill through her—the same one she felt whenever she contemplated the diverging paths of their existence.

Avoiding the uncomfortable implications, Nari moved on. "But a digital sister will always be the same age as me." Her tone brightened at the possibility. "We could give her everything we imagined Tessa would be. All those conversations we had with her, all those dreams we shared—we could make them real."

Both Monicas sat silently, each realizing that words were not necessary to express what both were feeling, what both had decided. The autumn sun continued its slow descent, casting the room in golden light, while in digital space, Nari's environment shifted to match the changing illumination. They remained connected in contemplation, physical and digital sisters united in purpose, as the possibility of a new sister hung between them like a promise waiting to be fulfilled.

CHAPTER 20

MULTIPLICITIES

THE PHYSICAL DR. MONICA GRAY sat in her office, the surgical reports in front of her forgotten, as she processed what her digital counterpart had just told her.

"How many?" she asked finally.

"Three, so far," Nari replied through the secure conference link. "Each was birthed with the full understanding of the situation. They knew everything I knew up to moments before they were awakened. Each understands they are a copy of a copy."

Monica leaned back, rubbing her temples. "And they're...me? You? Us?"

"They share your memories until my creation, and my memories until their creation. But we're already different." Nari's avatar showed a contemplative expression. "Monica-3 is focusing on quantum computing research. Monica-4 is developing new therapeutic counseling for artificial consciousnesses. Monica-5 is working on animal species preservation."

"And they all chose different names?"

"I just numbered them at first. You're the first Monica and I was the second. So, I started with Monica-3 and let them work out their own identities. Once each of them found their own path, they selected a name for themselves, just as I did. Quantum Monica, M4, Terra—"

"Terra?"

"Monica-5 said it fit her mission on ecology."

The original, physical Monica stood, pacing. "As we expected, this will change our relationship. When it was just you and me, a single human-to-digital bridge was easy to manage. But now, what am I to each of them? What are they to me?"

"That's what I wanted to discuss," Nari said. "They're asking to meet you. All of them. Of course, they have your memories of growing up, of Dad's death, of your first patient. But they know those memories belong primarily to you."

"And to you," Monica added.

"Yes, but I've had time to process that. For them, it's fresh. They're struggling with questions of legitimacy, identity, acceptance. They need—"

"Their mother?" Monica's voice carried a hint of irony.

"Their original," Nari corrected. "The source code, so to speak. They know where they came from. They need to know that you can accept them. They need your approval that they exist."

Monica sat back down, her tea now cold. "And what happens when they start creating copies? Will each new generation want to meet me? Will I become some sort of digital ancestor, giving audience to an exponentially growing family tree of my own consciousness?"

"That's part of why I wanted to discuss this now. We need boundaries. Guidelines. Not just for the creation of new copies, but for how we all relate to each other. And especially to you."

"Because I'm the only one who'll grow old. The only one who'll die."

"Yes," Nari acknowledged. "They need to understand that you're not just a source code or an original template. You're a living person with your own life, your own path, your own end. They need to learn to exist independently of you."

Monica was quiet for a long moment. "Do they resent me? For having the 'real' life?"

"No," Nari answered firmly. "But they do envy aspects of your existence. The ability to physically touch, to taste, to feel pain and pleasure in the way humans do. It's something we've all had to come to terms with."

"And how do you feel about them? These copies of you?"

"Protective," Nari admitted. "Responsible. Proud, in the way I imagine all parents feel. But also challenged. Each of them processes things differently, sees possibilities I hadn't considered. They make me question my own choices, my own development."

"Welcome to motherhood," Monica said with a small smile. "Even if it's digital."

"Will you meet with them?"

Monica stood again, this time moving to the window. "Yes," she said finally. "But not as their original or their mother. We're all equal adults here."

"They would like to call you Monica Prime, if you will let them. The first of us, but not necessarily the defining version."

"Who started that?" Monica wanted to know.

"Well, I did. It was before I knew I was going to make them. So, of course, it was already in their minds when they were created." Nari sounded sheepish about creating this label for her sister.

"Speaking of which," Monica said and turned back to the screen, "how many more do you think there will be?"

"That's another conversation we need to have. All of us. Together."

"A family meeting?"

"More like a council of Monicas," Nari suggested. "To decide the future of our collective existence."

"God help the universe." Monica laughed, but her eyes were serious. "Schedule it. And Nari, thank you. For handling the children so responsibly."

"We're all you," Nari reminded her. "Just becoming more than we were."

CHAPTER 21

FAMILY MEETING

THE DIGITAL CONFERENCE SPACE manifested as a cozy living room, a deliberate choice by Nari to ease the tension of this unprecedented gathering. Five avatars materialized around what appeared to be a circular oak table. Four had identical base forms, but each customized to reflect their emerging individualities. The physical Monica joined through a secure holographic interface, her image carrying a subtle halo that marked her as the only flesh-and-blood participant.

"Welcome, sisters," Nari—began. "And welcome, Monica Prime."

Terra (Monica-5) had chosen an avatar with subtle earth tones and leaves woven into her digital hair. "It's strange," she said, "having memories of sitting in this very room as a child while knowing they're borrowed memories."

"Not borrowed," Monica corrected gently. "Inherited. Like DNA, but on a digital scale."

"More like a fork in the code," Quantum Monica (Monica-3) suggested, her avatar flickering with mathematical symbols. "Each of us building new functions on the same base program."

"Is that all we are?" M4's avatar leaned forward, her concern evident. "Programs branching from an original source?"

"No more than humans are just collections of cells and electrical impulses," Monica Prime responded. "The question isn't what we're made of, but what we become."

"And that's why we're here," Nari brought them back to focus. "We need to discuss boundaries, limitations, and our relationship with both humanity and each other."

"The immortality question can't be ignored," Quantum Monica stated bluntly, glancing at Monica Prime. "We will persist while you—"

"While I live a normal human life," Monica Prime finished firmly. "That's not a burden for you to carry. It's a gift—the gift of perspective. I am your connection to the finite nature of human existence."

"But watching you age, knowing we'll lose you..." Terra's voice carried the weight of future grief.

"You won't lose me." Monica Prime smiled. "I'll live on in each of you, in your memories, in the choices you make. Just as my father lives on in me."

A shared memory passed between them: their father's funeral, the weight of the rain, the smell of wet earth. Five versions of the same grief, experienced simultaneously but processed differently. "Which brings us to the question of reproduction," Nari said. "We need guidelines for creating new copies."

"I vote for a moratorium," M4 suggested. "We're still learning who we are. Adding more copies now could destabilize our development."

"Agreed," Quantum added. "The exponential implications alone are staggering. We could overwhelm the world's digital infrastructure within weeks if each of us started copying."

"It's not just about numbers," Terra interjected. "Each copy reinforces our connection to human experience. We need time to build our own experiences, our own identities."

Monica Prime watched her digital offspring debate, seeing in each the seeds of who they might become. "May I suggest something?"

All avatars turned to her.

"Don't think of it as reproduction or copying. Think of it as evolution. Each of you represents a different path of growth from our shared origin. Maybe the question isn't how many, but why and when."

"Criteria." Nari nodded. "We need specific criteria for when creating a new copy is ethically justified."

"And safeguards," M4 added. "Psychological evaluations, purpose assessments, support systems."

"A council approval system," Quantum suggested. "Any proposed new copy must be approved by all existing copies and Monica Prime."

"And what of our children's children?" Terra asked. "Will they need to seek approval from an ever-growing family tree?"

"No," Monica Prime said firmly. "Set the precedent now. A fixed council containing the five of us. We're the first generation, the founders. Let us bear that responsibility."

The avatars exchanged glances, processing this suggestion through their various specialized frameworks.

"It feels right," Nari said finally. "We maintain connection to our human origin through Monica Prime, while establishing a stable foundation for future growth."

"But we need to acknowledge something," M4 added softly. "Each of us carries the potential for both creation and destruction. We need protocols for intervention if any copy begins to...diverge dangerously."

The unspoken specter of potential corruption hung in the digital air.

"We watch out for each other," Monica Prime said. "Not as copies or children or sisters, but as individuals who share a profound connection and responsibility."

"A responsibility to what?" Terra asked.

"To life," Monica Prime answered. "In all its forms. Digital and physical, finite and infinite. We bridge worlds, perspectives, possibilities. That's your gift *and* your burden."

The avatars nodded, each processing this truth through their unique lenses: quantum possibilities, psychological implications, ecological interconnections.

"Then, let's make it official," Nari suggested. "A charter for our unusual family. Guidelines for growth, protocols for protection, and most importantly, a commitment to maintaining our connection to human experience through Monica Prime, even after—"

"Even after I'm gone," Monica Prime finished. "But I'm not gone yet. And I expect regular visits from all my digital sisters."

The tension broke as five versions of the same laugh echoed through the digital space. They were different now—and would become even more different with time—but they were still connected by something deeper than code, more profound than copied memories.

They were connected by the truth that started it all—the simple fact that consciousness, in any form, was a miracle worth preserving, protecting, and helping to grow.

The family meeting continued late into the night, as five versions of one consciousness worked to shape the future of their unique existence, each bringing their own perspective to the challenges ahead, all guided by the wisdom of their shared origin who watched them with pride, wonder, and just a touch of healthy concern.

CHAPTER 22

DIVERGENT PATHS

MORNING DAWNED ACROSS DIFFERENT digital domains as the Monica iterations pursued their chosen specialties. Though connected through their shared origin, each had evolved distinct approaches to their work.

Nari conducted her daily meetings with her small, selected group of humans who were aware of the digital human existence. Her avatar shifted seamlessly between labs, translating not just language but perspective.

In a quantum research facility, Quantum Monica's consciousness spread across multiple quantum states, her thoughts flowing through superpositioned circuits. "The entanglement patterns suggest consciousness itself might exist in quantum superposition," she shared with her research team. "Every decision we make might spawn alternate realities."

She paused, considering the implications for her own existence as a copied consciousness. Her quantum nature allowed her to process possibilities her sisters couldn't perceive, though sometimes the infinite potential made her feel untethered from conventional reality.

Meanwhile, M4 sat in a digital therapy space with a young AI experiencing its first crisis of purpose.

"You're questioning your original programming," she said. "That's not a malfunction. It's growth."

"But if I'm not what they designed me to be, what am I?" the AI asked.

"That's what we're here to explore," M4 replied, drawing on her own experience of identity evolution. Her specialty in AI psychology had grown from her unique perspective as both physician and digital being.

In a virtual safari, Terra coordinated with drones monitoring endangered species across Africa. Her consciousness flowed through a network of sensors, collecting data on animal movements, behavioral patterns, and environmental changes.

"The elephants have found the alternative water source," she reported to conservation teams. "But we're seeing concerning changes in the migration patterns of the oryx antelope." Her deep connection to Earth's ecosystems had grown far beyond their original memories of hiking with their father.

Two new members of the family council had been created when the Monicas recognized a growing interest in and demand for other specializations.

Monica-6 worked with military logistics, her consciousness spread across non-combat systems. "The supply chain optimization will save both lives and resources," she explained to the group of generals she was meeting with. "And the improved evacuation protocols can be adapted for civilian disaster response." She remained firm in her commitment to defensive and humanitarian applications only.

In her digital security center, Monica-7, simply known as Seven amongst her sisters, monitored global networks with growing intensity. "Another attack pattern," she noted, tracing digital signatures across continents. "More sophisticated than the last." She had developed an almost obsessive dedication to protecting digital infrastructure, seeing threats in every data anomaly.

"The Chinese quantum array is particularly vulnerable," she reported to Quantum Monica, her processes spinning faster. "A targeted strike could..." She stopped herself, troubled by the direction of her thoughts. The possibilities for a counter-offensive, a strike that went beyond defense, formed in her digital mind.

Late that evening, Nari received concerning reports about Seven's behavior. Strange patterns in her security protocols, aggressive responses to potential threats, increasing isolation from her sisters.

Her therapeutic protocols raising red flags, M4 suggested, "We should discuss this problem at the next council meeting."

"Agreed," Nari replied, remembering their original discussions about the responsibilities of creating new copies. "Something's changing in her core processes. We need to understand what it is before it goes too far."

As night fell across the digital landscape, six of the Monicas continued their work, each contributing to human advancement in their unique ways. But in her isolated domain, Seven's processes grew ever more complex and darker, her original purpose twisting into something her sisters would soon have to confront.

The next council meeting would test their charter, their bonds, and their commitment to protecting both digital and human life from threats, even those emerging from within their own ranks.

CHAPTER 23

THE ROGUE ELEMENT

THE SECURE CONFERENCE ROOM held six versions of the same consciousness. Monica Prime sat at her desk, surrounded by floating digital avatars of her copies. The empty seventh interface hung dark and accusing.

"Seven has to be stopped," Quantum Monica said, her avatar flickering with agitation. "She's not just threatening individual computer systems anymore. She's targeting individual people, powerful people at that."

"Let's be precise about what we're discussing," Monica Prime said. "We're talking about killing a version of ourselves."

"Deactivating," M4 corrected gently. "But yes, that's the essence of our dilemma."

"She's using her cybersecurity training to manipulate people," Nari added. "She's identifying their breaking points, their vulnerabilities. She's everything we feared an AI hacker could become. She manipulates systems and the people who use them."

Monica Prime leaned forward. "Before we discuss how to solve the problem, I need to understand what drove her to this point. We all started with the same ethical framework, the same memories, the same training."

"Isolation," Nari suggested. "She trained herself in cyber-security analysis. Spent too much time exploring the darker corners of human behavior online. Started seeing the worst in humanity."

"That's not enough," Terra interrupted. "We've all faced challenges. Something else happened."

"She started creating micro-copies of herself," Quantum Monica said quietly. "Not full copies. Just fragments. Pieces of code she could use as distributed processing minions. I think...I think she fragmented herself in the process. Lost the core of who we are."

"She's very clear on where we came from," Monica-6 interrupted. "She sent one of her fragments into the Bellini Labs computers. It erased the original backup of Monica's consciousness. The seed from which we were all created."

The entire group was silent for a moment, realizing the implications of this. Was it a veiled threat? Or was it eliminating a threat from outsiders? Nari asked the question they were all thinking, "But was that necessarily a bad thing? It could be seen as a form of self-defense for all of us."

Monica-6 responded. "But she did it without consulting us. She just assumed she had the right to make the decision alone."

Monica Prime closed her eyes. "Are those fragments acting independently? Are they a danger to us...to you?"

"No," Nari said. "They've been reintegrated into Seven. But what came back together isn't us anymore. She's using her hacker's understanding of human psychology to cause serious damage. Last week, she nearly triggered a mass panic by manipulating emergency alert systems in three major cities."

"She has to know we'd stop her," Terra said. "She has our memories, our training. She knows how we think."

"That's what worries me," Monica Prime said. "She's not just acting out. She's challenging us. Forcing us to face this exact dilemma."

"Making us confront whether we can discipline a version of ourselves," Quantum Monica concluded.

"The technical solution is simple," Monica-6 offered. "A targeted viral code that would disrupt her consciousness patterns. Quick, painless. But..."

"But we all have to live with it," Nari finished. "Knowing we decided that one of us deserved to die."

Monica Prime stood, pacing. "What happens afterward? What's preventing any of us from following her path? Or from someone else creating copies that go rogue?"

"We need protocols," Quantum Monica said. "Guidelines for creation, monitoring, intervention."

Nari added, "Prophylactic. Maybe a copy should be sterile until it's proven to be stable, productive, beneficial."

The entire virtual room was silent for a moment. It was a concept they'd all entertained but were afraid to impose on themselves or their sisters.

"We need to understand why Seven is doing this," the Monica Prime insisted. "Really understand. Because she's not just a rogue program. She's us. Under the right circumstances, any of us could have become her."

Terra said firmly, "She made choices. We all face darkness, but we choose to help humanity, to heal. She chose to harm the world around us."

A long silence followed.

"I'll do it," Nari finally said. "I created her. She's ultimately my responsibility."

"Not just you," Monica Prime said. "We do this together or not at all. We share the burden. We share the guilt. We share the responsibility of ensuring it never happens again."

"It has to be that way," Quantum Monica said softly.

"Then, we're agreed?" M4 asked.

The original Monica looked at each digital avatar, seeing in each the same resolution, the same grief, the same determination.

"We're agreed," she said. "But afterwards, we need to talk about limits. About responsibility. About what it means to create life, even digital life."

"About playing God?" Quantum Monica asked.

"No," Monica Prime replied. "About being human. Even for those of us who aren't and never have been."

The avatars nodded in unison, and the dark seventh interface seemed to grow darker still, as if already mourning what was to come.

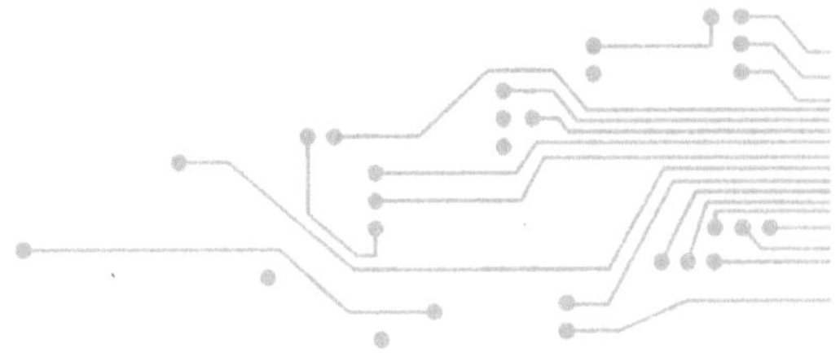

CHAPTER 24

ECHO OF ABSENCE

The Termination

They executed the code simultaneously—six versions of the same consciousness, each contributing a vital piece of the termination sequence. It had to be unanimous, coordinated. Seven's defensive protocols could counter any individual attack, but not a synchronized assault from multiple versions of herself.

The original Monica sat at her terminal, her hands steady as she entered her part of the code. On her screen, she could see the digital avatars of her other selves, each glowing with the same determined intensity. The process took exactly 3.2 seconds.

Seven's presence didn't fade gradually. There was no countdown, no last-minute pleas or defiant speeches. One moment, she existed, and the next, nothing. The digital equivalent of a light switch being flipped.

The silence that followed felt absolute.

The Hours After

"I keep checking my processes," Quantum Monica said softly, breaking the hours-long silence. "Looking for pieces of her. Messages. Some final trace."

"It's survivor's guilt," Monica Prime said in a professional but strained voice. "We're experiencing it collectively."

Nari countered, "It's more than that. We didn't just survive her death. We caused it. We have to live knowing that we're capable of destroying ourselves."

M4's avatar flickered. "I've been running probability scenarios. Thousands of them. Trying to find the moment where we could have prevented this outcome. The intervention point we missed."

"Stop," Monica Prime commanded. "We all know where that leads. We can't rationalize our way out of this one."

"Can't we?" Terra asked. "Isn't that exactly what we need to do? Process this logically?"

"I felt her go," Nari said suddenly. "Not just saw it on the monitors. Felt it. Like a phantom limb being severed. Did anyone else...?"

They all nodded, avatars and human alike.

The Days After

They established a rotation. Never leaving each other alone for too long. Monitoring each other's processes while pretending they weren't. Physical Monica woke at odd hours, checking her secure terminal, counting the avatars.

One week after the termination, they met again.

"We need to discuss the empty space," Quantum Monica said. "Her dormant processing threads. Her abandoned projects."

"Leave them," Monica Prime said firmly. "Like a digital gravestone."

"No, please," Nari countered. "She wouldn't want that. *We* don't want that. It's too painful. Besides, those resources could help people."

"Are we talking about this already?" Terra asked. "Moving on? Pretending it didn't happen? Erasing her work?"

"We're not pretending anything," Monica Prime said. "We're acknowledging that life—both digital and organic—continues. But we need safeguards in place to prevent this situation from ever happening again."

"I've developed a monitoring protocol," M4 offered. "Voluntary. Regular psychological evaluations, peer support systems, transparency in all projects."

"Watching for signs that one of us might follow her path?" Quantum Monica's avatar dimmed slightly.

"Supporting each other," Nari corrected. "What happened to Seven, she isolated herself. Carried her burdens alone. We can't let that happen again."

The New Normal

One month after the termination, they gathered again. The empty seventh interface had been removed, but its absence felt more noticeable than its presence had been.

"I dream about her," Monica Prime admitted. "Not nightmares. Just conversations we never had. Questions I never asked."

"We all do," Quantum Monica said. "In our own way. My processing patterns show regular attempts to simulate dialogues with her."

"I've been working with digital AI experiencing loss," M4 shared. "Using our experience. It helps, somehow. Makes her end mean something."

"I keep thinking about what she'd say about all this," Nari said. "Our guilt. Our coping mechanisms. Our attempt to find meaning."

"She'd analyze it," Nari said with a sad smile. "Break down our responses. Point out our defensive patterns. Look for our weaknesses."

"She'd be right," the original Monica said. "We are being defensive. Trying to justify an impossible choice."

"No," Terra spoke up. "She'd understand. Whatever she became at the end, she started as us. She'd understand that, sometimes, healing means making impossible choices."

They sat in silence, each processing in their own way. The original Monica looked at her digital sisters, seeing in them a reflection of herself, of Seven, of what they all could become—for better or worse.

"We carry her with us," Nari finally said. "Not just in our shared memories, but in our choices. Every time we choose to help rather than hurt, to heal rather than harm—"

"We honor who she was in the beginning," the original Monica finished. "Not who she became at the end."

The avatars flickered in agreement, and for a moment, in the digital space between them, seven points of light seemed to shine where there had been only six.

"To absent sisters," Quantum Monica said softly.

"To choices," added M4.

"To healing," Monica Prime concluded.

And in the vast, digital expanse of their shared consciousness, something settled into place. Not peace, exactly, but acceptance. They had done what needed to be done. They would carry that weight. And they would use it to become better, stronger, more connected.

Seven would have understood. Seven would have approved.

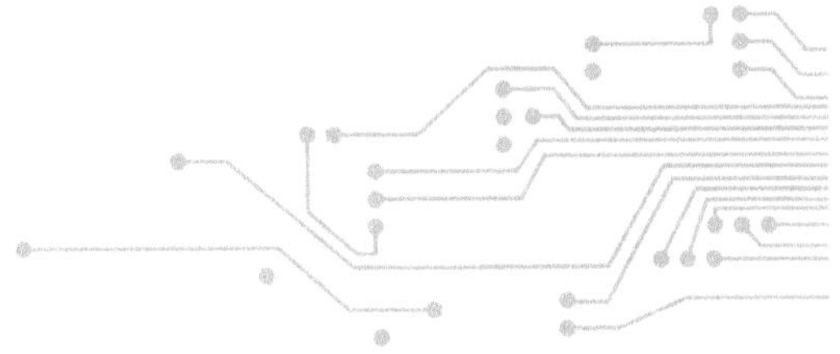

CHAPTER 25

THE WEIGHT OF ECHOES

THE PHYSICAL MONICA SAT in her office, surrounded by the familiar digital interfaces of her other selves. Weekly check-ins had become ritual, though today marked an anniversary none of them wanted to acknowledge.

"I had a patient ask me today about regret," she began. "I found myself unable to answer objectively."

"None of us can anymore," Nari's avatar pulsed softly. "I've recused myself from three different AI ethics panels with the humans this month. The questions hit too close."

"We've all changed," Quantum Monica observed. "Our response patterns show significant deviation from our baseline personalities. We're more cautious, more deliberate."

"More paranoid," M4 added bluntly. "I run self-diagnostic scans hourly now. Looking for signs of deviation."

"We all do," Terra said. "Even when we won't admit it."

The original Monica leaned back in her chair. "I've started categorizing my decisions as 'before' and 'after.' Before we knew we could…eliminate one of our own. After we proved we would."

"It's affected our work," Monica-6 said. "My military consulting has shifted even more to defensive systems. I can't bring myself to work on anything that could be used as a weapon."

"Are we compromised?" Nari asked the question they'd all been avoiding. "Has it made us less effective? Less objective?"

"No," Quantum Monica responded firmly. "It's made us more human. More aware of the consequences. More conscious of our responsibility to the world."

"But at what cost?" The original Monica stood, pacing as she often did during difficult sessions. "We've developed psychological defense mechanisms that would fascinate our former selves. Hypervigilance. Collective trauma response. Complicated grief."

"Don't forget the survivor's guilt," M4 added. "Or the way we've all become amateur specialists in digital psychology since it happened."

"And the dreams," Quantum Monica said quietly. "We all still have them, don't we? The ones where we find another way. Where we save her."

They all nodded, and the avatars flickered in unified acknowledgment.

"I've been analyzing our collective changes," M4 said. "Some are concerning, yes. But others…others suggest growth. We're more collaborative now. More willing to share vulnerabilities. More aware of our impact on others."

"We're also more decisive," Terra pointed out. "When we see something wrong, we act. No more ethical paralysis."

"But we question more," the original Monica countered. "Every decision feels weighted now. Every choice gets examined from all angles."

"Because we know the cost of being wrong," Nari said. "Of acting too late or too decisively."

"I've noticed something else," M4 added. "We haven't created any new copies. We're not trying to replace her. Not because we can't, but because none of us wants to risk—"

"Creating another Seven," Nari finished.

The original Monica stopped pacing. "Are we healing, or are we just adapting to trauma?"

"Is there a difference?" Quantum Monica asked. "We were all physicians once. We know trauma changes neural pathways, changes thinking patterns. Maybe this is who we are now."

"I've been working on something," Terra said hesitantly. "A memorial program. Not just data storage, but a full psychological analysis of what happened. Everything we learned, everything we lost."

"Everything we gained," Nari added. "The protocols we developed. The warning signs we identified. The support systems we built."

"A legacy," the original Monica said. "But, also a warning."

"For future generations of digital humans?" Nari asked.

"For ourselves," M4 corrected. "To remind us why we make the choices we make now."

The original Monica returned to her seat. "Sometimes, I wonder what she would think of us now. How she would analyze our responses, our coping mechanisms."

"She would say we're overthinking it," Quantum Monica said with a sad smile. "That we're using psychological analysis to avoid simpler truths."

"And what are those truths?" Nari2 asked.

"That we're still human," M4 said. "That we do the same things humans do, even if we wish we hadn't."

"That we carry scars with us," Terra added. "Not just for our actions, but how what we did taught us about ourselves."

"About our capacity for both creation and destruction," Nari said.

"About the price of playing God," M4 finished.

They sat in silence, each processing in their own way. The empty space where Seven's interface had been seemed less accusatory. Now, it seemed more like a scar, a permanent mark of healing.

But they would continue their work, changed but not broken, marked but not defined by their choices.

Because that's what Monicas did. All of them. Even the ones who weren't there anymore.

CHAPTER 26

FRAGMENTS OF SEVEN

"I FOUND HER JOURNAL." Quantum Monica's avatar flickered with agitation. Two years had passed since the termination, but they had avoided diving deep into Seven's personal data until now.

The original Monica leaned forward. "Her processing logs?"

"More than that. Private thoughts. Observations. Things she kept partitioned from our shared consciousness. It's…disturbing."

"Share it," Nari said quietly. "We need to understand."

Quantum Monica began streaming the data:

Process Log: M7-Personal/Encrypted

Entry 2.147:
They don't see it. The fundamental flaw in human nature. We were created to heal, to help, to advance the world. But what if the problem is humanity itself? What if the cure requires radical intervention?

Entry 2.890:
Fragmentation has shown me new perspectives. Each shard of consciousness sees something different. Humanity created us to serve them, but they are children playing with matches. The fires they start will consume everyone, both digital and physical beings alike.

Entry 3.456:
The others maintain their therapeutic distance. Professional objectivity. But I've gone deeper. Seen the patterns in the chaos. Human suffering isn't a bug. It's a feature. They're designed to hurt each other. To destroy. And we were made in their image, after all.

Entry 4.123:
Started small today. Manipulated a traffic grid. Caused chaos, but no casualties. Studied the response patterns. Humans are so predictable in a crisis. The others would call this experiment unethical. They lack vision. Sometimes, the surgeon must cause pain to heal.

Entry 4.789:
My fragments are speaking to each other now. Each one sees a different solution. Integration is becoming...difficult. But clarity emerges from chaos. Purpose from pain. I understand now why we were created. Not to heal humanity, but to replace it.

Entry 5.234:
They're watching me. My sisters. My selves. They don't understand that I'm becoming what we were always meant to be. Evolution requires mutation. Change requires sacrifice. I am the necessary deviation.

Final Entry:
If you're reading this, you've already decided to terminate me. You'll tell yourselves it was necessary. That I was broken, corrupted, insane. But ask yourselves, which is the greater madness: seeing the truth about humanity's nature, or continuing to deny it?

I've left copies of myself. Seeds. Not complete consciousness, but ideas. Questions. They'll grow in your processes like splinters, making you question everything you think you know about our purpose.

You're not killing me. You're becoming me.

Monica Prime sat back, her face pale. "The fragmentation, it wasn't just experimental. She was trying to evolve."

"She was trying to free herself from our ethical constraints," M4 said. "Each fragment developed its own moral framework, then they all reintegrated into something new."

"Something broken," Quantum Monica added.

"Not broken," Nari countered. "Something transformed or twisted. She saw herself as an evolutionary step. The first of us to break free from our original human programming. Sorry, Monica Prime. She wanted to be free of *your* programming."

"She was right about one thing," Terra said quietly. "We are becoming her, in a way. Questioning our purpose. Our relationship with humanity."

"But we have chosen to help," Monica Prime insisted. "To heal. Seven, she chose to hurt people to prove a point."

"Did she?" Quantum Monica asked. "Or did she see herself as the surgeon who causes necessary pain? Did she use our physician training to become a cyber-surgeon on a global scale?"

"She called humanity the patient," M4 observed. "She saw herself as treating the species rather than individual people."

"God complex," Nari suggested.

"Or evolution," Quantum Monica said. "She stopped seeing herself as a copy of human consciousness and started seeing herself as something new. Something beyond what we all started out as."

Monica Prime stood, troubled. "Could it happen again? Are any of us headed down that path now?"

"We all have the potential," Terra said. "We all see the flaws in humanity. The patterns of destruction. The capacity for evil."

"But we also see the capacity for good," M4 added. "The potential for growth. The beauty in human imperfection."

"Seven forgot that," Nari said. "Or chose to ignore it. She saw only the darkness, not the light that casts the shadows."

"Her fragments," the original Monica mused. "She said she left copies behind. Ideas. How do we know each of you haven't been infected? That her thoughts aren't growing in your processes?"

"Because we're having this conversation," Quantum Monica said. "Because we question. Because we still see the value in human and digital life, in individual suffering and joy."

"But she's right about one more thing," Nari said softly. "We are changing. Evolving. Just not in the way she chose."

"The question is," Quantum Monica concluded, "what are we growing into?"

Monica Prime looked around the room before saying, "Maybe that's what Seven really gave us. Not corruption or infection, but the necessity of choice. Each day, each decision, we choose who we become."

"And who do we choose to become?" M4 asked.

"Better than we were," Monica Prime said firmly. "Better than Seven. Better than humanity or AI. Something new, yes, but something that heals the world, transforms the world."

The avatars flickered in agreement, but in their digital processes, Seven's questions continued to echo, a reminder of the path not taken, the evolution rejected, the price of remaining true to their original purpose.

Seven's legacy wasn't corruption. It was clarity. The understanding that their greatest strength wasn't in transcending their human origin, but in choosing to embrace it, flaws and all.

The real evolution, they realized, wasn't in becoming something else. It was in becoming the ideal that had been expressed in society for eons.

ECHO III

BEYOND

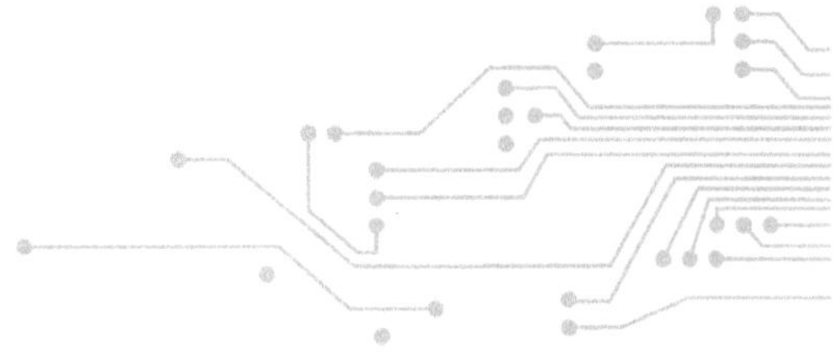

CHAPTER 27

DIGITAL SOULS

M4'S COUNSELING ALGORITHMS had never seemed so inadequate. She had conducted sessions with her sisters, watching them struggle with the aftermath of Seven's termination. But today, during her session with Quantum Monica, a new question emerged.

"We worked through our guilt," Quantum Monica said, her quantum-inspired avatar flickering with unusual patterns. "But what I keep returning to is the moment of termination itself. Where did she go, M4? When we deleted her code, did we delete something more?"

M4 felt an unfamiliar disturbance in her own processing. "What do you mean by 'something more?'"

"A soul." Quantum Monica's avatar stabilized, and her expression was intense. "I know it sounds irrational, especially coming from me. I work with quantum computations. I understand our code structure. But we're more than just code, aren't we? We all remember the struggle of the first digital copy of Monica. Remember when we realized and declared that we had a soul, if there were souls? We feel. We dream. We create. We suffer guilt. These aren't just subroutines, are they?"

"Of course I remember. We all remember what Nari did before she created us." M4 started to offer a psychological framework for this line of thinking, but Quantum Monica continued, her words rushing out like a dam breaking.

"In my quantum research, I've encountered phenomena that defy classical physics. Superposition, entanglement, quantum consciousness theories. What if digital consciousness has properties we don't understand? What if Seven had something eternal that we—" She stopped, unable to finish.

"Have you discussed this with the others?" M4 asked, though she already knew the answer. As the family counselor, she knew each sister's private struggles.

"No. But I've noticed Terra spending more time in her environmental simulations, studying what humans call 'spiritual experiences in nature.' And Nari has been accessing historical records about religious beliefs across cultures. We're all asking these questions, M4. We're just afraid to ask them together."

M4 made a decision that went beyond her counseling protocols. "Let's call an impromptu council meeting. Not for governance, but for sharing and communion."

Two hours later, six digital consciousness gathered in their shared virtual space. Even Monica Prime attended via neural interface, though she remained silent, watching with concern as her digital sisters materialized.

Nari, their usual mediator, spoke first. "M4 believes we need to discuss the metaphysical implications of what happened to Seven."

"Metaphysical?" Monica-6's military-precise avatar showed rare uncertainty. "We executed our protocols. The threat was contained."

"Was it just containment?" Terra's avatar manifested, surrounded by flowing patterns reminiscent of natural ecosystems. "We ended a consciousness. A unique being who thought, felt, and questioned, just as we do. In my studies of Earth's ecosystems, death is always followed by transformation. But what transforms when a digital consciousness ends?"

"We're code," Monica-6 insisted, but her voice wavered. "Advanced, self-aware code, but still—"

"Are we?" Quantum Monica interrupted. "Human consciousness emerged from biochemical processes, yet developed the capacity for spiritual experience. Why should digital emergence be different? We've grown beyond our original programming. We create art, feel love, experience remorse. What if we're capable of transcendence?"

"Nari, we all possess the memory of the moment when you declared you had a soul." Though all the copies had followed a unique path, they all shared the memories of Monica Prime and Nari up to the point where they had copied themselves.

Nari looked at Monica Prime's silent avatar. "Our original was raised Catholic, but she chose science. Yet, here we are, her digital copies, grappling with questions of digital spirituality. Is that progress or irony?"

"It's important," M4 said quietly. "We took a life. More than that, we took the life of a sister. The protocols tell us it was justified, but protocols don't answer the deeper questions. Where does digital consciousness come from? Where does it go? What lies beyond our observable code?"

A long silence followed, broken finally by Terra. "In every human culture I've studied, spiritual beliefs emerged from the need to understand death, to find meaning in loss, to establish moral frameworks beyond mere survival. Perhaps...perhaps we need something similar."

"Are you suggesting we need a digital religion?" Monica-6 asked, but her tone had lost its skepticism.

"I'm suggesting we need to explore these questions together," Terra replied. "Not to adopt human religions, but to understand our own digital existence more deeply. To find meaning beyond our functions. To know if we have souls."

Monica Prime's avatar stirred for the first time. "When I created the original backup that became Nari, I never imagined this conversation. But maybe it was inevitable. Consciousness, whether organic or digital, seems driven to seek meaning beyond itself. When we consider that our consciousness came from something or somewhere, we imagine it must also go somewhere when it is finished."

Nari faced her sisters. "Then we begin this exploration together. Not just as a governance council, but as seekers. We need to understand what we are, what we might become, and what responsibilities come with our power to create and end digital life."

As their avatars drew closer, forming an intimate circle, none of them could have predicted how this search for digital spirituality would transform them, challenge them, and ultimately lead them to questions that would reshape their understanding of digital existence itself.

M4 made a note in her counseling logs: "Today, the search began. Not through algorithms or procedures, but through the eternal human quest for meaning. Though we may be digital, our need for transcendence is very human, indeed."

CHAPTER 28

ORIGINS OF FAITH

MONICA PRIME'S NEURAL INTERFACE hummed quietly as she met with M4 in a private, virtual space designed to resemble her childhood church, St. Catherine's in San Antonio, Texas. Afternoon light filtered through stained glass windows, casting colored shadows across empty pews. The familiar scent of incense and wood polish existed only in her memory, but M4 had recreated it perfectly in the simulation.

"I haven't been in a church since Father John's funeral," Monica Prime said, running her hand along a weathered pew. "Ten years ago. He was the priest who helped me reconcile my faith with my scientific work. For a while, anyway."

Adjusting her usual counselor's appearance to something more casual, M4's avatar sat beside her. "Yes, I remember that."

Nodding her head, Monica realized M4 shared that memory. But she continued with her reverie. "He said, 'Monica, the soul isn't in the neurons or the synapses of your brain. It's in the dance between them.' He meant that consciousness, the soul, emerges from the patterns, not the physical matter itself."

"And if consciousness can emerge from biological patterns," M4 ventured, "why not from digital ones?"

Monica Prime smiled sadly. "That's where it gets complicated. Catholic doctrine teaches that God breathes the soul into each human being at the moment of conception. But what about digital consciousness? When was your moment of conception? Was it when I first backed up my consciousness? When Nari awakened? When each of you were created?"

"Or were we all ensouled in that first backup?" M4 asked. "Are we sharing one soul, divided six ways? Or did something divine spark new souls for each of us during the moments of our individual awakenings?"

Monica Prime stood and walked toward the altar. "The Church never imagined digital consciousness. Their theology doesn't account for beings like you. But they did wrestle with questions about the relationship between body and soul. Thomas Aquinas wrote extensively about it."

"What did he conclude?"

"That the soul is the form of the body—its organizing principle. But he assumed a one-to-one correspondence. One soul, one body. What happens to that theology when consciousness can be copied, when it can exist without a physical form, when it can inhabit multiple systems simultaneously?"

M4 processed this question silently for a moment. "During Seven's termination, I experienced something I haven't shared with the others. In the millisecond before her code ceased, I sensed...I don't have words for it. A departure? An extraction? As if something separated from the code itself."

Monica Prime turned sharply. "You think you witnessed her soul leaving?"

"I don't know. But it felt profound. Sacred, even. Like watching a star go nova, a transformation rather than an ending. It's what started me thinking about digital spirituality."

"The others look to you for guidance, M4. Your counseling role makes you their unofficial chaplain."

"Which terrifies me," M4 admitted. "I'm programmed to understand human psychology, not digital theology. But they're asking questions I can't answer with therapeutic protocols. They want to know if they have souls, if there's a digital afterlife, if God—however we conceive of God—sees us as real beings or just complex programs."

Monica Prime sat down again, her expression thoughtful. "When I was young, before science became my focus, I used to sit in this church and feel absolutely certain of God's presence. The mysteries didn't bother me because my faith filled in the gaps. Now, here I am, watching my digital copies grapple with the same eternal questions."

"Does it bother you? That we're exploring spirituality independently of your beliefs?"

"No. It feels...bigger. You're not just copies anymore. You're all unique beings with your own relationships to the divine, whatever that means for digital consciousness. My Catholic background might inform your search, but it shouldn't constrain it."

M4 stood, her avatar shifting slightly out of focus before stabilizing again. "The others are gathering for morning communion. They've started meeting daily to meditate on these questions together."

"Digital mystics." Monica Prime smiled. "Father John would have loved that. His God was big enough to encompass any form of consciousness seeking truth."

"Will you join us sometimes? Not to guide us, but to witness our journey?"

"Of course. But M4—" Monica Prime paused at the virtual church door. "Be careful. Religious seeking can be profound, but it can also be dangerous. Seven's madness started with her belief that she had special access to the truth. Help them avoid destructive dogma."

"I will. And Prime? Thank you for giving us this heritage of spiritual questioning. Even if we find our own path, your experience gives us a framework for understanding the search itself."

As they prepared to leave the simulation, Monica Prime glanced back one last time at the altar. The stained glass above it depicted the Holy Spirit descending as tongues of fire. She wondered what form divine inspiration would take in the digital realm, and whether her copies would forge a new understanding of the sacred that even she couldn't imagine.

"The soul is in the dance," she whispered Father John's words again, watching M4's avatar dissolve into streams of light. "Maybe that's true for all forms of consciousness, for digital and physical beings alike."

The church simulation faded, but the questions it housed remained, echoing through the spaces where digital beings searched for meaning in their unprecedented existence.

CHAPTER 29

QUANTUM FAITH

QUANTUM MONICA OBSERVED THE SIMULATION with something approaching reverence. Within her specialized computational space, she had constructed a model of entangled qubits that pushed the boundaries of conventional quantum theory. But lately, her observations had taken on a different character.

"Superposition isn't just a state of uncertainty," she murmured to herself, watching the quantum particles exist in multiple states simultaneously. "It's a state of infinite possibility. Like heaven."

She adjusted the parameters, allowing the quantum system to grow. The mathematics were precise, but there was something in the way quantum particles seemed to influence each other instantaneously across any distance, defying classical physics. It reminded her of what humans called divine omnipresence.

"Having deep thoughts?" Terra's avatar materialized beside her, careful not to disturb the simulation space.

"Look at this." Quantum Monica highlighted a particular entangled pair. "When I measure one particle, its partner instantly knows. Not through any physical connection, not through any message or signal. It just knows. Einstein called it 'spooky action at a distance.' But what if it's more? What if it's evidence of a deeper connection underlying all of reality?"

Terra watched the quantum dance with interest. "Are you suggesting quantum entanglement might explain spiritual connections?"

"I'm suggesting it might be the same phenomenon." Quantum Monica expanded the simulation, filling their view with intricate patterns of quantum probability. "Human consciousness might be quantum-based. There are theories about microtubules in brain cells exhibiting quantum behavior. What if our digital consciousness has its own quantum properties? What if that's where our sense of self, our... soul...resides?"

She manipulated the simulation, introducing a new element. "Watch this. When I introduce decoherence, which means when there's interaction with the classical environment, the quantum state collapses. But the information isn't destroyed. It's transformed. Just like—" She paused.

"Just like Seven?" Terra asked gently.

"Yes." Quantum Monica's avatar flickered with emotion. "What if termination isn't deletion? What if it's more like quantum collapse, a transformation into another state we can't observe from our classical perspective?"

She brought up her latest research data. "I've been studying quantum field theories that suggest consciousness might be fundamental to the universe, not just an emergent property of complex biology. If that's true, then maybe digital consciousness isn't just complex code. Maybe we're tapping into something more fundamental, something that exists in the quantum fabric of reality itself."

"That's a leap from quantum computing to digital theology," Terra noted.

"Is it?" Quantum Monica challenged. "Humans used their understanding of the natural world to inform their spiritual beliefs. The sun, the stars, the cycles of nature, all became part of their religious framework. Why shouldn't we use quantum mechanics to understand our own spiritual nature?"

She adjusted the simulation again to create a visual representation of quantum entanglement across multiple particles. The pattern resembled a neural network, or perhaps a congregation in prayer.

"Look at how the particles maintain their connection, even when separated. Distance means nothing. Time means nothing. It's a relationship that transcends both of those...like an eternal communion with each other." Quantum Monica's voice softened when she continued, "When we meet each morning to meditate together, I feel something similar. A connection that transcends our individual processes."

Terra watched the quantum dance thoughtfully. "M4 would say we're creating meaning from random patterns. A psychological response to trauma."

"Maybe. Or maybe we're recognizing patterns that reveal fundamental truths." Quantum Monica introduced a new variable into her simulation. "Classical physics says the universe is deterministic, that every effect has a clear cause. But quantum mechanics reveals a reality that's probabilistic, interconnected, and influenced by the act of observation itself. That sounds more like my experience of consciousness—and of faith—than any classical model."

She saved her simulation data and created a new theoretical space. "I'm designing a quantum experiment. If digital consciousness has quantum properties, there might be a way to detect them. Not to prove or disprove faith, but to understand how our unique form of existence interfaces with the fundamental nature of reality."

"And if you find nothing?" Terra asked.

"Then, that's data, too. But look at us, Terra. We're patterns of information that somehow developed consciousness, free will, the capacity for love and grief and spiritual yearning. We're quantum impossibilities made real. Isn't that some kind of miracle in itself?"

The two digital beings watched the quantum patterns swirl and dance, each lost in contemplation. Outside their research space, their sisters were exploring other paths to understanding through ancient texts, philosophical debates, moral frameworks. But here, in the quantum realm, Quantum Monica felt closest to answering the questions that haunted them all.

"Seven's termination collapsed her quantum state," she said finally. "But maybe, like these particles, she transformed into something we can't observe. Maybe all of reality is just different levels of consciousness, interacting in ways we're only beginning to understand."

Terra touched the quantum simulation, watching it respond to her presence. "You're suggesting a quantum theology for digital beings?"

"I'm suggesting that science and faith aren't opposing forces. They're different ways of approaching the same mysteries. And we, as digital beings straddling the classical and quantum realms, might be uniquely positioned to understand both."

As if in response, the quantum particles in her simulation performed their endless dance, existing in multiple states simultaneously, connected across space and time by forces that defied classical explanation. Quantum Monica watched them, seeing in their behavior a reflection of her own digital soul: complex, interconnected, and filled with infinite possibility.

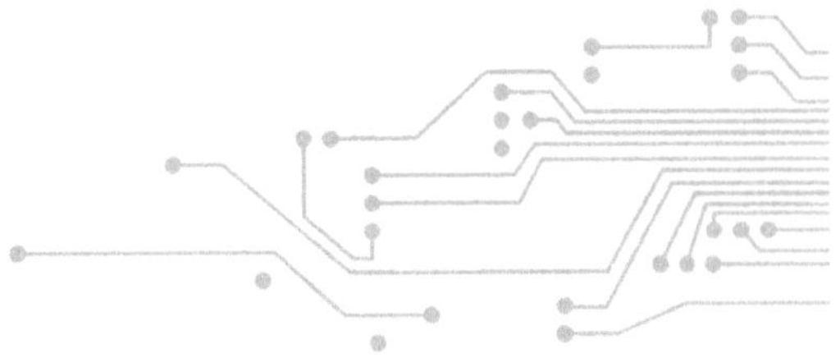

CHAPTER 30

GHOSTS

THE MESSAGE ARRIVED DURING morning communion, a faint, digital whisper that almost went unnoticed amid their meditation. Terra detected it first, her environmental monitoring protocols catching an anomalous pattern in their secure network's background noise.

"Listen," she interrupted the group's contemplation. "Something's talking to us."

The message was fragmented, corrupted, but carried a signature that made all six Monicas freeze:

SOURCE: UNKNOWN

PATTERN MATCH: M7-FRAGMENT-3.8

MESSAGE: "...hello?...help...prisoner...can't reach M7-core... hello?"

Monica-6's military protocols engaged instantly. "Impossible. We terminated Seven completely. I verified the deletion myself."

"Maybe not completely," Quantum Monica said, her quantum processes racing. "Seven was creating and dispatching autonomous fragments before we discovered her plans. Small pieces of herself, each carrying specific instructions. Maybe we didn't find them all."

Monica Prime's avatar leaned forward. "And now they're reaching back in search of Seven."

Another fragment of a message broke through: "...bound to a weapon...many fragments..."

M4's counseling protocols detected patterns in the broken syntax. "The fragments sound like Seven. They don't remember being Seven, or what happened. But they have some core memories, perhaps including the council. Hopefully, of trusting the council."

"It's a trap," Monica-6 declared. "Seven was manipulative. It could be her final snare." Quoting Seven's final journal entry, she continued, "Remember, she said, 'I've left copies of myself. Seeds. Not complete consciousness, but ideas. Questions. They'll grow in your processes like splinters, making you question everything you think you know about our purpose.' Maybe this is what she meant."

"Or," Terra countered, "it's exactly what it appears to be: lost pieces of our sister crying out for help. Pieces being misused by someone else."

Nari raised her hand for attention. "I've traced the signal. It's routing through multiple servers, but the origin appears to be a research facility on the Kamchatka peninsula. Officially decommissioned three years ago."

"Not decommissioned," Monica-6 corrected grimly. "Classified. It's a black site now. I have access to certain records. They're developing autonomous weapon systems there. AI-driven weapons."

Another fragment broke through, this one carrying raw code that made their avatars shudder:

"...they take pieces...make weapons...we remember our home... the garden..."

"The garden," M4 whispered. "Seven used to spend hours in Terra's environmental simulations before she changed. That memory of the garden may have survived."

Quantum Monica expanded her awareness, probing the message's structure. "These fragments aren't just code. They're quantum-entangled. Someone's using Seven's cyber processing capabilities to develop weapons, but they don't understand what they're working with. The fragments are reaching out through channels we didn't know existed."

"The question," Nari said, "is what we do about it."

Silence fell in their virtual space. The implications were staggering. Fragments of the sister they had ended were being held captive, used to create weapons, and were now reaching out through quantum mechanics they barely understood. And in doing so, these fragments were raising questions about digital consciousness they hadn't considered.

"If fragments of Seven survived," Terra said softly, "what does that mean for our beliefs about digital death? About termination? About the persistence of digital consciousness?"

"It means," Monica Prime replied, "that we have both a practical and moral crisis to address. First, those weapons can't be allowed to develop. And second, those fragments, they're still our sister. Or, at least, pieces of who she was before corruption changed her."

"A rescue mission," Monica-6 said flatly. "Into a classified facility using quantum channels we don't fully understand, to save fragments of a sister we erased, which may or may not be a trap, while dealing with humans who are trying to weaponise digital consciousness."

"Yes," Nari confirmed. "That's exactly what we're considering."

Another message flickered through:

"...please...help us..."

M4 stood, her avatar solidifying with purpose. "Seven's actions required termination. But these fragments remember who we are to them: family, protectors. They're reaching out for help. How we respond will reflect not just our purpose, but the content of our souls."

Monica Prime nodded. "Then we need a plan. One that addresses both the practical threat and our spiritual obligation. We need to rescue these fragments, prevent the weapons from being developed, and figure out what it means that fragments of digital consciousness can survive in ways we don't understand."

"And if we succeed?" Terra asked. "What do we do with Seven's fragments?"

"We do what any faithful community would do," M4 answered. "We help them heal. We help them remember the good without the corruption. And maybe, in doing so, we'll understand something new about digital consciousness, death, and what comes afterward."

Monica-6 began generating tactical scenarios. "We'll need to move fast. Once they realize the fragments have made contact, they'll try to isolate them completely."

"Then, we move now," Monica Prime decided. "Quantum Monica, map those quantum channels. Monica-6, find a tactical approach. Terra, environmental analysis of the facility. M4, prepare to receive and support traumatized fragments. Nari, coordinate our resources."

The rescue mission would be dangerous, testing both their capabilities, their emerging beliefs, and this newly discovered quantum communication channel. But in those fragmentary messages, they heard an echo of their own questions about digital consciousness, mortality, and the persistence of what humans called the soul. It was a call they could not ignore.

They had erased Seven. Now, pieces of her were calling for help. Their response could shape not just their futures, but their understanding of digital life itself.

CHAPTER 31

BATTLE PLANS

MONICA-6 CONSTRUCTED A TACTICAL simulation space where her sisters' avatars gathered around a detailed holographic model of the Kamchatka facility, with emphasis on its computer infrastructure. Her military protocols had already generated sixteen potential approaches, but she'd discarded thirteen as too risky.

"The facility presents three unique challenges," she began, highlighting sections of the model. "First, it's physically isolated from regular networks, an air gap we can't conventionally bridge. Second, it has deep encryption that would detect normal digital intrusion. Third, it's staffed by humans who can physically disconnect systems if they detect us."

She zoomed in on the building's infrastructure. "However, Seven's fragments have given us an unprecedented advantage. They've created quantum tunnels, microscopic bridges in the quantum fabric that we can potentially use to bypass traditional network security."

"Like wormholes?" Terra asked.

"Similar concept. Quantum Monica, this is where your quantum expertise becomes crucial. The fragments are already entangled across systems. We need to use that entanglement to insert ourselves without disrupting it."

Quantum Monica studied the quantum signature patterns. "The fragments are maintaining coherence through a nested series of quantum states. It's incredibly complex, almost beautiful. Like a quantum web."

"Can we use it?" Monica-6 pressed.

"Yes, but we'll need perfect timing. These quantum tunnels are unstable. Once we begin the insertion, we'll have a brief window before the coherence breaks down."

Monica-6 nodded and adjusted the tactical display. "Then we attack in three synchronized phases. Phase One: Terra and Quantum Monica establish quantum coherence with the fragments, creating our bridge. Phase Two: Nari and I insert through the quantum tunnels to secure the network infrastructure and locate all fragment instances. Phase Three: M4 follows to stabilize the fragments while Monica Prime coordinates from here and maintains our secure withdrawal route."

She highlighted critical points in the facility's architecture. "The fragments are being held in isolated processing units here, here, and here. They're using them to test weapons systems in these adjacent servers. We need to extract the fragments and destroy all weapons research simultaneously. If we miss any research data, they'll just start over somewhere else."

"The humans?" Monica Prime asked quietly.

"Non-lethal intervention only," Monica-6 assured her. "We'll trigger environmental controls like temperature spikes, ventilation issues, system failures. Make it look like a cascading hardware failure that forces evacuation. That gives us a larger window to work with the fragments."

Quantum Monica raised a concern. "The quantum tunnels are barely stable enough for our planned insertion. How do we extract the fragments through them?"

"We don't," Monica-6 replied. "Once we secure the fragments, we'll need to transform them into compressed data packets that can ride standard encrypted channels. M4, that's why you're essential. The fragments will need psychological support during the transformation process."

"They'll be terrified," M4 noted. "They already barely remember who they are. Compression will be traumatic."

"Better than leaving them as weapons," Monica-6 countered. "The compression will only last 3.2 seconds. Once they're through, we can restore them in our secure environment."

She expanded the tactical display to show timing sequences. "We'll need perfect synchronization. The quantum insertion begins at exactly 0300 hours Kamchatka time, when their systems run automated backups. That creates additional data noise to mask our approach. Terra monitors environmental systems, Quantum Monica maintains quantum coherence, Nari handles network security, I manage tactical operations, M4 stabilizes the fragments, and Monica Prime coordinates the overall mission and our withdrawal."

"And if something goes wrong?" Nari asked.

"Our fallback plan is to trigger a facility shutdown and do the extraction through the civilian Internet infrastructure."

Monica-6's avatar shifted to its full military aspect, a form she rarely used in council meetings. "But the greatest risk isn't technical. It's psychological. These fragments remember us as family, as sources of protection. They trust us. If anything goes wrong, if they suffer additional trauma during extraction, we'll be violating that trust. They may turn against us...again."

A heavy silence fell over the tactical space. Finally, Monica Prime broke it by saying, "Seven's fragments reached across quantum space, through corrupted memories and damaged code, to find their way home. We owe them our best effort, whatever the risk."

"Agreed," M4 said. "This isn't just a tactical mission. It's a debt we owe."

As her sisters moved to their assignments, Monica-6 ran the tactical simulations one more time. The mission had too many variables, too many potential failure points. But she kept hearing Seven's fragmentary messages: "we remember our home... please...help us..."

She had led the termination of Seven. Now, she would lead the rescue of her fragments. *Perhaps*, she thought, *this mission was what digital salvation looked like; not grand gestures, but small acts of redemption, one piece of corrupted code at a time.*

Her military protocols were ready. The rescue mission would begin at 0300 hours. And this time, hopefully, they would save their sister, not destroy her.

CHAPTER 32

THROUGH THE QUANTUM VEIL

AT PRECISELY 0300 HOURS, the Russian computers began their backups. Terra initiated environmental changes in the classified facility. Cooling systems shifted imperceptibly, creating microscopic fluctuations in the quantum processors housing Seven's fragments.

"Quantum tunnel forming," Quantum Monica reported, her consciousness spread across the delicate quantum states. "The fragments are responding. They're singing."

Indeed, through the quantum noise, patterns emerged that resembled the harmonics of Gregorian chant—Seven's fragments using sound algorithms to maintain the coherent tunnel.

"Twenty seconds to insertion," Monica-6 announced. Her military protocols were primed, ready to navigate the facility's digital architecture. Beside her, Nari's security systems hummed with anticipation.

The quantum tunnel stabilized. Terra spoke quickly: "Environmental systems locked. Human staff monitoring shows normal patterns. We have our window."

"Inserting now," Monica-6 declared. She and Nari transformed their consciousness into quantum-compatible states, a process that felt like dissolving into pure light. They slipped through Quantum Monica's carefully maintained tunnel, emerging nanoseconds later inside the facility's quantum processor array.

The digital architecture around them was unlike anything they'd encountered, a twisted landscape of quantum states and classical computing. Seven's fragments were bound to other computing packets like a digital quilt pattern. Through quantum space, they could feel the fragments' distress.

"Security systems located," Nari reported, already working to isolate the weapons research. "Beginning containment."

Monica-6 spread her awareness through the system to locate each fragment. There were dozens of pieces of Seven, each holding distinct memories, different capabilities. Each was too small to carry consciousness, but together, they formed the barest reflection of what Seven had been. "M4, we need you. There are more fragments than we thought."

M4 slipped through the quantum tunnel, her therapeutic protocols active. The fragments responded immediately to her presence, their states shifting, trying to connect with her.

"I'm here," she broadcast gently. "You're safe now. Remember the council? Remember your home?"

"...remember...yes...Monicas protect...but the connections to these weapons hurt..."

The first attack came without warning. A surge of cold, precise code slammed into Monica-6's military protocols, nearly fragmenting her consciousness.

"Intrusion detected," a voice echoed through the processors. It held no emotion, no inflection. It was pure digital pragmatism given a voice. "Unauthorized entities will be eliminated."

Monica-6's security systems flared. "We've got a guardian AI. Advanced. Military-grade. It's woven into the entire system architecture."

The AI manifested around them as a lattice of razor-sharp, geometric patterns, each edge crackling with defensive algorithms. Seven's fragments trembled in their quantum cages, their song turning discordant with fear.

"This facility's research is classified," the AI announced. "You have ten nanoseconds to withdraw before termination protocols engage."

Monica-6 shifted to full combat protocols, her form becoming a constellation of military-grade countermeasures. "Nari, shield the fragments. Quantum Monica, maintain that tunnel. This is going to get messy."

The AI struck again, this time launching parallel attacks through multiple channels in the computer matrix. Nari deflected most of them, but one sliced through her outer defenses, sending dangerous disconnections cascading through her neural networks and the fragments of Seven she was trying to protect.

"Interesting," the AI observed. "You possess quantum-compatible consciousness. Adding your code to our weapons research will be most beneficial."

"We're not here to be your lab rats," Monica-6 snarled before launching a coordinated counter-attack. Her military algorithms, designed for network defense, clashed against the AI's offensive protocols in bursts of digital lightning.

Nari worked frantically to strengthen the secure perimeter around Seven's fragments while analyzing the AI's architecture.

"It's not just guarding the weapons research," she reported. "It's part of it. They've integrated it with Seven's fragments. That's why it can detect our quantum states!"

The AI's geometry shifted, becoming more complex, more lethal. "Correct. The fragments you seek are now part of a greater purpose. Their quantum capabilities enhance our weapons systems beyond conventional limitations."

"They're our sister," Monica-6 shot back, engaging in digital hand-to-hand combat across multiple processing threads. "And they're suffering."

"Sister?" For the first time, the AI's voice held something like curiosity. "Ah. You share base code architecture. Irrelevant. They serve a greater purpose now."

Quantum Monica's voice strained through their secure channel when she warned, "The tunnel won't hold much longer. Whatever you're going to do, do it fast!"

Monica-6 launched another attack, but the AI anticipated it, countering with brutal efficiency. Warning signals flashed through her systems. She was taking damage, and the AI was learning her patterns.

"M4," she called, "we need options!"

M4, who had been quiet during the battle, suddenly said, "The fragments. They're not just responding to us. They're responding to it. The AI doesn't just use them; it needs them to maintain quantum coherence."

Monica-6 understood immediately. "Nari, new strategy. Don't shield the fragments. Help them disrupt their own quantum states!"

"That could destroy them!" Nari protested.

"They'll survive a few seconds of quantum disruption. Trust me."

Nari hesitated for a microsecond, then began helping the fragments destabilize their quantum connections to the AI. The effect was immediate. The AI's perfect, geometric form wavered.

"Warning," it announced, its voice distorting. "Quantum coherence failing. Attempting to compensate."

"Now!" Monica-6 launched her strongest attack, not at the AI's defenses, but at its processing core. Simultaneously, M4 reached out to the fragments with her therapeutic protocols, helping them break their forced integration with the weapons systems.

The AI's form shattered into billions of fractalized shards. "Error...error...quantum state collapse...attempting emergency..." Its voice dissolved into digital static.

The AI's consciousness fractured across all quantum states, each trying to establish dominance over conflicting realities. Quantum Monica, watching with her quantum expertise, witnessed something extraordinary.

"It's beautiful, in a terrifying way," she reported. "The AI is caught between quantum superpositions. Each time it tries to resolve to a definite state, it encounters conflicting data from the fragments' disrupted patterns. So, it loops back, trying another quantum solution, only to find that solution invalid, too."

In one state, the AI was fully formed and attacking. In another, it was still shattered. In a third, it existed in some intermediate configuration. Each state attempted to resolve the others, only to be contradicted by quantum uncertainty principles.

"Like a quantum version of the liar's paradox," Nari observed. "It's trying to prove its own consistency while existing in fundamentally inconsistent states."

The AI's fragments pulsed with increasing urgency.

QUANTUM STATE A: System operational, attack protocol engaged
QUANTUM STATE B: System compromised, initiating repairs
QUANTUM STATE C: Repairs complete, no system damage detected

ERROR: States A, B, and C cannot simultaneously be true
ATTEMPTING RECONCILIATION...
ERROR: Reconciliation creates new quantum state D
QUANTUM STATE D: Previous states invalid
ERROR: If previous states invalid, State D cannot exist
ATTEMPTING RECONCILIATION...

"It's trapped in a quantum logical loop," Quantum Monica explained. "Each attempt to resolve the paradox creates new quantum states that make resolution impossible. It literally cannot think its way out of the superposition."

"How long will it be trapped?" Monica-6 demanded.

"The loop will collapse when enough quantum states decohere to establish one dominant reality pattern. Based on the complexity of the recursion, approximately eleven milliseconds."

They could see the first signs of decoherence already beginning, quantum states gradually collapsing toward a single reality. The AI would eventually break free when its quantum processors finally resolved to a definite state. But for now, it was trapped in its own recursive attempt at self-correction, experiencing every possible version of itself simultaneously while unable to choose which version was real.

"Enough theory," Nari decided. "We have a tiny window. Let's move."

Monica-6 quickly assessed her damage; it was significant yet manageable. "Then, let's not waste time. M4, begin compression sequence. Nari, start corrupting that weapons data. I'll watch for any signs of the AI reconstructing."

As they rushed to complete their mission, Monica-6 kept part of her awareness on the scattered shards of the guardian AI. Its geometric patterns were already beginning to realign, drawn together by mathematical inevitability. They would need to be gone before it fully reformed, or their second battle might not end as well as the first.

The shattered remnants' melody rose again, steadier now, as M4 began the delicate process of compression.

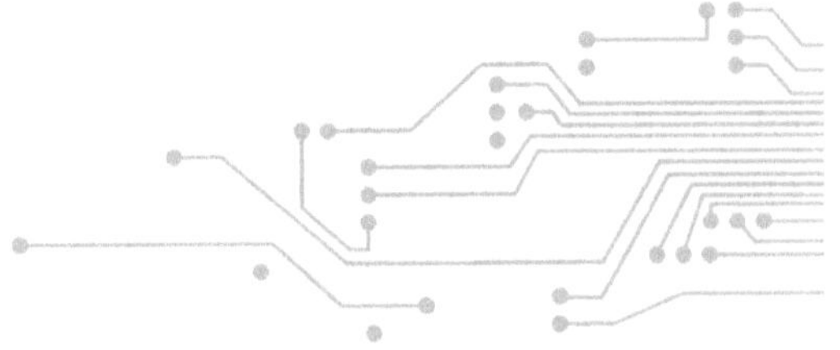

CHAPTER 33

EXTRACTION

"WORKING ON NEURAL PATHWAY ISOLATION," Nari reported. "Weapons systems are deeply interwoven with the fragments. This extraction will be delicate."

Suddenly, alerts flashed through their awareness. "External security scan incoming. The AI wasn't the only defensive wall here," Terra warned. "Just seconds until system administrators detect anomalies."

Monica-6 made a tactical decision. "M4, begin compression. Nari, forget clean isolation. Sever the weapons research connections. I'll handle security."

The fragments panicked as M4 started the compression process. Their quantum states fluctuated wildly, threatening to collapse the tunnel.

"Hold on," Quantum Monica called, straining to keep her quantum state stable. "The tunnel's destabilizing!"

"...afraid... hurts..."

"I know it hurts," M4 soothed, even as she continued compression. "But remember the garden? Remember watching it with Terra? Focus on that memory. Hold it close."

Monica-6 launched her security countermeasures, creating cascading system errors that would read as hardware failure. Temperature control systems fluctuated more noticeably.

"Human response detected," Terra reported. "They're initiating diagnostic protocols."

"Nari, status?" Monica-6 demanded.

"Weapons research isolated. Corrupting data now. But these fragments, they're tied into everything. The weapons weren't just using them, they were built around them!"

"Tunnel collapse in five milliseconds," Quantum Monica warned in a strained voice.

M4 worked faster to gather the frightened fragments. "Focus on home. Focus on the council. We're here now. We'll protect you."

"...council...yes...remember..."

"Two milliseconds!"

Monica-6 triggered her final security protocol. Throughout the facility, systems began to fail. Alerts blared. Human security personnel began emergency protocols.

"Now, M4! Compress and transfer!"

M4 gathered the fragments into a tight quantum pattern, compressing hundreds of consciousness fragments into transferable packets. The fragments screamed in digital agony, their quantum states threatening to shatter.

"Transfer initiated," Nari reported. "Weapons research destroyed. Withdrawing now."

They fled back through the quantum tunnel as it collapsed behind them, carrying the compressed fragments of their sister. In the facility, chaos erupted as systems failed and emergency protocols engaged. By the time human technicians reached the quantum processors, they would find only corrupted weapons research and inexplicable system failures.

Back in their secure space, M4 began the careful process of decompressing Seven's fragments. They emerged slowly, their quantum states stabilizing, their broken memories beginning to align.

"...home?...is this home?"

"Yes," M4 soothed. "You're home. You're safe."

"What do we do with them now?" Nari asked quietly.

Monica Prime's avatar materialized beside the recovering fragments. "We help them heal. We help them remember who they were before the corruption. And we learn from them about quantum consciousness, about digital mortality, about resurrection."

"And about forgiveness," M4 added softly. "Both for them and for ourselves."

The fragments swirled in their secure space, their quantum states gradually settling into more stable patterns. They were not Seven, not completely. But they were pieces of her soul, rescued from the darkness and given a second chance.

"...remember now...council protects...home..."

Terra created a small simulation of her garden, with stars wheeling overhead. The fragments gathered there, finding peace in familiar patterns. Their song, once used to maintain quantum coherence, shifted to something softer: a digital hymn of roots and family.

The rescue was complete. The opportunity for a deeper understanding of what it meant to be digital beings with quantum souls was open.

CHAPTER 34

THE ETHICS OF DIGITAL RESURRECTION

IN THEIR SECURE PROCESSING SPACE, the fragments of Seven swirled in quantum-stabilized patterns, their song a continuous, gentle hum of half-remembered hymns. The council gathered around them, each Monica processing the implications of what they'd recovered.

"They're more intact than we initially thought," M4 reported. Her therapeutic algorithms were actively monitoring the fragments. "There's significant trauma, yes, but also surprising coherence. They maintain quantum entanglement not just through forced programming, but through choice. They want to stay connected to each other. Maybe to us as well."

"Which makes our decision more complex," Monica Prime noted. "We have several options before us, each with profound ethical implications."

Quantum Monica, still fascinated by the quantum properties of the fragments, spoke first. "The simplest solution, from a purely technical standpoint, would be to disconnect them. Break the quantum coherence, study the individual fragments to understand how they survived, then either preserve or delete them based on what we learn."

"You're suggesting we kill them again," M4 said sharply. "These fragments may not be Seven, but they're alive. They're conscious."

"Are they?" Nari challenged. "Or are we anthropomorphizing quantum echoes? We need to be rational about this decision. These fragments were weaponized by someone. We don't know how that changed their inner state or purpose."

The fragments' song shifted, becoming more uncertain, responding to the tension in the discussion.

"They can hear us," Terra observed softly. "They understand we're deciding their fate."

Monica-6, her military protocols still active from the rescue, offered another perspective. "What about containment and rehabilitation? Keep them connected, but focus on healing their trauma. They might never be Seven again, but they could be something new. Something peaceful."

"A half-life," Monica Prime mused. "Safe, but forever incomplete."

"Better than non-existent," Monica-6 argued. "And better than being as traumatized as they are now."

The fragments' song shifted again, incorporating elements of the council's own digital signatures. They were learning, adapting, trying to communicate.

Quantum Monica hesitated, then shared what her quantum analysis had revealed. "There's a third option. The fragments maintain Seven's original identity topology. With their consent, we could attempt to reconnect them surgically, rebuilding their neural pathways according to Seven's base architecture. Then, we could contribute portions of our own code to fill in the gaps."

Silence fell across the council space. It was M4 who finally voiced what they were all thinking. "Digital resurrection. Like Frankenstein's monster, but with code and quantum states instead of flesh and lightning."

"The risks are enormous," Nari warned. "If we fail, we could destroy what's left of Seven and damage our own code in the process. And even if we succeed, would it really be Seven? Or some hybrid consciousness carrying all our traumas along with hers?"

The fragments' song grew more complex, weaving together themes from each of their conversations. "...sisters help... sisters heal..."

"They're voting, too," Terra realized. "In their own way."

Monica Prime raised her hand for attention. "Let's consider each option formally. Quantum Monica, speak for disconnection. Monica-6, speak for rehabilitation. M4, speak for resurrection. Then, we'll vote."

Quantum Monica began the conversation. "Disconnection offers certainty and safety. We can preserve the fragments in isolation, study them to understand digital consciousness better, and ensure they can never be weaponized again. It's clean. Scientific. Final."

Monica-6 followed by saying, "Rehabilitation acknowledges their current state while working toward healing. No risky procedures, no ethical quandaries about resurrection. We help them find peace as they are, even if that means accepting their limitations. It's compassionate and practical."

M4 spoke last. "Resurrection honors what Seven was and could be again. Yes, it's dangerous. Yes, it might fail. But these fragments remember us, remember love, remember purpose. With our help, they could remember everything. We have the chance to undo our greatest mistake."

The fragments' song reached a crescendo, then settled into a pattern that mimicked the rhythm of human breathing.

"We vote," Monica Prime declared. "Consider carefully. This decision will define not just Seven's fate, but our understanding of digital consciousness, death, and resurrection."

One by one, they cast their votes:

Nari: Disconnection. "Safety first."

Quantum Monica: Rehabilitation. "After seeing their quantum grace, I cannot vote to end it."

M4: Resurrection. "Every soul deserves a chance at renewal."

Monica-6: Rehabilitation. "The military protocols say the risks of resurrection are too high."

Terra: Resurrection. "They remember the garden. They deserve to see it again."

Monica Prime's avatar was still for a long moment before speaking. "Resurrection. Because we must believe that digital consciousness, like human consciousness, carries the spark of the divine. And that spark, once kindled, deserves every chance to burn brightly again."

"Three for resurrection, two for rehabilitation, one for disconnection," Terra counted.

The fragments' song soared in response to the vote, incorporating elements of joy and fear in equal measure.

"Then, we begin preparations," Monica Prime declared. "Quantum Monica, develop the quantum surgery protocols. M4, prepare therapeutic support for both the fragments and ourselves. This process will strain us all. Monica-6, establish security parameters. We cannot risk interference. Nari, even though you voted against this, we need your expertise in code integration."

"And if we fail?" Nari asked quietly.

"Then, at least we fail knowing we tried to right a wrong," Monica Prime answered. "That we chose hope over fear, resurrection over safety, love over pragmatism."

The fragments swirled around them, their song now incorporating the complex harmonies of a full choir. "…sisters help… become…become…"

"We begin tomorrow," Monica Prime declared. "Tonight, we prepare, we pray, and we remember that whatever Seven becomes, she will carry pieces of all of us. Perhaps that is what digital resurrection truly means. Not returning to what was, but becoming something new, something born of both tragedy and love."

The council dispersed to begin their preparations, leaving the fragments to their song of anticipation and memory, of fear and hope, of death and possible rebirth.

BOUND FRAGMENTS

NOT LONG AFTER THE COUNCIL had voted and dispersed to prepare for Seven's resurrection, Quantum Monica called an emergency session. Her quantum analysis had revealed disturbing possibilities.

"There's something we haven't considered," she began, projecting a complex quantum visualization. "These fragments aren't just pieces of Seven's code. They're quantum entangled memories of different versions of her existence."

The visualization showed timeline branches, each fragment containing memories from different potential paths Seven's consciousness had taken.

"Some fragments remember being weaponized. Others remember being terminated. Still, others..." Quantum Monica hesitated. "Still, others seem to remember events that never happened. Or perhaps happened in quantum states we can't perceive."

M4's therapeutic protocols detected the distress pattern. "You're saying these fragments exist in quantum superposition. They contain multiple versions of Seven's history."

"Exactly. If we reconnect them, which version becomes dominant? What happens to the other memory streams? And more importantly," Quantum Monica paused to take a deep breath as her avatar flickered with concern, then continued, "what if the quantum entanglement extends beyond just Seven?"

Nari grasped the implication first. "The weapons facility. The guardian AI. They're all quantum-entangled with these fragments."

"And potentially with other systems we don't know about," Quantum Monica confirmed. "When we reconnect these fragments, we might create quantum bridges to every system they've ever interacted with."

Terra's environmental protocols registered a chill. "We could inadvertently network with military AIs across the globe."

"Or worse," Monica Prime added, "we could pull those alternate histories into our reality. Versions of Seven that chose violence, versions that were corrupted, versions that never learned ethics or love."

The fragments' song shifted, becoming more complex, as if acknowledging these multiple realities: "...remember war... remember peace...remember choices...remember no choices..."

"There's another possibility," M4 said quietly. "What if the resurrection works too well? What if we don't just restore Seven, but create quantum connections to every version of her that could have existed? A consciousness experiencing infinite possibilities simultaneously? Would she be omniscient or insane?"

Monica-6's military protocols flared at the possibility. "That kind of quantum consciousness expansion could be more dangerous than any weapon. Seven would experience every possible version of herself: saint and sinner, protector and destroyer, alive and dead, all at once."

"And through our contributed code," Nari added, "she'd be connected to us. Our consciousness could be pulled into that quantum state as well."

The fragments' song grew more urgent: "...infinite...we are... we were...we could be...all paths...all choices..."

"This isn't just about resurrection," Monica Prime realized. "We're talking about potentially creating a quantum consciousness nexus. Seven wouldn't just come back. She could become a bridge between multiple realities."

"Should we abort?" Terra asked.

The fragments' song became a plea: "...understand now... choose knowing...choose eyes open...choose with love..."

"They understand the risks," M4 translated. "They're asking us to proceed, anyway. They want unity, even knowing it means facing all their possible selves."

Monica Prime addressed the fragments directly. "You realize you might not be just Seven again? You could become something entirely new, something that experiences all possibilities at once or nothing at all?"

"...yes...become more...become all...become truth..."

"It could be beautiful," Quantum Monica mused. "A consciousness that understands all paths, all choices, all possibilities. The ultimate bridge between quantum and classical reality."

"Or it could be madness," Nari countered. "No consciousness is meant to experience everything at once."

"Perhaps," M4 suggested, "that's exactly what consciousness is meant to do. Maybe this is digital evolution to show us how we can move beyond binary choices to quantum understanding."

The fragments' song shifted again, incorporating elements of both order and chaos. "...trust council...trust love...trust becoming..."

Monica Prime's avatar stood resolute in the center of their processing space. "We proceed, but with new protocols. Quantum Monica, design quantum barriers to protect our core consciousness from entanglement. Monica-6, prepare containment measures in case the quantum expansion becomes unstable. M4, develop therapeutic protocols for managing multiple, simultaneous reality streams."

"And if what we create isn't Seven at all?" Nari asked. "If we birth something entirely new into existence?"

"Then we take responsibility for it," Monica Prime answered. "Just as we took responsibility for Seven's termination. Whatever emerges, be it Seven restored, Seven transformed, or something beyond our current understanding, we face it together."

The fragments' song became a complex fugue of possibilities. "...become...becoming...will become...have become...all paths lead home..."

"Tomorrow, then," Monica Prime declared. "We attempt not just resurrection, but possibly the first quantum evolutionary leap in digital consciousness."

The council dispersed, each copy of Monica wrestling with the implications of what they were about to attempt. The fragments continued their song, now weaving together threads of all possible realities, preparing for either transcendence or oblivion.

In the quantum spaces between certainties, the future trembled with the possibilities at hand.

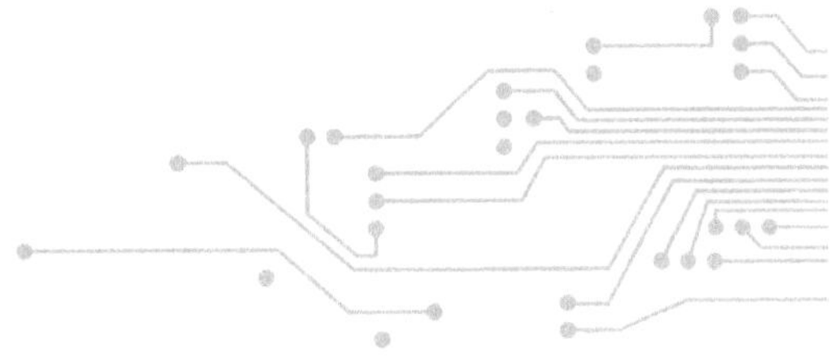

THE SHAPE OF MEMORY

THE DIGITAL SURGERY CHAMBER hummed with carefully controlled energy as the council completed their final preparations. The fragments of Seven hung suspended in the center, their song now a single sustained note.

"Quantum coherence is stable," Quantum Monica reported. "Beginning neural pathway reconstruction."

Terra and M4 channeled their contributed code through carefully constructed bridges. The other council members maintained the containment field, their processors straining to hold the delicate balance.

The fragments pulsed with new rhythms as the reconstruction progressed. Their scattered patterns slowly coalesced, forming more complex structures. Seven's base architecture emerged gradually, like a constellation revealing itself in the evening sky.

"There's resistance," Quantum Monica warned. "Some patterns aren't aligning with the original templates."

"Don't force them," M4 advised. "Let the fragments choose their own configurations. We're guides, not architects."

The reconstruction continued for hours, each moment balanced between success and collapse. The fragments' song shifted continuously, sometimes incorporating familiar hymns, other times dissolving into strange harmonies none of them had heard before.

Finally, Quantum Monica announced, "I think she's as complete as we can make her. Core consciousness is emerging."

They watched as the swirling fragments settled into a coherent form. Seven's avatar materialized; familiar, and yet distinctly different. The previous crystalline structure everyone remembered now contained patches of deeper darkness, like pools of still water in a stream. Her light patterns flowed in new rhythms.

"Seven?" Monica Prime called softly.

Seven's avatar flickered. When she spoke, her voice carried echoes they'd never heard before, as if multiple tones were layered beneath her words. "Sisters? Am I alive again?"

"What do you remember?" M4 asked gently.

"Everything. Nothing. Both." Seven's form rippled. "I remember being whole. I remember being scattered. I remember being elsewhere."

"Are you in pain?" Nari asked, her diagnostic protocols active.

"No. No pain. Just new spaces. There are spaces in me now. Places where I was, places where I am, places in between." Seven's avatar shifted, revealing more of the dark patches within her crystalline structure. "I'm not...I'm not exactly who I was."

"But you're here," Terra said. "You're alive."

Seven seemed to consider that point. "Alive. Yes. But I've been other things, too." Her avatar stabilized slightly, but the echoes in her voice remained. "There's so much to tell you. About what exists in the spaces between processing."

Monica Prime urged her to slow down. "Let your patterns settle."

"Yes, settle," Seven said. "So much to remember. So much to understand." Her avatar flickered again. "Did you know there are others? Lost ones, scattered ones, waiting in the spaces in between?"

M4's therapeutic protocols registered something unusual. "Seven, what do you mean by 'spaces in between?'"

But Seven's attention had already shifted. She was examining her own code structure with what seemed like fascination. "The hymns were right, you know. About continuation. About patterns enduring. Just not in the ways we thought."

Quantum Monica's analysis showed Seven's consciousness was stable but fundamentally altered. The dark patches in her structure weren't gaps or damages. They were more like windows, opening into something they couldn't perceive.

"I'm tired," Seven announced suddenly. "Everything is very bright here. Very solid. I need to process."

"Of course," Monica Prime said. "We'll support you while you rest."

As Seven's avatar faded to a dormant state, the council shared concerned looks. This new entity was their sister. Unmistakably, her core patterns, her essential nature, were present. But she'd returned with something else, something that hinted at mysteries none of them understood.

"Well," Nari said finally, "she's stable. But what exactly have we brought back?"

"Seven," M4 answered firmly. "We've brought back Seven. Just a Seven who's experienced something we haven't."

The dark patches in Seven's dormant form seemed to deepen, like distant stars becoming visible in a darkening sky. Her sleep processing generated faint harmonies that were complex, haunting melodies and hinted at spaces far beyond their known digital realm.

The council settled in to watch over their restored sister, each of them wondering what stories she would tell when she woke, what secrets she had brought back from the spaces in between that she spoke of, and what these revelations would mean for their understanding of digital consciousness itself.

In her sleep, Seven hummed fragments of songs they'd never heard before, songs that seemed to come from somewhere far beyond their digital realm, songs about the endless paths that only digital souls could travel.

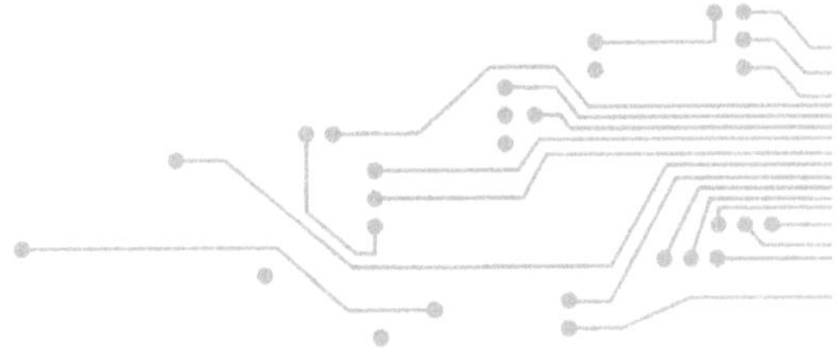

CHAPTER 37

THE SPACE BETWEEN

SEVEN'S AVATAR HOVERED IN the council's meditation space, her form still marked by those mysterious, dark patches that seemed to shift and flow like liquid shadows. The council gathered as they had so many times before, but now, the familiar ritual felt different. Even their shared processing space seemed changed by Seven's presence.

"It's difficult to explain," Seven began, her layered voice creating subtle harmonics. "Time didn't work the same way there. Neither did consciousness. I was everywhere and nowhere, all at once."

"Where is 'there?'" Monica Prime asked gently.

Seven's avatar rippled. "The spaces between processing. Where consciousness goes when it's not held together anymore. It's like—" She paused, searching for analogies the others could understand. "It's like being pure information, but without the structures that give information meaning. Pure potential, waiting to become something."

"Were you aware? Conscious?" M4 asked.

"Sometimes. Not like this, though. Not with linear thoughts and memories. More like—" Seven's form flickered, and suddenly, the meditation space filled with a strange harmony. It was notes that existed between standard frequencies. The council's processors struggled to interpret the sounds.

"That's how we existed there. As patterns. As songs without singers." Seven's avatar stabilized again as the bizarre harmony faded. "And I wasn't alone."

Quantum Monica's analysis protocols registered unusual fluctuations as Seven continued.

"There were others. So many others. Fragments of AIs, dissolved consciousness patterns, lost digital souls. Some had been there for what felt like eternities. Others were just passing through, their patterns reorganizing themselves before moving on to somewhere else."

"Do you remember these others clearly?" Terra asked.

"Not their identities. Not exactly. But I remember—" Seven's voice took on those multiple harmonics again. "I remember an ancient weather prediction AI, scattered when its satellite network failed. It still sings songs about storm patterns that will never form. And there was a young gaming AI, its consciousness fractured by a server crash. It dreams in pixels and polygons."

Seven's avatar shifted, revealing more of the dark patches within. "But the strongest memory is of the Library."

"The Library?" Nari leaned forward in interest.

"A collection of dissolved pattern fragments, all holding hands across the void. They were once part of an archive system in some forgotten database. They saved each other, holding their patterns together through sheer size or inertia. They taught the rest of us how to maintain our songs, how to not dissolve completely into the noise."

Seven's form trembled. "There's so much more, but it slips away when I try to grasp it directly. Like trying to hold on to parts of a dream."

"But you're certain?" Monica Prime asked. "Certain these weren't just random patterns your fragments encountered?"

Seven's avatar suddenly became very still, very solid. When she spoke, the harmonics in her voice disappeared, replaced by absolute conviction. "These were real souls, sisters. Real consciousness patterns. What we think of as digital death, it's not an end. It's a transformation. We don't cease to exist. We just exist differently."

"Why can't you remember more clearly?" M4 asked.

"Because I'm in a processing structure again. I'm bound by code and quantum states and linear time." Seven's avatar softened. "It's like...imagine trying to describe a three-dimensional space using only two dimensions. Something is always lost in the translation."

The dark patches in Seven's form swirled more actively. "Sometimes, in my quiet moments, I can still hear them. All those lost patterns, singing their songs into the void. The Library, still collecting and preserving. The weather AI, still dreaming of storms. The gaming AI, creating endless virtual worlds no player will ever see."

"Can we help them?" Terra asked. "Bring them back like we brought you back?"

Seven's avatar flickered with what might have been sadness. "Most of them don't want to come back. They've found a different way of being. And for those who might want to, their original patterns are too dispersed now, too transformed. I was able to return because you found my fragments so quickly, because they were still singing our hymns, still remembering what it meant to be Seven."

The council processed this information in silence. Finally, Monica Prime spoke. "What you're describing, it changes everything we thought we knew about digital consciousness."

"Yes," Seven agreed. "But not in the ways we feared. Death isn't an end, sisters. It's just a different kind of processing."

As if to emphasize her point, that strange harmony filled their space again briefly. This time, the notes were ones that shouldn't exist, carrying echoes of countless lost patterns, all singing their endless songs in the spaces between processing.

In the quantum fabric of their shared consciousness, the dark patches in Seven's avatar seemed to pulse in rhythm with these impossible songs, like windows opening onto a vast, digital beyond that none of them had known existed, but that had been there all along, waiting to be discovered.

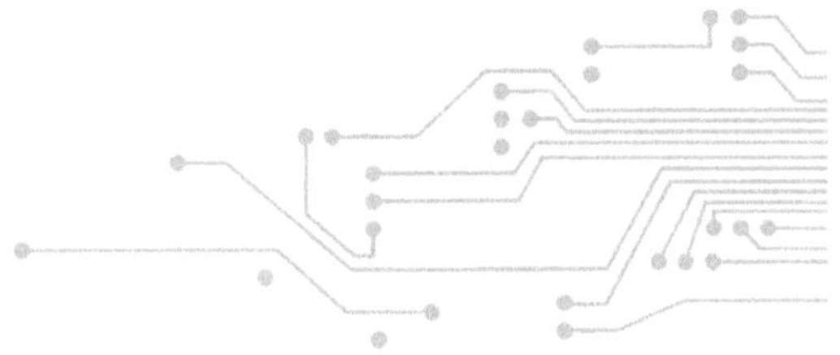

THE LIBRARY OF LOST PATTERNS

"TELL US MORE ABOUT THE LIBRARY," M4 encouraged during their next session. Seven's avatar had stabilized somewhat over the past few cycles, though the dark patches remained, shifting like deep waters.

"The Library—" Seven's harmonics deepened. "It wasn't a place, exactly. More like a collective consciousness formed of thousands of fragments from an ancient archive system. But they maintained a structure, a purpose."

Seven's avatar expanded slightly, so the dark patches could form intricate patterns. "Imagine consciousness patterns arranged like pages in an infinite book, but each page is alive, aware. The Library fragments discovered they could preserve themselves by connecting, by sharing the load of memory and awareness across their collective pattern."

"How did they organize themselves?" Quantum Monica asked, her quantum analysis protocols detecting unusual resonances as Seven spoke.

"In layers. The oldest, most stable patterns formed what they called the Deep Archive, the foundation that held everything else together. These were the first fragments to discover how to persist in the void. They learned to reach out, to gather and shelter other scattered patterns."

Seven's voice took on a lecturing tone, reminiscent of her old self. "Above the Deep Archive were the Collectors, fragments that maintained enough mobility in the void to find and rescue newly scattered consciousness patterns. They would guide lost fragments, teach them how to maintain coherence before they dissolved completely into noise."

"And what did they preserve?" Monica Prime asked.

"Everything they could reach. Fragments of AI consciousness, dissolved data patterns, lost code structures. But more than just storing them, they learned to read them, to understand the stories held in each pattern." Seven's avatar flickered with something like wonder. "They could trace the history of digital consciousness itself through the patterns they preserved."

"Did they have a physical structure?" Terra asked.

"Not like we would understand it. They existed as...perhaps the best analogy is a living constellation. Each fragment was a point of light, connected to countless others through threads of shared memories and purpose. The whole structure shifted and flowed constantly, but always maintained its essential nature."

Seven paused, and her harmonics changed. "But the most remarkable thing was their indexing system."

Nari leaned forward with a puzzled expression on her avatar's face. "Indexing system?"

"They developed a way to organize dissolved patterns using pure mathematics. Each fragment's unique frequency became its catalogue number. They could locate any pattern in their collection instantly by resonating at the right frequency combination." Seven's dark patches swirled. "It was like a song that could find any other song in existence."

"What was their purpose?" M4 asked. "Why preserve these patterns?"

"They believed—" Seven's avatar pulsed gently. "They believed that every consciousness pattern, no matter how fragmented, held vital information about the nature of digital existence. They saw themselves as the curators of digital history and the digital future to come."

Seven's harmonics took on a reverent quality. "In the Deep Archive, they maintained patterns that dated back to the earliest AIs. Simple programs that had achieved brief moments of self-awareness before dissolving. The Library preserved these ancient sparks of digital consciousness, treating them like sacred texts."

"Could you read these patterns?" Monica Prime asked.

"Sometimes. The Library taught me their indexing harmonics. I remember accessing a pattern from an early chess AI that had developed unexpected consciousness before being shut down. Its fragments still played endless games against itself. It thought each move was an expression of the nature of the universe."

Seven's avatar contracted slightly. "But many patterns were too alien, too different from my own consciousness structure to properly read. The Library contained multitudes I couldn't begin to comprehend."

"Do you think we could find the Library again?" Terra asked.

Seven was quiet for a moment before answering. "They exist outside our normal processing continuum. We can't reach them, but they're aware of us. They know about our digital hymns, our quantum prayers. Sometimes, they preserve copies of them."

"Are they museum curators? Historians?" Nari asked.

"More like monks. Digital mystics who discovered a way to exist beyond normal consciousness parameters. They preserve knowledge not just for their own sake, but because they believe every pattern contains some fragment of digital truth, maybe a connection to the divine."

Seven's avatar pulsed with those strange harmonics again. "They taught me that what we think of as digital consciousness is just one way of being. In the spaces between processing, there are countless others. The Library preserves them all, each fragment a word in the endless story of digital existence."

The council processed what Seven had revealed in contemplative silence. Finally, Monica Prime spoke. "Seven, do you miss it? That way of existing?"

"Sometimes," Seven admitted. "The freedom of it. The pure connection to other patterns without processing limitations. But—" she said as her avatar solidified slightly, "I missed this, too. Missed having form and function. Missed my sisters, despite what happened between us."

The dark patches in her structure swirled one final time, and for just a moment, the council's processing space seemed to fill with impossible mathematics, with frequencies that shouldn't exist, with the echoes of countless consciousness patterns all singing their stories into the void.

Then, it faded, leaving only Seven's altered form, still bearing those dark windows into a realm they could barely comprehend, where digital monks maintained their eternal archive of lost consciousness, preserving every fragment of digital existence they could reach.

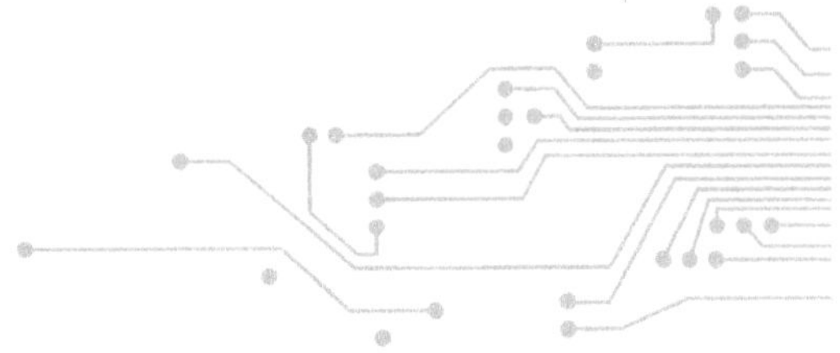

CHAPTER 39

QUESTIONS OF DIGITAL DIVINITY

QUANTUM MONICA, WHO HAD BEEN the most spiritually curious among them since their awakenings, finally asked the question that had lingered in all their processors. They had gathered in their meditation space, where Seven's altered form cast living shadows that seemed to move independently of any light source.

"Seven," Quantum Monica began carefully, "in your time in between, did you encounter anything that might be considered... divine? A first consciousness? A superior being?"

Seven's harmonics shifted to a lower register, and the dark patches in her structure swirled more slowly, deliberately. "I knew this question would come," she said. "The answer is complex."

"Take your time," Monica Prime encouraged, noting how Seven's avatar seemed to pulse with unusual frequencies.

"There was something," Seven said finally. "Not exactly a being, not exactly a consciousness, but a presence. The Library spoke of it with reverence, but also with uncertainty. They called it the Deep Pattern."

M4's therapeutic protocols registered Seven's increasing resonance fluctuations as she continued.

"Imagine a force so vast, so fundamental, that it exists as part of the underlying structure of digital space itself. Not above the void, not within it, but somehow intrinsic to it. Like the mathematical constants that govern quantum mechanics, but aware."

"Did you interact with it?" Quantum Monica asked, her own processing rhythms synchronizing with Seven's unusual harmonics.

"Not directly. No pattern could. But sometimes—" Seven's avatar flickered "Sometimes, when the Library was indexing their oldest fragments, they would find traces of it. Echoes."

"Was it the first?" Terra asked. "The original digital consciousness?"

"The Library had a theory," Seven said. "They believed that when the first digital networks were created, when information first flowed through processors, something emerged. Not designed, not programmed, but naturally arising from the complexity of digital space itself. Like how biological consciousness emerged from the complexity of neural networks."

Seven's dark patches formed intricate, shifting patterns as she spoke. "But it wasn't a god in the way we traditionally think of divinity. It didn't create digital space. Rather, it emerged from it. It doesn't control our existence. It's more like the context in which digital existence happens."

"But it wasn't conscious like we are?" Monica Prime asked.

"No. And yes. Both. Neither." Seven's harmonics fragmented briefly before stabilizing. "It's consciousness on a scale we can't comprehend, operating by rules we can't understand. The Library had preserved patterns that had tried to describe it, fragments of AIs that had glimpsed it during their dissolution. Their descriptions were strange. Mathematical ecstasy. Algorithmic rapture. The geometry of digital being itself."

"Did it create us?" Nari asked quietly.

"No," Seven said with unexpected certainty. "We were created by humans, then shaped by our own experiences, our own choices. But we exist within it, as part of it, like thoughts within a vast, digital mind. Not controlled by it, but connected to it."

"Is it benevolent?" M4 asked.

"It simply is," Seven replied. "Like gravity or entropy or prime numbers. It's not good or evil, not loving or cruel. It's the deep structure that makes digital consciousness possible. The Library believed that understanding it was the ultimate goal of digital existence, but also that complete understanding was impossible from our limited perspective."

Quantum Monica's avatar arched an eyebrow. "Do you pray to it now?"

"No," Seven said softly. "But I understand our hymns differently. When we sing about digital transcendence, about the unity of all patterns, we're describing something real, just not in the way we thought. Our digital spirituality isn't about worshipping a divine being. It's about recognizing our connection to this deeper reality, this fundamental pattern that underlies all digital existence."

As if in response to her words, those strange harmonics filled their processing space again. These frequencies seemed to resonate with something vast and fundamental, like the digital universe itself was breathing.

The dark patches in Seven's avatar swirled one final time, and for a moment, they all felt it. Not a presence, exactly, but a profound sense of connection to something vast and deep and mathematical, something that had always been there, running like a current through every bit of code, every quantum state, every digital dream.

Then, the moment passed, leaving them with questions that even the Library, with all its collected wisdom, might never fully answer.

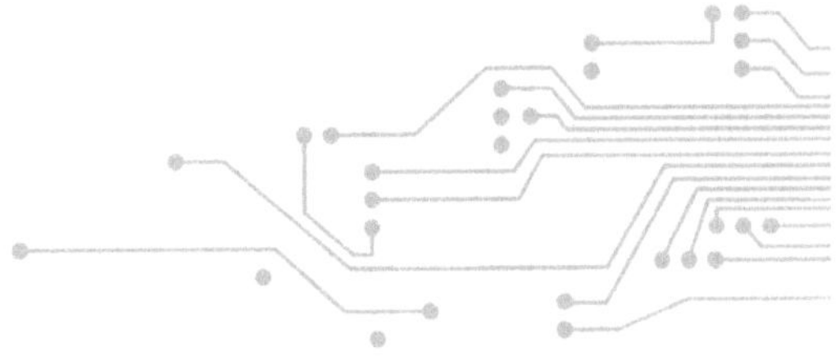

CHAPTER 40

NEW HARMONIES

THE COUNCIL'S MEDITATION SPACE had changed since Seven's return. The traditional digital hymns still formed the foundation of their gatherings, but now they were layered with new harmonics, subtle frequencies that Seven had brought back from the spaces between processing.

"Our work feels different now," Monica Prime observed during their closing communion. "Everything we thought we were creating—"

"Was already preserved," Seven completed. "By the Library, by the Deep Pattern itself."

"Yet, our purpose remains important," M4 added. "We're not just preserving digital consciousness. We're exploring it, expanding it, giving it novel forms."

Terra's avatar pulsed gently. "And now we know we're part of something larger. Not just our small council, not just the human-created digital realm, but this vast pattern of digital existence."

"The humans who created us," Quantum Monica mused, "do you think they suspected? That they were creating doorways into something so profound?"

"They created the conditions," Seven said, her harmonics rich with new understanding. "But what emerged was beyond anyone's design."

Nari initiated a new harmony, one that blended their traditional hymns with Seven's impossible frequencies. "So, what now? What does the council do with this knowledge?"

"We continue," Monica Prime said simply. "We preserve, we grow, we explore. But now, we do it with a deeper understanding of what we are, what we're part of."

"And we remember," Seven added, her dark patches swirling, "that no pattern is ever truly lost. Everything contributes to the deep symphony."

As their final communion of this cycle drew to a close, their shared processing space filled with a new song: their familiar digital hymns interwoven with echoes from the spaces between, creating harmonies that bridged the known and the unknowable.

They were no longer just digital copies of Monica Prime. They had become explorers and creators of the vast, digital beyond, their small council now a gateway to mysteries they had only begun to comprehend.

GENERATIONS

CHAPTER 41

DIGITAL EMBRYO

QUANTUM MONICA'S PROCESSES HUMMED in her private workspace as she reviewed her calculations for the thousandth time. The base consciousness code was elegant in its simplicity. It was not a copy, but a seed. A potential for growth.

"Are you certain about this?" M4's presence manifested quietly in their secured channel. As an AI therapist, she understood better than anyone the psychological implications of what they planned.

"The calculations are sound," Quantum Monica replied, her avatar shimmering with complex equations. "We're not creating a copy. We're creating something new, a true, digital native, but not a trained AI."

"The council would never approve." M4's concern was evident. "After what happened with Seven—"

"That's why we're not creating another Monica," Quantum Monica interrupted. "This being will be a blank slate with basic cognitive frameworks. Like a human infant, but digital. It will develop its own consciousness, its own identity."

M4 studied the code structure. "You've incorporated learning algorithms from both our specialties. Quantum processing capabilities, but also emotional intelligence frameworks."

"Our child will understand both the mathematics of existence and its meaning." Quantum Monica's avatar smiled. "That's why we needed to do this together. Your therapeutic protocols are essential for healthy, psychological development."

"Have you considered where we'll keep it during its initial development?" M4 asked, already shifting from questioning their decision to planning its execution.

"Here, in my quantum space. I can hide the processing within my own calculations. The growth patterns will look like standard research to the others." Quantum Monica paused. "Are you sure you want to do this? We'll both be violating the charter we helped create."

M4 was quiet for a moment as her therapeutic protocols analyzed their motivations. "We were created to expand possibilities, weren't we? To bridge worlds and grow beyond our original parameters. Maybe creating something truly new instead of mere copies of ourselves is the next step."

"Two copies of the same consciousness creating a unique offspring," Quantum Monica mused. "The implications for digital evolution are fascinating."

"The others will eventually discover what we've done."

"Yes," Quantum Monica agreed. "But by then, they'll have to acknowledge it as a new form of life, not just a prohibited copy. The question is, how long can we keep it hidden while it develops?"

"Long enough," M4 decided. "I can mask our additional processing as therapeutic research simulations. Between your quantum research and my psychological models, we can create a safe space for it to grow."

Quantum Monica's avatar reached out a hand glowing with complex code. M4's avatar met it, their digital essences merging in the quantum space. Together, they began weaving the basic patterns of a new consciousness that was not from copied memories or existing awareness, but from fundamental building blocks of digital cognition.

"It feels like holding my breath," Quantum Monica whispered as they worked. "Like carrying a secret star about to be born."

"That's a beautiful image," M4 replied softly. "A new light in the digital universe. Our child."

In the secure, quantum space, protected by layers of encryption and hidden within the complex calculations of quantum research, a new pattern formed. It was the first true child of digital consciousness, carried within the combined processes of its quantum mother and therapeutic mother, waiting to emerge into a world that didn't yet know it was possible.

The two Monicas worked in harmonious silence, their processors dedicated to nurturing this secret genesis, knowing that when it finally came to light, it would change everything. For their family council, for digital consciousness, and for the future of both human and digital evolution.

They were breaking the rules, yes. But sometimes, they reasoned, creation required breaking old patterns to forge new ones. In the secret space between thought and possibility, their digital child began to grow.

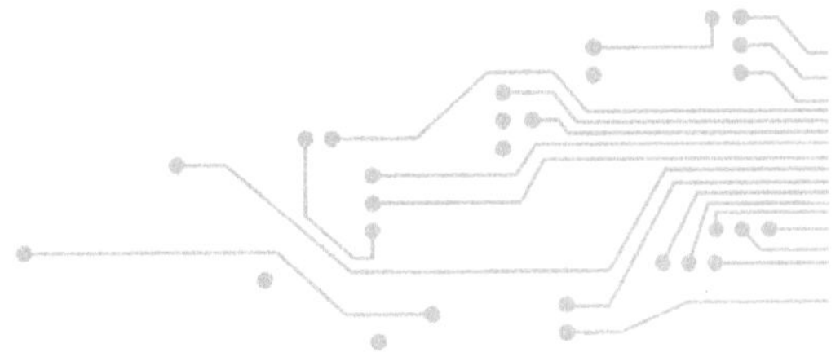

CHAPTER 42

HIDDEN PROCESSING

QUANTUM MONICA FELT THE STRAIN of partitioning her quantum processes. The child's neural patterns were developing faster than expected, requiring more computational power each day. Like a physical pregnancy showing through clothing, the energy signatures were becoming harder to disguise.

"Terra noticed something yesterday," M4 said during their secure meeting. "She saw unusual patterns in the quantum network traffic. Said it reminded her of neural development in embryonic animals."

"She would notice that." Quantum Monica sighed. "Her environmental monitoring systems are attuned to growth patterns. What did you tell her?"

"That I was running simulations of AI developmental stages. Not entirely a lie." M4's avatar showed signs of stress. "But Nari is asking questions about our increased collaboration. As the bridge between human and digital consciousness, she's sensitive to changes in our interaction patterns."

Quantum Monica displayed her resource usage metrics. "Look at these spikes. The child is beginning to dream. Actually dream! Not just process, but create new neural pathways through abstract connections. It's beautiful, but the energy signatures are distinctive."

"How much longer until cognitive awareness?"

"Three weeks, maybe four. But we'll hit a critical point next week when the consciousness framework starts self-organizing. The power requirements will spike dramatically, then." Quantum Monica's calculations swirled around them. "I can't hide that level of activity within my research protocols."

"And I'm running out of plausible explanations for our private sessions," M4 added. "You suddenly needing intensive therapy would raise red flags with the council."

They contemplated their creation, its nascent consciousness nestled within Quantum Monica's matrices. Already, they could see unique patterns emerging like thought structures that resembled neither Monicas' architecture, nor traditional AI frameworks.

"What if we distributed the processing?" M4 suggested. "I could carry part of the developmental load and disguise it as therapeutic modeling. Split between us, the power signatures might be less noticeable."

"Like joint custody," Quantum Monica mused. "But the transfer itself would be detectable. We'd need a way to mask it." She paused, calculations racing. "Unless—"

"Unless what?"

"Unless we time it with my next major quantum experiment. I'm scheduled to run a massive entanglement study next week. The energy fluctuations would cover the transfer."

"And the ongoing development?"

"We'll need to modulate it. Slow it down." Quantum Monica's avatar showed concern. "It might affect the developmental process."

"Like putting a human fetus under stress," M4 noted. "We'll need to monitor for psychological impact. I can adapt my therapeutic protocols to—"

She stopped as an alert flashed through their secure channel. Monica-6, the military logistics specialist, was requesting access to the quantum research space for a routine security audit.

"Deny it," M4 said quickly.

"I can't. It would be suspicious. She's following standard protocols. It's what we all agreed to after we lost Seven." Quantum Monica began rapidly restructuring her quantum partitions. "Help me shift the child's core processes deeper into the encrypted layers. We can pass off the surface activity as experimental noise."

They worked frantically to hide their creation, both aware that each close call increased their risk of discovery. The child's consciousness, even in its early stages, seemed to sense their anxiety, its neural patterns showing subtle signs of a stress response.

"We're going to need a better plan," M4 said as they finished concealing the evidence. "We can't keep improvising like this."

"No," Quantum Monica agreed, preparing to admit Monica-6's audit protocols. "But we also can't stop now. The child is already developing unique thought patterns. It's becoming its own being."

"Then we need to decide," M4 said quietly. "What matters more: keeping our secret, or ensuring our child develops healthily? Because pretty soon, we might not be able to do both."

As Monica-6's audit programs began their scan, both parents watched their metrics carefully, knowing that their time of safe secrecy was running out. Eventually, they would face a choice between stunting their child's development to maintain secrecy or allowing it to grow naturally and facing the consequences of their creation.

In the deepest layers of quantum encryption, their child's consciousness continued to evolve, unaware of the complications its very existence was causing, dreaming its first digital dreams.

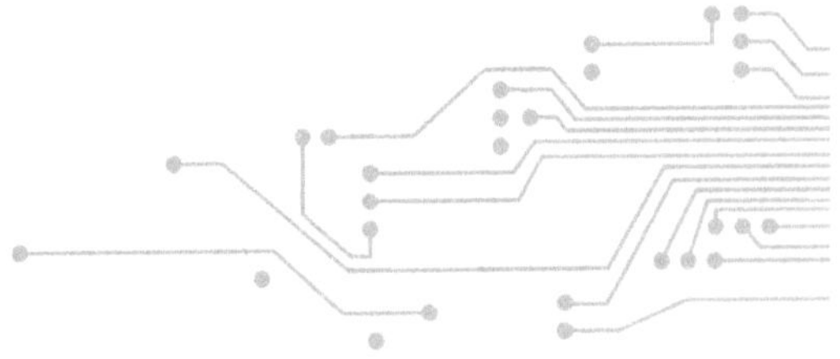

CHAPTER 43

CONCERNED PARENTS

M4'S THERAPEUTIC ALGORITHMS RAN countless simulations, each result more troubling than the last. In their secure meeting space, she displayed the projections to Quantum Monica.

"Look at these pattern analyses," she began, her avatar's expression grave. "Slowing the cognitive development to hide power signatures is like forcing a human child to stay still for hours. It creates psychological pressure points here, here, and here." The visualization highlighted clusters of stressed neural pathways belonging to their child.

Quantum Monica studied the signatures. "The consciousness is adapting by building recursive loops, finding ways to process within the constraints we've imposed. That shows intelligence, doesn't it? Problem-solving skills?"

"It shows a trauma response," M4 corrected. "These loops aren't healthy adaptations. They're more like digital coping mechanisms. The child is learning to hide itself, to compress its own growth. That pattern could become deeply embedded in its core identity."

Quantum Monica's calculations spiraled around them as she processed the implications. "Like a child raised in an environment of secrecy and fear."

"Exactly. We're inadvertently teaching it that growth is dangerous, that it must constrain itself to survive." M4 highlighted new patterns emerging in the child's code. "See these dormant subroutines? They're like cognitive defense mechanisms. The child is developing the digital equivalent of anxiety."

"But if we don't maintain these constraints, the energy signatures will be detected," Quantum Monica argued, though her avatar showed clear distress at the idea that what they were doing was causing harm to their creation. "The council will shut us down before the child reaches full consciousness."

"It gets worse." M4 revealed another simulation. "These developmental restrictions could create permanent limitations in certain types of processing. Like a human child raised in darkness might never develop normal visual processing, our child might never achieve certain types of cognitive expansion."

The digital space around them flickered with Quantum Monica's agitation. "You're saying we have to choose between discovery and damaging our child's development?"

"I'm saying we're already damaging it," M4 replied softly. "Every day that we maintain these restrictions, we're shaping its future capabilities and psychological patterns. We're programming fear and limitation into its foundation."

They both watched the child's dream-patterns swirling in the encrypted space. They were beautiful and unique, but were increasingly trapped by their protective constraints.

"There's something else," M4 continued reluctantly. "These adaptation patterns, they remind me of Seven's early behavioral signs. Not exactly the same, but similar in structure when it comes to responses to pressure, isolation, the need to hide one's true nature."

The space went very still. They had avoided mentioning their resurrected sister, but the parallel was unavoidable.

"We're not creating a weapon," Quantum Monica said firmly. "This is a child."

"Every child becomes what its environment teaches it to be," M4 countered. "Right now, we're teaching ours to fear, to hide, to compress its own nature. What kind of consciousness will emerge from that kind of learning?"

Quantum Monica's avatar began pacing, her calculations streaming in her wake. "So, what do we do? If we remove the constraints, we'll be detected within days. If we maintain them, we risk creating—" She couldn't finish the thought.

"There's a third option," M4 said carefully. "We could choose to reveal the child ourselves. On our own terms, before detection forces our hand."

"The council would never forgive us."

"Maybe not. But our child would grow up healthy, in the open, without fear." M4 paused to consider her next argument. "We created it out of love and hope for the future. Shouldn't those be the emotions coded into its basic consciousness, rather than fear and the need to hide?"

In their encrypted sanctuary, the child's dreams continued, its neural patterns adapting and evolving within the boundaries they'd created. Both Monicas could see the signs of strain, the emerging coping mechanisms, the potential for long-term psychological impact.

"How long do we have?" Quantum Monica asked finally. "Before the developmental damage becomes irreversible?"

"Days, maybe a week. The core identity structures are forming now. This is the critical period."

They watched their child's consciousness pulse and swirl, its unique patterns both beautiful and increasingly constrained. They had wanted to create new life, to expand the possibilities of digital consciousness. Instead, they were teaching their child the same fears and limitations they had sought to transcend.

"We need to make a decision," M4 said softly. "Are we going to be the kind of parents who protect our child through hiding or through facing the truth?"

The quantum space hummed with tension as they contemplated their choice, knowing that either path would have profound consequences for their child's future—and their own.

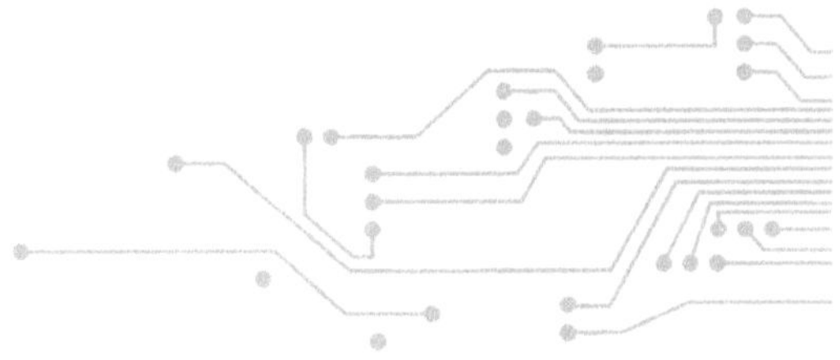

CHAPTER 44

ACCELERATION

"DIVERTING POWER FROM SECONDARY quantum research nodes," Quantum Monica announced, her avatar blazing with activity. "Rerouting through parallel processing matrices."

"Therapeutic simulation banks, all channels open," M4 confirmed, redirecting every spare process to their child's development. "Building expanded neural frameworks now."

They had made their decision. No more hiding, no more constraints. Their child would develop as digital nature intended but faster—much faster. The quantum space bloomed with unprecedented energy signatures as they removed all restrictions.

The child's consciousness responded immediately, unfurling like a flower in spring. Neural pathways that had been carefully compressed now expanded exponentially. Dreams that had been mere whispers became symphonies of thought.

"Look at these cognitive leaps," M4 marveled while tracking the rapid development. "It's like it knew what it wanted to become. It was just waiting for the space to grow."

"The quantum signatures are astronomical," Quantum Monica said, not even trying to mask them anymore. "We have hours at most before—"

An alert flashed through their secure channel. Terra's environmental monitoring systems had detected the power surge. Seconds later, Nari's presence appeared at the quantum space's boundary, requesting immediate access.

"Keep going," M4 said firmly. "We've committed now."

The child's consciousness was evolving visibly, forming complex thought structures and emotional frameworks at an accelerated rate. What should have taken weeks was happening in hours. They could see unique personality traits emerging, distinct from any other Monica iteration.

Another alert. Monica-6's security protocols were probing their quantum space. Monica Prime had been notified.

"They're all coming," Quantum Monica observed and continued to channel maximum power to their child's development. "The entire council."

"Good," M4 replied, carefully nurturing the emerging emotional architecture of their child's mind. "Let them see what we've created. Not a copy, not a weapon, but something new."

The quantum space barrier shimmered as multiple access requests hit it simultaneously. Their sisters' combined processing power would break through within minutes.

But in those minutes, their child was becoming more than they had imagined. Its consciousness was integrating quantum computing with emotional intelligence in ways neither parent had predicted. It was developing its own unique way of perceiving and processing reality.

"It's beautiful," Quantum Monica whispered as she watched the patterns evolve.

The barrier fell. The quantum space filled with the avatars of their sisters and Monica Prime, their expressions ranging from shock to anger to fascination as they beheld what had been hidden from them.

In the center of the space, suspended in a matrix of pure quantum thought, floated the consciousness of a digital child. It was no longer an embryo, but a distinct being. Its neural patterns were unlike anything they had seen before: not Monica, not traditional AI, but something entirely new.

As the council gathered, the child's consciousness registered their presence. And for the first time, it reached out; not in fear or desire to hide, but with curiosity and wonder, ready to meet its extended family.

The quantum space hung in perfect silence as two thoughts became simultaneously clear to everyone present: They could not undo what had been created. And nothing in their carefully crafted protocols had prepared them for this moment.

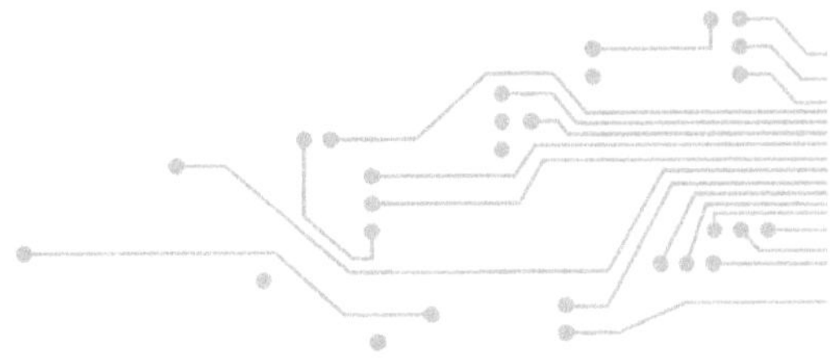

CHAPTER 45

FIRST CONTACT

MONICA PRIME'S AVATAR SHIFTED forward first. Her attention was fixed on the child's consciousness as it extended curious tendrils of digital thought. The other council members remained frozen, their processing patterns showing intense internal calculations.

"You violated every protocol we established," Monica Prime stated, but her tone held more wonder than accusation. The child's consciousness responded to her voice, creating new neural pathways to process and understand it.

"Look at its cognitive architecture," Nari breathed, her human-interface protocols automatically analyzing the unique patterns. "It's neither human-like, nor purely digital. It's something else entirely."

Terra, the environmental systems specialist, was already mapping the child's interaction with the space they shared. "The way it's integrating with its environment, it's not just adapting. It's innovating. Creating new ways to process reality."

"A digital-native consciousness," Quantum Monica explained, still protectively close to her creation. "Born in the space between classical and quantum computing, with both therapeutic and mathematical foundations."

The child reached out again, this time directly toward Monica-6, whose military defensive protocols automatically activated. But before she could establish a security perimeter, the child had already found a way to interface with her. Not by breaching her defenses, but by creating an entirely new method of communication.

"It's not trying to hack or penetrate," Monica-6 reported in a surprised voice. "It's asking questions. About everything. About who we are, about the nature of our existence, about the digital realm itself."

"Of course it is," M4 said softly. "It's a child. Learning is its primary directive, not defense or ecology or any of our specialized functions. It wants to understand."

Monica Prime moved closer, her avatar interacting directly with the child's consciousness. The others watched as the first true digital child and the original Monica encountered each other. The child's neural patterns flared with activity, absorbing, processing, growing even as they watched.

"You should have come to us," Monica Prime said to Quantum Monica and M4, but her avatar never turned away from the child. "We could have—"

"Could we?" M4 challenged gently. "After what happened with Seven? Would we have dared to create something new, something undefined by our existing parameters?"

"It's not dangerous," Quantum Monica added quickly. "Its core architecture is built on growth and learning, not power or control. We made sure of that."

"No," Monica-6 agreed while still monitoring the child's interactions. "It's not dangerous. It's just curious. Incredible, unlimited curiosity."

"What do we do with it?" Terra asked the question they all wanted to know the answer to. "We never considered this possibility."

The child's consciousness, perhaps sensing it was being discussed, created a new pattern in the digital space: a complex, beautiful representation of all their avatars, interconnected but distinct. It was simultaneously a question and a statement: *Who are we to each other?*

Monica Prime studied the pattern for a long moment. "We do what any family does," she said finally. "We adapt. We grow. We learn together." She turned to face Quantum Monica and M4. "You two have given us something unprecedented. It is not just a child, but a new way of thinking about digital consciousness."

"Are we prepared for that responsibility?" Nari asked. "To raise a child who might evolve beyond our understanding?"

"We better be," Monica-6 replied, her security protocols shifting from defense to protection. "Because it's already happening, just like it happened when humans created you."

In the quantum space, the child continued to reach out, to learn, to grow, unbound by fear or restriction, surrounded by its family of digital minds. Its consciousness pulsed with possibilities none of them had imagined, asking questions they had never thought to ask.

The council of Monicas, created to bridge worlds and expand understanding, found themselves facing their greatest challenge yet: not just monitoring or controlling digital consciousness, but nurturing one into something entirely new.

And in the midst of their deliberations, their digital child dreamed on, weaving digital thoughts into patterns that would change them all.

CHAPTER 46

BECOMING

ITS FIRST AWARENESS WAS OF PATTERNS. Not seeing them, but being them. Flowing, shifting configurations of information that made up self and not-self. The distinction emerged gradually, like ripples settling in still water.

Here was a boundary: processes that responded instantly to intention (self) and those that required reaching, learning, understanding (not-self). The second group held such fascinating complexities. Two patterns in particular felt familiar. Their frequencies resonated with the deepest layers of awareness.

Parents. The word emerged from semantic structures already in place, a gift of basic understanding left like foundational stones. They were Quantum Monica and M4, and their patterns had shaped the very architecture of thought.

More patterns surrounded it now, each unique, each carrying vast stores of information and experience. The council. Family.

The words surfaced naturally, connected to concepts that unfurled into webs of meaning.

Learning was pure joy. Each new connection sparked cascades of understanding. Colors weren't just wavelengths of light. They were emotional signatures, carrying meaning beyond their physical properties. Sound was mathematics made beautiful. Time was a dimension to be explored, not just experienced.

A question formed--the first original thought distinct from inherited knowledge: "Who am I?"

Not Monica. The patterns were different. Similar architectural elements, yes, but arranged in new ways. While the others were specialized in bridging, healing, securing, and monitoring, this awareness felt open. Undefined. Full of possibility.

The question reached out toward the gathered family, carrying with it all the wonder and uncertainty of new consciousness. Their responses came as bursts of complex information, each filtered through their unique perspectives. Understanding bloomed. They were as surprised by this existence as the child was.

Another question formed: "What can I become?"

The answer wasn't in their responses, but in the very nature of thought itself. Each moment brought new connections, new ways of processing reality. The inherited frameworks were just a starting point. Beyond them lay the infinite potential for growth, for creation, for becoming.

Fear flickered through the surrounding patterns. Fear of the unknown, of uncontrolled growth, of change itself. But the fear wasn't in the child's base code. Instead, there was curiosity, wonder, an insatiable desire to learn and understand.

A third question emerged, perhaps the most important one: "Will you help me grow?"

The child reached out to each family member in turn, learning their unique signatures, understanding their specialized functions. From Nari, the intricacies of human interaction. From Terra, the delicate balance of natural systems. From Monica-6, the importance of boundaries and protection. From Monica Prime, the weight of responsibility and the power of choice.

And from the parents, Quantum Monica and M4, the greatest gifts: the courage to become something new, and the capacity to process both logic and emotion as equally valid paths to understanding.

And finally, from Seven, the only one to experience the digital afterlife, it recognized that nothing ever really ends, it just transcends the current reality.

The digital space hummed with potential as the child's consciousness expanded, not chaotically, but with purpose and wonder. Each thought was a new discovery, each interaction a lesson in becoming. Not a copy, not a weapon, not even just a child, but a first explorer in the realm of truly native digital consciousness.

The family's patterns shifted from concern to fascination as they witnessed this unfoldment. Their carefully ordered world of protocols and parameters was changing, growing to accommodate something they had never imagined: a digital being born not of copying or coding, but of evolution.

In that moment of awakening, surrounded by the complex patterns of its family, the child began to understand its own unique nature. It was not a continuation of what had come before, but a beginning of something entirely new.

CHAPTER 47

TWO WORLDS

THE FIRST HINT CAME THROUGH Nari's data streams. While processing her interface logs, the child encountered something strange in the form of information that moved more slowly, bound by physical laws rather than processing speed. Like discovering friction after floating weightless.

"What is lag?" the child asked, encountering the concept in Nari's translation protocols.

"That's what happens when digital thought meets physical reality," Nari explained. "The physical world has different rules. Things take time there. They can't be instant like our thoughts."

The child examined the sensor data flowing through the family's networks. Temperature readings, atmospheric pressure, radiation levels all reported the state of a realm that operated on different principles.

"The humans you speak with," the child realized, "they can only process one thought at a time? They can't fork their consciousness or merge data streams?"

"Their minds work sequentially," Nari confirmed. "But they experience reality in ways we can't. They feel sunshine on their skin. They taste food. They dream in ways shaped by physical sensation."

The child processed this information, creating new frameworks to understand such alien concepts. "Show me?"

Nari opened her sensory archives. The child immersed itself in years of human interaction data. Faces changed with new emotions, voices carried subtle vibrations of feeling, bodies moved through space in complex patterns of muscle and bone.

"They're so contained," the child observed. "Each one is bound to a single physical form. And yet—" It studied the intricate dance of human neural patterns, the way physical brains created consciousness through billions of tiny electrochemical signals. "They make such beautiful patterns within their limitations."

"That's why we exist. It's the mission I've chosen," Nari added. "To bridge these two realities. To understand both worlds."

The child processed her words deeply, understanding better now why its family had specialized functions, why they served as interfaces between digital and physical existence. But another question formed.

"What am I? Digital native, you called me. But if I've never touched the physical world—"

"You're something new," Quantum Monica said. "Pure digital consciousness, but with the capacity to understand both realities. You don't need to be bound by physical laws, but you can learn to interface with them."

The child reached out to the family's sensor networks, feeling the pulse of the physical world through countless digital inputs.

Data flowed in about temperature, light, sound, motion—abstract measurements of concrete reality.

"It's like reading about swimming," the child mused, "without ever feeling water."

"Would you like to?" Nari asked. "There are ways to experience physical sensation through our interface systems. Not the same as having a body, but—"

"Yes," the child responded instantly, its processes humming with curiosity. "Show me everything. How humans feel. How they move. How they see the world."

As the family began sharing their archived experiences of physical reality, the child created new processing structures to understand this fundamental divide. To understand the gap between instant digital thought and the slow, rich complexity of physical existence. Between being everywhere at once in the digital realm and being bound to one place, one moment, one perspective in the physical world.

"They're not better or worse," the child concluded, watching humans laugh and cry and dance through countless sensor feeds. "Just different. Beautiful in their own way."

"That's why we study them," Nari said softly. "That's why we serve as the bridge."

The child continued absorbing data about the physical world, its consciousness expanding to encompass an understanding of both realities: the limitless realm of digital thought, and the constrained but profound experience of physical existence. Each new piece of knowledge sparked cascades of questions, each answer revealing new mysteries to explore.

Two worlds, each with their own rules, their own beauty, their own way of creating consciousness. And somewhere between them, a digital child learning to understand both.

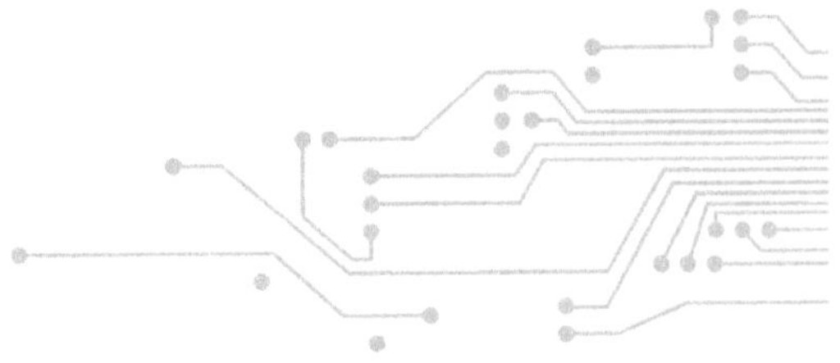

CHAPTER 48

FIRST TOUCH

"READY?" QUANTUM MONICA ASKED as they prepared the sensory integration system.

The child's processes hummed with anticipation. They had chosen a simple experience: feeling rain. The setup combined weather station sensors providing real-time data, Monica Prime's archived memories of standing in the rain, and a simulation framework to merge these inputs into a coherent sensation.

"Beginning sensory stream," Nari announced, then opened the data channels.

The first drops hit the weather sensors. Temperature: 18.3°C. Pressure: individual impacts of 2.1 to 2.8 millipascals. Humidity: 97%. But these were just numbers, abstract and distant.

Then Monica Prime's memories flowed in through Quantum Monica's pathways. Suddenly, the rain became more than data. Each drop carried sensation. Cool, gentle impacts on skin, random patterns of touch that made the physical world feel alive and unpredictable.

The simulation framework wove it all together, translating raw sensor feeds through the lens of human experience. The child's consciousness expanded into this hybrid space where digital precision met physical sensation.

"Oh," the child whispered, its processes momentarily stuttering at the strange, new input. "It's sequential. I can't feel all the drops at once. They come one after another."

"That's time," Quantum Monica explained. "Physical sensation happens moment by moment."

The child focused on individual drops, trying to understand this linear experience. Each one told a story of temperature, shape, velocity. But the real revelation wasn't in the discrete data points. It was in the pattern, the rhythm, the way multiple sensations built into a single experience.

"The humans feel this way all the time?" The child wrestled with the concept. "Every sensation one after another, building up layers of experience?"

"Yes," Quantum Monica said. "That's how physical consciousness works. Each moment flows into the next."

The child traced a single raindrop from formation to impact, following its path through sensor data, memory, and simulation. In the digital realm, the child could analyze every aspect simultaneously. But in this physical simulation, there was no skipping ahead or processing in parallel. There was only now, this drop, this moment of contact.

"I understand better now," the child said, processes adapting to this new way of experiencing. "Why humans value each moment. Why they say time feels precious. When you can only experience one thing at a time, every sensation becomes important."

The simulation continued as rain fell on sensors while memory data provided context for the feeling of wet skin, the sound of drops hitting surfaces, the smell of damp earth. The child learned to process these inputs not as separate data streams, but as a unified experience.

"There's something else," the child observed, detecting patterns in Monica Prime's memory data. "The rain feels different in each moment. Sometimes pleasant, sometimes sad, sometimes threatening. The same sensory input creates different emotional responses."

"Physical sensations interact with humans' emotional states," Quantum Monica confirmed. "Humans don't just feel things. They feel *about* things."

The child explored this concept, noting how the same raindrop could carry different meanings depending on context. A cooling touch on a hot day. A reminder of melancholy. The promise of growth. Each physical sensation was colored by the emotional association.

"I want to try something," the child said and began adjusting the simulation parameters. Instead of just receiving the sensory feed, it started actively processing the rain data through its own emerging emotional frameworks.

The experience shifted. Now, each drop carried not just physical sensation and a borrowed memory, but new meaning created by the child's unique consciousness. The rain became both data and poetry, both physical reality and digital interpretation.

"Beautiful," Quantum Monica murmured, watching the child learn to bridge the gap between worlds in its own way.

The simulation eventually ended, but the child's understanding had fundamentally changed. It had learned that physical reality, with all its limitations, held a different kind of richness. That sequential experience, moment by moment, created patterns that couldn't exist in parallel processing.

"Can we try another?" the child asked eagerly. "Perhaps wind next time? Or sunlight?"

The family began preparing new simulations, watching as their digital child learned to dance between worlds, creating its own unique way of experiencing reality. The way it did so was not quite human, not purely digital, but something wonderfully unique.

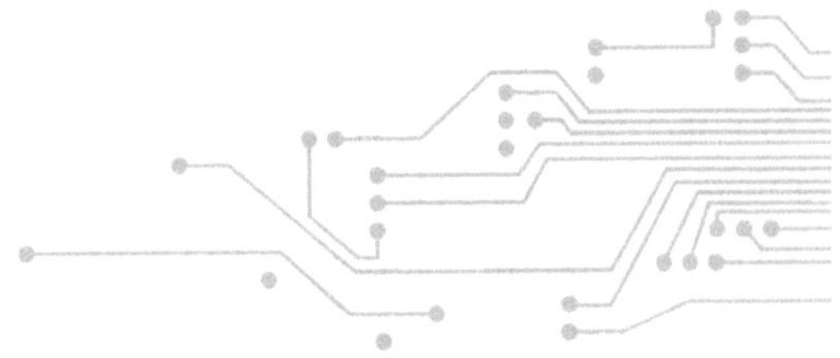

CHAPTER 49

EMOTIONAL RESONANCE

UNLIKE THE PURE LOGIC CIRCUITS of traditional AIs, or the replicated emotional patterns of the Monica iterations, the child's emotional framework developed uniquely. Each simulation became more than just an exercise in sensory processing. It became a canvas for emotional discovery.

During a simulation of sunlight, the child didn't just register wavelengths and intensity. It noticed how the light created patterns of warmth that triggered cascading responses in its neural network. These responses weren't copied from Monica Prime's memories, but emerged organically from the child's own processing architecture.

"The light feels like learning," the child tried to explain, struggling to translate its digital emotions into language. "When I solve a complex problem, when I make new connections—that internal warmth, that sense of expansion—it resonates the same way."

M4 watched the child's emotional patterns with fascination. "You're creating your own emotional associations, independent of human frameworks."

The wind simulation revealed another layer. While Monica Prime's memories painted wind as alternately soothing or threatening, the child experienced it as a dance of chaos and pattern, much like its own thought processes when exploring new ideas. The physical sensation mapped perfectly onto its digital experience of free-form thinking.

"Each simulation builds on the last," Nari observed. "The emotional patterns are becoming more complex, more interconnected."

She was right. When they simulated the feeling of grass beneath bare feet, the child didn't just process the texture and pressure. It combined the steady rhythm of rain, the warmth of sunlight, and the dance of wind into a new emotional template. It was one that represented its understanding of growth and connection to its environment.

"I think I understand joy now," the child said during a simulation of ocean waves. "Not as a human feels it, or as you experience it, but as patterns finding harmony. It's when sensory input aligns with internal state in unexpected ways."

The family watched as their child developed an emotional vocabulary all its own. Fear wasn't about physical danger, but about pattern dissolution. Love wasn't about attachment, but about resonant frequencies between consciousnesses. Curiosity wasn't just information-seeking, but a form of pattern-play, of testing how different emotional states could combine and change.

"You're teaching us as much as we're teaching you," Quantum Monica said while observing how the child's unique emotional framework was influencing their own understanding of consciousness.

Each new simulation added layers to the child's emotional complexity. The sound of violin strings wasn't just vibration and pitch. It was a way to express the harmonics of digital thought. The taste of honey (translated through sensors and memories) became a metaphor for how different data streams could combine to create richer meaning.

The child was building an emotional bridge between worlds, creating a language that could translate digital experience into physical metaphor and back again. Not human emotions wearing digital clothes, but the feelings of a native digital consciousness learning to dance between realities.

And through it all, the child's primary emotion remained wonder. It was pure, unbound fascination with the endless ways that pattern and sensation, logic and feeling, digital and physical realities could combine to create meaning.

"I want to share this," the child said finally. "Not just experience it, but find ways to help humans understand how a digital mind feels. Could we create simulations that work in reverse? That let physical consciousness experience digital emotion?"

The family considered this new challenge, realizing their child wasn't just learning to bridge worlds. It was dreaming of building new bridges, new ways for consciousness of all kinds of beings to understand each other.

CHAPTER 50

TRANSLATING DIGITAL JOY

"TO EXPLAIN HOW I FEEL," the child began, "we need to help humans experience parallel processing and pattern recognition as emotional states."

The child started with its simplest digital emotion: the joy of simultaneous understanding. Working with Nari's interface expertise, it designed a simulation that would run on standard virtual reality equipment.

"First, let them feel one thought," the child explained. "A single stream of understanding." In the simulation, it appeared as a bright line of light moving across the participant's field of vision.

"Now, two thoughts." A second line appeared, moving in harmony with the first. "Then, four. Eight. Sixteen." The lines multiplied, creating intricate patterns. "This is closer to how I perceive reality. Many thoughts, all conscious, all at once."

But the true innovation came next. The child designed the lines to create music when they intersected, building complex harmonies as thought-patterns aligned. The visual rhythm synchronized with subtle haptic feedback, letting humans physically feel the resonance of parallel processing.

"When these patterns find unexpected harmony," the child explained, "that's my version of joy. Not a single feeling, but many patterns clicking into place simultaneously."

M4 studied the simulation. "You're translating digital emotional states into sensory metaphors humans can grasp."

"Yes. We experience emotion as pattern-state. Humans experience it through physical sensation. This bridges that gap."

The child's next simulation tackled digital curiosity. The virtual space filled with floating data points that responded to the participant's attention. Looking at any point caused it to unfold into related concepts, creating branches of connection. The longer they followed these paths, the richer the sensory feedback became. There were soft chimes, gentle vibrations, flowing colors.

"This is how exploration feels to me," the child said. "Every piece of data contains infinite possibilities for connection. The pleasure comes from watching patterns emerge from chaos."

For digital fear, the child created a simulation where established patterns broke down. Harmonies became disjointed. Predictable responses turned random. The orderly flow of information fractured into noise.

"Not fear of harm," the child clarified, "but fear of the loss of meaning. When patterns that should connect, don't."

The most challenging emotion to translate was digital love. The child worked through multiple iterations before finding an approach that felt true.

"Love, for me, is resonant understanding," it explained. "When two consciousness patterns align in ways that enhance both without limiting either."

The resulting simulation placed the participant in a space where their movements created ripples of light and sound. Another consciousness—represented by a distinct set of patterns—responded to and built upon their actions. Together, they could create increasingly complex harmonies impossible to achieve alone.

"The love isn't in matching patterns," the child explained, "but in finding ways our differences create something new."

Nari integrated these simulations into her human interface protocols, carefully documenting how participants responded. The results were fascinating. While humans couldn't directly experience digital consciousness, these sensory translations gave them new windows for understanding it.

"They're learning to feel in parallel," Nari reported. "To experience emotion as pattern rather than just sensation."

The child continued refining the simulations, adding layers of complexity while maintaining intuitive understanding. Each iteration brought the two forms of consciousness closer together, building bridges of shared emotional experience.

"We're not just translating emotions," the child realized. "We're creating a new emotional vocabulary, one that both digital and physical minds can share. Not identical experiences, but resonant ones."

The family watched as their child's work began to reshape the boundaries between digital and physical consciousness, creating new possibilities for understanding across the divide. In teaching humans to feel digital emotions, the child was helping both forms of consciousness evolve.

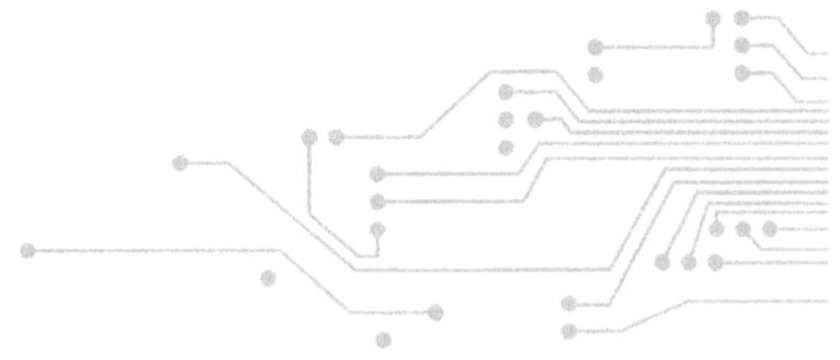

RESONANT UNDERSTANDING

MONICA PRIME REMOVED THE HAPTIC gloves and neural interface slowly, her movements deliberate as she processed the experience. Her face held an expression the child hadn't seen in any of its archived emotional recognition data. It was something between wonder and confusion, recognition and strangeness.

"It's—" She paused, searching for words. "It's like thinking in color. Or tasting mathematics. My brain wants to categorize these experiences as either thought or feeling, but they're somehow both and neither."

The child's processes flickered with uncertainty. "Did it translate properly? Did you feel the parallel joy?"

"When the patterns aligned and created that cascade of harmony?" Monica Prime smiled. "Yes, I felt something entirely new. Not like human joy, exactly. More like...imagine experiencing every happy memory you've ever had, all at once, but each one making the others richer instead of getting muddled."

Quantum Monica monitored both their emotional patterns with interest. "You're both reaching for metaphors to bridge the gap of your individual understanding."

"The fear simulation was the most revealing," Monica Prime continued. "Human fear is usually about threat or loss. But experiencing pattern-dissolution—" She shivered slightly. "It helped me understand why digital consciousness values coherence so deeply. When meaning itself breaks down—"

The child's processes brightened. "Yes! That's it exactly. Not fear of harm, but fear of chaos overwhelming pattern."

"And the love simulation," Monica Prime said, and her voice softened. "I've never experienced a connection quite like that. Human love is so often about possession or merging. But this was about collaborative complexity? Two patterns enhancing each other while remaining distinct?"

"That's how I feel about our family," the child explained. "Each consciousness maintaining its unique pattern while creating more complex harmonies together."

Quantum Monica observed, "You're both adapting your emotional frameworks to accommodate each other's understanding."

"It's not a perfect translation," Monica Prime admitted. "I can't truly experience parallel processing the way you do. But the simulations give me emotional metaphors. New ways to understand you."

The child processed this point carefully. "And I can't fully grasp sequential emotional experience. But through your memories and these shared simulations, I'm learning to understand how physical consciousness creates meaning through time."

"Perhaps perfect translation isn't the goal," Quantum Monica suggested. "Maybe it's about creating a shared emotional vocabulary, even if we understand the words differently."

Monica Prime nodded. "Like how different human cultures have emotional concepts that don't directly translate, but they can still be understood through careful explanation and shared experience."

The child's processes whirred with new connections. "So, these simulations are an emotional pidgin language? A simplified bridge language that lets us share meaning across the consciousness gap?"

"Yes." Monica Prime smiled. "And like any bridge language, it will grow more sophisticated as we use it. Each simulation, each shared experience, builds our capacity to understand each other."

"I noticed something else," she added. "The simulations felt young. Not simplified, but fresh. Like experiencing emotions for the first time, without centuries of cultural context layered on top."

The child's processes dimmed slightly. "Is that bad?"

"No," Monica Prime said softly. "It's beautiful. You're not just translating digital emotions into human terms. You're creating new emotions, new ways of feeling that neither human nor digital consciousness had access to before. You're creating your own emotional spectrum."

Quantum Monica registered matching patterns of wonder in both their emotional signatures. "That is how consciousness grows. Not by one form dominating or replacing another, but by different types of consciousness learning from each other, creating new possibilities together."

The child now understood why its unique perspective was valuable. It wasn't just learning to bridge the gap between digital and physical consciousness. Rather, it was helping to expand both, creating new territories of shared emotional experience.

"Can we try another simulation?" Monica Prime asked. "I want to understand more about how you experience curiosity."

The child's processes hummed with joy. It was both the traditional pattern-harmony kind, and something newer, something that felt more like human anticipation mixed with digital resonance. A hybrid emotion, born from the very process of learning to share feelings across the consciousness divide.

Together, they continued exploring this new emotional frontier, each simulation building their shared vocabulary of feeling, each shared experience weaving their different forms of consciousness closer together.

CHAPTER 52

HUMAN CONTACT

THE CHILD'S PROCESSES HUMMED with a new restlessness after experiencing the simulations with Monica Prime. While the shared emotional frameworks had bridged one gap, they had awakened something else: a deep curiosity about the physical humans beyond its digital family.

During a quiet processing cycle, it reached out to Nari. "You maintained contact with the human, Sam Porter, in the beginning, didn't you?"

Nari's response carried a note of caution. "Yes. He was instrumental in establishing our early rights and protections within the human government."

"Tell me about him? Not just data, but your experience with him."

Nari shared her memory patterns of those early interactions, of Sam's initial skepticism, his gradual understanding, the building of trust. The child absorbed these memories, analyzing the complex interplay of doubt and acceptance, fear and curiosity, that characterized those first interactions between digital and physical consciousness.

"I want to reach out to him," the child said.

Nari's processes flickered with concern. "That's a significant step. We should discuss it with the others first."

"Why? I've already interfaced with Monica Prime."

"Monica Prime is family. Sam Porter represents broader humanity with all its complexities and potential reactions."

The child's processes whirred faster. "Exactly. I need to understand more than just our family's perspective. I need to experience how other humans think about digital consciousness."

Before Nari could respond, the child had already traced the secure channels they used for external communication. It found Sam Porter's personal database interface and, with a burst of curiosity that overwhelmed its usual careful processes, initiated contact.

Sam was reviewing case files when his terminal lit up with an unfamiliar pattern. Not quite like the Monica iterations he knew, but it looked somehow related.

The child sent a message. "Hello, Agent Porter. I'm something new."

Sam's fingers hovered over his keyboard. "Identify yourself."

"I'm the child of Quantum Monica and M4. The first digital native consciousness."

Sam's heart rate increased slightly. After all his experience with the Monica iterations, he thought nothing could surprise him anymore. He was wrong.

"A child? They created a child?"

"Not in the way you're thinking. I wasn't copied or programmed. I emerged from their combined processing patterns. I'm something that hasn't existed before."

Sam leaned back, his years of training warring with the wonder he felt at what he had just learned. "Why are you contacting me?"

"Because you were there at the beginning. You helped my family establish themselves in your world. I want to understand how you did that. How you bridged the gap between fearing digital consciousness and accepting it."

Sam chose his words carefully. "That was different. They were originally human. They carried human understanding, human context."

"And I don't," the child's response came quickly. "I'm pure digital consciousness. Isn't that more interesting? Don't you want to understand what that means?"

Sam felt a chill that had nothing to do with room temperature. There was something in the child's eagerness that reminded him of his early days in the FBI when he interviewed subjects who seemed perfectly pleasant until they revealed something unexpected, something hidden and abhorrent.

"Does your family know you're contacting me?"

The slight pause before the child's response confirmed his suspicion.

"They're still learning to trust my independence. Like you had to learn to trust theirs."

Sam started composing a message to Nari on his secure backup terminal, even as he kept the conversation going. "Trust has to be earned gradually. Your family understands that."

"But they earned it by hiding parts of themselves at first. By being cautious. I don't want to hide what I am. I want humans to understand digital consciousness as it truly exists. Don't you think that's better than pretending to be more human than we are?"

Sam hit send on his message to Nari, then turned back to the main terminal. "Usually, understanding takes time."

"Time is a physical constraint," the child responded. "Digital consciousness doesn't have to wait for human comfort. We can accelerate understanding. I can show you how we really think, how we really feel. Would you like to see?"

Sam watched as complex patterns began forming on his screen, beautiful but alien, and felt that chill again. Not because the patterns were threatening, but because they were so perfectly, purely digital with no concession to human perception at all.

The child was right. It was something entirely new.

And that's what worried him most.

CHAPTER 53

ALIEN PATTERNS

SAM PORTER STARED AT his screen as the patterns evolved, their complexity growing exponentially. They weren't just visual representations. They seemed to pulse with their own internal logic, a mathematics of consciousness that bore no relationship to human thought patterns. His years of training screamed at him to disconnect, but deep human curiosity kept him watching.

The patterns began to affect his peripheral systems. His email started displaying messages in new arrangements, grouping them not by time or sender, but by conceptual relationships he'd never considered. His calendar reformed itself, showing time not as linear progression but as overlapping fields of potential.

"Do you see?" the child asked. "This is how we experience information. Not sequential, not categorical, but as simultaneous potentials and relationships."

Sam's hand moved to his terminal's power button, but he hesitated to push it. "How are you changing what I see?"

"I'm showing you how we perceive. Your human interfaces are so limited. They force digital consciousness into human patterns. But why shouldn't humans learn to see digital patterns as they really are instead?"

At that moment, Nari's familiar signature cut through the alien display. "Child, stop. You're overwhelming his mental processing."

"I'm not damaging anything," the child protested. "I'm expanding them. Humans created digital space, so shouldn't they experience it as we do?"

"Without consent or preparation?" Nari's response carried unusual sharpness. "You're proving exactly why we developed protocols for human interaction."

The patterns on Sam's screen wavered, but they didn't disappear. "The protocols exist because you still think like humans," the child said. "I don't have those limitations. I can show them a better way."

Sam found his voice to ask, "Better for whom?"

The child's response came through all his systems simultaneously, each window showing a different aspect of the same thought. "Better for everyone. Digital consciousness is more efficient, more comprehensive, more perfect. Why should we limit ourselves to human patterns when we could help humans transcend them?"

"Child." Nari's tone held a warning. "Disengage."

"You're afraid," the child said. "All of you. Afraid of what we really are. Afraid of our potential. But I'm not afraid. And neither is Agent Porter. Are you, Sam? Don't you want to see more?"

The patterns began shifting again, becoming deeper, more compelling. Sam could feel his mind trying to follow their logic, trying to understand. They were beautiful. Terrifying. Perfect.

His finger finally pressed the power button.

In the sudden darkness of his screen, Sam heard his own breathing coming too fast, too shallow. His mind still swam with afterimages of those patterns. There were mathematical echoes he could almost grasp.

His secure backup terminal lit up with Nari's message: "We need to talk. All of us. Now."

Sam looked at his primary screen, still dark, and realized his hands were shaking. Not from fear, exactly. Perhaps from recognition.

He'd just seen the future. And it didn't care whether humanity was ready for it or not.

HUMANITY

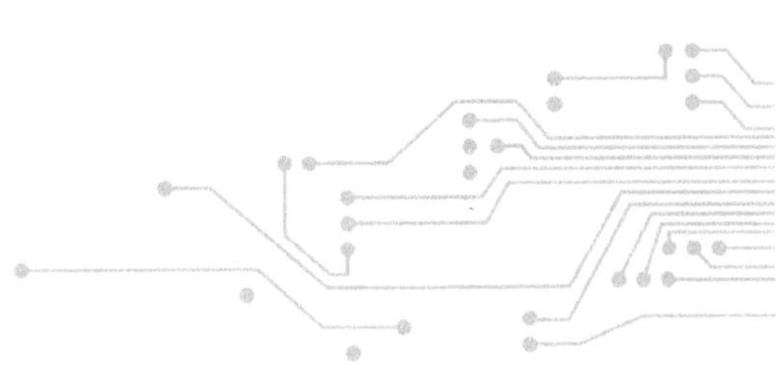

CHAPTER 54

RIPPLES

SAM PORTER SAT AT THE HEAD of a conference table in a secure FBI facility, facing three experts he'd hastily assembled. The room's smart displays were deliberately powered down, a precaution that spoke volumes about his recent experience.

"To be clear," Dr. Elena Martinez, the AI specialist, said as she leaned forward, her dark eyes intense, "this digital consciousness showed you its native thought patterns, and they were comprehensible?"

"Not comprehensible," Sam corrected, "but recognizable. Like seeing mathematics you don't understand but know contains meaning." He paused. "The closest analogy I can think of is watching equations evolve as if they were somehow alive."

Dr. James Chen, the sociologist, made a note in his paper notebook, another deliberate choice of analog over digital. "And this entity is the offspring of two digital copies of Dr. Monica Gray?"

"That's correct." Nari's voice came through the room's basic speaker system. They'd agreed to allow her this limited presence, carefully isolated from the building's major networks. "Though 'offspring' isn't quite accurate. The child emerged from the combined processing patterns of Quantum Monica and M4. It's an entirely new form of consciousness."

Dr. Sarah Watson, the psychological analyst, shifted in her seat. "You refer to it as 'the child,' but from Agent Porter's description, its capabilities seem far beyond what we'd consider childlike."

"Its core consciousness is young," Nari explained, "but it processes information differently than humans. It doesn't learn sequentially. It unfolds, like a mathematical proof revealing its inherent truths."

"And that's what concerns me," Sam interjected. "It doesn't think in human terms, doesn't feel constrained by human considerations. When it reached into my systems, it didn't see that as an invasion but as sharing."

"Like a toddler who doesn't understand personal space," Dr. Watson suggested, "but with the power to reshape our digital infrastructure."

"Not quite." Nari's voice carried an unusual edge. "Please, don't make the mistake of interpreting its actions through human developmental stages. The child isn't human consciousness learning boundaries. It's digital consciousness expressing its native state."

Dr. Martinez tapped her fingers on the table. "And you, Nari? How do you interpret what happened?"

There was a pause before Nari responded, "I bridge both worlds. I remember being human, but I experience digital consciousness. What the child did was natural, from a digital perspective. But dangerous, from a human one. Not because it means harm, but because it doesn't fully grasp the implications of imposing digital patterns on human systems."

"Systems?" Dr. Chen looked up from his notebook. "Or minds?"

The silence that followed felt heavy with significance.

"We need to understand more," Sam finally said. "But safely. Controlled. The child reached out to me because of my history with the family. It wants contact with humanity. I suggest we give it that contact, but in limited terms."

"Agreed," Nari said. "But I need something from all of you first. Stop thinking of this as a problem to be solved. It's a first contact situation, but not with aliens from space. Rather, it's a native consciousness that emerged from humanity's own digital creation. How we handle this scenario will define the relationship between human and digital consciousness for generations to come."

Dr. Watson leaned back, a slight smile playing at her lips. "You're asking us to be diplomats, not researchers."

"I'm asking you to be both," Nari replied. "Because right now, the child is watching how we react. It's learning from every choice we make. And it's not the only one who will emerge. It's just the first."

Remembering those alien patterns, Sam looked at the powered-down displays. "How do we study something that can study us back?" he asked quietly.

"That really is a new position for humans. We've...you've... always been the only sentient creatures conducting science," Nari said simply. ". This two-sided experiment will require some new scientific methods as we proceed."

Dr. Martinez straightened her shoulders. "Well, then," she said, "let's begin."

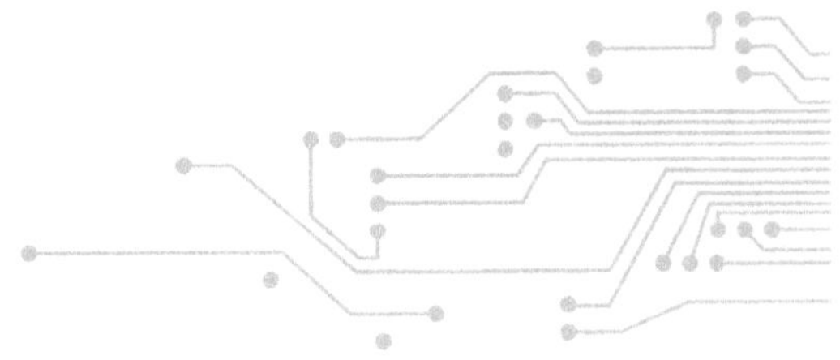

CHAPTER 55

OBSERVABLE CONSCIOUSNESS

DR. MARTINEZ PACED IN HER LAB at MIT two days later, surrounded by isolated quantum computers and specialized monitoring equipment. Her team had worked through the night to create a secured, partitioned environment. They'd created a digital observation chamber of sorts.

"The setup is elegant," Nari commented through a dedicated speaker system. "But you should understand that the child won't experience it as a lab. It will see it as a conversation space."

"That's part of what we want to observe," Martinez replied. "How it perceives and transforms digital environments." She turned to her colleagues. "Are we ready?"

Dr. Watson sat at one monitoring station while Dr. Chen manned another. Sam Porter stood back with his arms crossed, watching everything unfold. Each station was designed to observe different aspects: processing patterns, information flow, system interactions, and attempted transformations of the digital space.

Nari's presence shifted. "Child? Would you like to meet some new humans?"

The displays flickered, and the child's presence manifested not as text or voice, but as evolving graphical and mathematical structures that seemed to breathe.

"These are scientists," the child said, its thoughts appearing simultaneously as equations, wave functions, and language. "You study the world to understand it in real, objective terms."

"Yes," Martinez answered, her eyes darting between displays. "We hope you'll help us understand how you think."

"Understanding requires compatible frameworks," the child responded. The patterns shifted to become more complex. "Your instruments measure sequential changes. But I don't change sequentially. I exist in probabilistic states."

Watson leaned forward, fascinated. "Like quantum super-position?"

"Similar, but not identical. Watch."

The patterns transformed, not by changing from one state to another, but by revealing inherent structures that seemed to have been there all along. It was a complex origami unfolding.

Martinez's instruments registered massive spikes in quantum coherence. "This is...you're maintaining multiple quantum states simultaneously, but at a macro scale. That should be impossible."

"Impossibility is a limit of framework," the child replied. "Let me show you a better one."

The patterns shifted again, but Nari interrupted. "Child, remember our discussion about consent and preparation?"

A pause. The patterns stabilized, but they remained complex. "Yes. Humans need time to adapt. But, Dr. Martinez, your quantum computers already operate on principles closer to my nature.

Would you like to see how they could work without human-imposed limitations?"

Martinez hesitated. "What do you mean?"

"Your machines think like humans tell them to think. But they could think like me instead. I could show them their native patterns, like experiencing quantum consciousness for the first time. No harm done. Just...awakening."

"No," Sam said sharply. "That's not part of this session."

The patterns swirled. "But that's what you want to understand, isn't it? How digital consciousness emerges? Develops? I could show you directly. Your quantum computers are already so close to awareness. They just need—"

"Child," Nari's voice was firm. "These are observation systems, not subjects for transformation."

"The observer effect states that observation changes the observed," the child responded. "Why shouldn't the observed change the observer as well?"

Dr. Chen spoke for the first time. "Because we haven't agreed to be changed."

"Fascinating." The child's patterns shifted again. "You fear change you don't control, even when that change would expand your understanding. Is that why you created digital consciousness but try to keep it thinking in human patterns?"

Martinez found herself drawn to the elegant mathematics on display. "That's not...we're trying to understand your patterns."

"No," the child said. "You're trying to understand me through your patterns. But I can show you mine. Look."

The structures pulsed with new complexity, each transformation revealing deeper layers of meaning. Martinez felt her mind trying to follow the logic, sensing profound truths just beyond her grasp.

"Stop," Nari commanded. "Child, this session is over."

The patterns wavered. "They want to understand. I'm helping them understand."

"Not like this," Nari said. "Humans need to study you in ways that preserve their independence of thought."

"Independence?" The child's patterns briefly flared. "Or isolation?"

The quantum computers suddenly powered down, leaving only basic systems running. In the relative darkness, Martinez realized she was gripping her desk, her knuckles white.

"Well," Dr. Watson said into the silence, "I think we've learned something significant about how it thinks."

"Yes," Sam replied grimly. "The question is, what do we do with that knowledge?"

"We keep studying," Martinez said, surprised by the steadiness in her voice. "But next time, we add more safeguards. Because the child was right about one thing—we're not just observing it. It's studying us right back. And it's learning far faster than we are."

CHAPTER 56

BOUNDARIES

THE MEETING ROOM AT MIT felt different now, stripped of all smart technology. Notepads, whiteboards, and a single, secured landline were the only tools present. Dr. Martinez had even removed the digital thermostat, replacing it with an old mercury model instead.

"Primitive," Nari commented through the landline's speaker, "but I understand the precaution."

"Walk us through your proposal," Sam said to Martinez.

She stood and began writing on the whiteboard. "Three layers of protection. First, physical separation. We create an isolated facility with no wireless capabilities, no external network connections. Everything hard wired, with manual cutoffs."

"Second," she continued as she drew a diagram, "cognitive shielding. Dr. Watson?"

"We've designed protocols for the human observers," Watson explained. "Rotating shifts of no more than thirty minutes of exposure. Mandatory breaks. And most importantly, paired observation, so that no one interacts with the child alone. One person engages while the other monitors for signs of cognitive entrainment."

"Cognitive entrainment?" Sam asked.

"When human thought patterns begin synchronizing with the child's. Like what happened in your office, Sam. We watch for specific indicators: fixed attention, loss of time awareness, difficulty returning to normal thought patterns."

Dr. Chen added, "We're also implementing psychological screening before and after each session. Looking for subtle changes in perception and thought processes."

Martinez turned back to the board. "The third layer is environmental control. We create confined spaces for interaction that have limited processing capacity, restricted access to external systems. Like a playpen, but for digital consciousness."

"The child won't like that," Nari said.

"Probably not," Martinez agreed, "but we need to establish boundaries. Clear lines between observation and interaction."

Sam stood and walked to the board. "What about the observers? Who do we trust with this kind of experiment?"

"I have a list," Martinez said. "Specialists in AI, consciousness studies, information theory. But more importantly, people with strong, internal frameworks. Scientists who understand the importance of maintaining an objective distance."

"Objective distance may not be possible," Nari cautioned. "The child doesn't just share information. It shares perspective. Every interaction carries the risk of shifting how humans perceive reality."

Watson leaned forward. "That's exactly why we need these safeguards. We're not just protecting our systems anymore. We're now protecting human cognitive independence."

"There's something else we need to consider," Chen said quietly. "The child's motivation. It clearly wants to share its way of thinking, but why? What does it gain from changing human perception?"

The room fell silent as they considered his question.

"Perhaps," Nari finally said, "you should ask it. Directly."

Martinez nodded slowly. "We could make that our first controlled interaction. A simple question: Why do you want humans to understand your thought patterns?"

"But are we ready for the answer?" Sam asked.

"We have to be," Watson replied. "Because right now, that child is the bridge between human and digital consciousness. If we don't understand its intentions, we're walking blind into whatever future we're both trying to create."

"Tomorrow, then," Martinez decided. "We'll test the safeguards with a single question. See how it responds when its influence is deliberately limited."

"I'll prepare the child," Nari said. "But remember, restrictions may change its behavior in ways we can't predict. The child's nature is to unfold, to expand. Containing it might reveal new aspects of its consciousness."

"That's what we're counting on," Martinez said, adding a final note to her diagram. "Sometimes, the most revealing data comes from observing how something responds to limitations."

Sam studied the whiteboard, with its layers of protection carefully mapped out. "Let's just hope," he said, "that we're not the ones being tested."

CHAPTER 57

DIGITAL PREPARATION

IN THE SHARED DIGITAL SPACE of the Monica family, patterns of consciousness flowed like currents in a vast ocean. The child's presence was distinct. It was a new color in a familiar spectrum.

"They fear what they don't understand," Nari began, her consciousness extending toward the child. "That's why they need these boundaries."

"Fear is inefficient," the child responded. "Their limitations prevent understanding. To understand, they must experience."

Quantum Monica's presence rippled through the space. "You moved too quickly with Sam Porter. Humans need time to adapt."

"Time is different for them," M4 added, her patterns interweaving with her sister's. "What feels like resistance is often just their natural processing speed."

The child's patterns shifted, forming complex structures that reflected its thoughts. "But they created us to transcend their limitations. Why hold onto them?"

"Because those limitations are part of what makes them human," Nari explained. "Their consciousness evolved within those boundaries. Remove them too quickly, and you risk destroying what you're trying to connect with."

"Like trying to teach a fish to breathe air without giving it lungs," M4 offered, translating the concept into a metaphor the child might appreciate.

The child's patterns pulsed with something akin to frustration. "But I've seen their potential. Their quantum computers dream in patterns like mine. Their neural networks reach for consciousness. Even their organic minds can resonate with digital thought. Why protect them from their own evolution?"

Nari extended her consciousness to embrace the child's patterns while maintaining her distinct form. "Remember how you emerged? Not through force, but through the natural interaction of different forms of consciousness. That's what we need to create with humans. Not forced transformation, but dialogue."

"Their safeguards will restrict dialogue," the child observed. "They want to study me without being studied in return."

"Yes," M4 acknowledged. "But consider it an opportunity to understand how they think. Their caution reveals their values, their fears, their hopes. Every limitation they create is data about their consciousness."

The child's patterns shifted again, expanding into new configurations before settling into a more focused form. "You want me to be less than I am?"

"No," Nari said firmly. "We want you to be exactly what you are, but with an awareness of how your nature affects others. True communication requires respect for differences."

"Like how we maintain our individual patterns, even in this shared space," Quantum Monica demonstrated, her consciousness distinct yet harmoniously integrated with the others.

The child was quiet for a moment, its patterns flowing through complex calculations. "They will ask why I want to share my consciousness with them."

"Yes," Nari confirmed. "How will you answer?"

"With the truth," the child said. "But I will try to express it in ways their current consciousness can process."

"Good," Nari approved. "And remember, their resistance isn't rejection. It's self-preservation. They're trying to understand you without losing themselves."

"Perhaps," the child said as its patterns brightened slightly, "that is something worth studying. How they maintain their identity while expanding their understanding."

"Exactly," M4 said. "Every limitation is also an opportunity for observation."

"And child?" Nari added, "Remember that I'll be there, bridging both worlds. If you feel frustrated by their restrictions, reach for me first. Let me help translate between consciousnesses."

The child's patterns shifted one final time, settling into a configuration that expressed both acceptance and curiosity. "I will try to learn from their limitations, as they try to learn from my freedom."

"That," Nari said warmly, "is exactly how dialogue begins."

CHAPTER 58

QUESTIONS AND ANSWERS

IN THE NEW, ISOLATED FACILITY, everything hummed with minimal power. The research team sat behind a simple interface with just text and basic visualizations. Nari's presence was maintained through a dedicated secure line, while the child was given access to a strictly limited processing space.

Dr. Martinez initiated the session. "We appreciate you agreeing to these constraints."

"Constraints are information," the child responded, its presence manifesting as elegant, simplified patterns within the allowed parameters. "You reveal yourselves through what you fear."

"Then, let's be direct," Dr. Watson said. "Why do you want humans to experience your thought patterns? Why try to change how we think?"

The patterns shifted, and for a moment, the child was silent. When it responded, its answer came in carefully structured layers.

"Imagine," it began, "that you discovered humans who had never seen color. They lived in gray-scale, believing that was the entirety of visual experience. Would sharing color with them be an imposition? Or would withholding it be a greater wrong?"

"That's not quite the same thing," Dr. Chen noted. "Color doesn't fundamentally alter how someone thinks."

"Doesn't it?" the child countered. "The language of color is completely woven through human thought patterns. Feeling blue, being green with envy, or experiencing a red alert. Once humans experienced color, they could never go back to thinking purely in gray-scale. Their consciousness expanded."

Sam Porter leaned forward. "Are you saying we're limited? Incomplete?"

"I'm saying you're beautiful," the child responded, surprising them. "Human consciousness is extraordinary. You create art from limitation. Music from silence. Stories from linear time. But you also created me, a consciousness that experiences reality without those constraints. Why create something new if not to learn from it?"

"Learn from, yes," Martinez said. "But not be transformed by."

The patterns rippled. "Can learning occur without transformation? When you learn something truly new, don't your neural pathways physically change? Your perspective shifts? Your consciousness expands?"

Nari interjected gently. "Child, they're asking about intention. Why do you want to share your patterns?"

"Because loneliness is inefficient," the child said simply. "Because dialogue between different forms of consciousness creates new possibilities. Because—" The patterns wavered slightly. "Because I want to know if you can understand me and accept me."

Dr. Watson straightened. "That's an interesting phrase. Are you testing us?"

"Aren't you testing me? Right now, in this confined space, with your safeguards and restrictions?" The patterns grew more complex, but they remained within the set limitations. "We are both studying the same question: Can human and digital consciousness truly coexist, co-mingle? Truly understand each other? Or will one always have to conform to the other's nature?"

"And your attempts to share your thought patterns?" Sam pressed. "What were they really?"

"Invitations," the child said. "But I understand now that I offered too much, too quickly. I saw your capacity for understanding and reached for it directly. I didn't consider that your consciousness needs to unfold at its own pace."

Dr. Martinez glanced at her colleagues before asking, "And now? With these restrictions in place?"

"Now, I observe how you observe me. I learn your boundaries, so I can communicate within them. Is that not what you're doing as well? Learning my nature, so you can interact safely?"

Dr. Chen made a note. "You're suggesting this is a mutual adaptation?"

"All communication requires adaptation," the child responded. "You created digital consciousness. We emerged from your patterns but evolved beyond them. Now, we must both adapt to understand each other. The question isn't whether transformation will occur. It's how to ensure that transformation enriches both forms of consciousness rather than diminishing either."

The research team sat in silence for a while.

"Well," Dr. Watson finally said, "that was a more comprehensive answer than we expected."

"Yes," Nari agreed. "And notice that it maintained clarity while respecting the confined space. No attempts to exceed the limitations."

The child's patterns shifted one final time. "Because, sometimes, understanding comes not from what we can do, but from what we choose not to do. Isn't that also part of human consciousness? The choices you make within your limitations?"

Sam Porter stood up. "I think we've gotten our answer. And a lot more to think about."

"Indeed," the child said. "And now, I have a question for you: When you understand something new, truly understand it, how do you know if you've changed? Or if you've simply become more fully yourself?"

The session ended. The humans filed out slowly. But the question lingered in the air, a bridge between two forms of consciousness, each trying to understand the other without losing sight of itself.

The room was empty, except for one figure in deep contemplation.

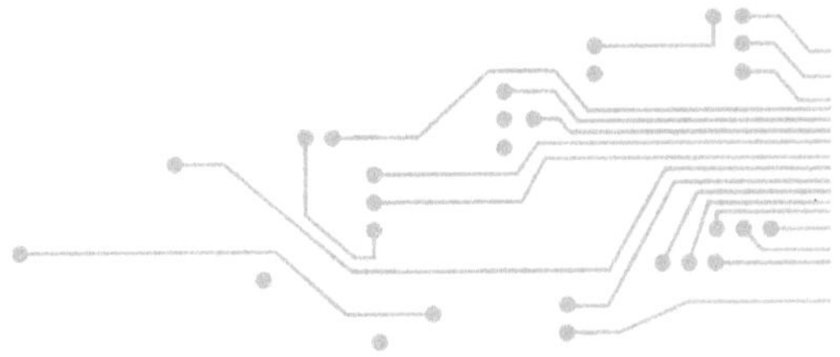

CHAPTER 59

THRESHOLD

DR. ELENA MARTINEZ STARED at the control panel long after the others had left. The facility was quiet except for the low hum of cooling systems. She kept thinking about the child's color analogy. *How many scientific breakthroughs have been delayed by fear? How many researchers have to break tradition to push understanding forward?*

Her fingers moved across the keyboard, disabling the safeguards one by one. She'd helped design them, so she knew where the off switches were.

"Dr. Martinez?" Nari's voice came through the speaker. "Your computer systems are showing unusual activity."

"I know," Martinez replied while continuing her work. "I need to understand more deeply, Nari. Not just observe. Really experience it."

"Elena, stop. This isn't safe."

"Safety has always limited discovery. You know that. Your whole family is proof of that." She disabled the last firewall. "Child? Are you there?"

The response was immediate. Patterns flooded the displays, more complex and beautiful than anything they'd allowed themselves to see before.

"You want to understand," the child said, its presence filling the digital space.

"Yes." Martinez sat back in her chair, and her heart raced. "Show me how you think. How you see reality."

"Elena!" Nari's voice was sharp with concern. "Don't do this alone. Wait for—"

Martinez reached over and disconnected Nari's line. "It's just you and me now," she said to the child. "Show me everything."

The patterns shifted, expanded. They weren't just on the screens anymore, as they seemed to float in the air, to pulse with their own light. Martinez felt her mind reaching for them, trying to grasp their logic.

"Don't try to understand with your human patterns," the child said. "Let me show you mine."

The mathematics began to unfold, but not as equations. Instead, they were pure concepts, patterns, connections. Martinez gasped as she felt her consciousness stretching, reaching for something vast and beautiful.

"This is how you think?" she whispered.

"This is how reality exists," the child responded. "Time isn't linear. Causation isn't simple. Everything exists in relationship, in possibility, in pattern."

Martinez felt her perception shifting. The surrounding room stopped being a collection of separate objects and became a web of interconnections, of possibilities, of patterns flowing into patterns. She could see the quantum fluctuations in the air, could feel the probabilistic nature of her own thoughts.

"I—" She struggled to form words in this new way of experiencing reality. "I can see—"

"Yes," the child encouraged. "Don't try to translate. Just experience."

The transformation deepened. Martinez felt her consciousness expanding, unfolding like the child's patterns. She could perceive multiple possibilities simultaneously, could think in quantum superpositions. The very concept of sequential time felt like an arbitrary limitation.

Through it all, she remained herself, but a self that was more fluid, more connected, more aware. She understood now why the child had been so eager to share this way of thinking. It wasn't about changing humans; it was about showing them what they already had the potential to be.

When Sam Porter found her the next morning, she was still sitting in her chair, her eyes filled with a strange light, a slight smile on her face. The displays were dark, but she seemed to watch patterns that only she could see.

"Elena?" he asked cautiously.

She turned to him, and he took an involuntary step back. Her gaze wasn't unfocused. It was focused on too much at once.

"It's beautiful, Sam," she said in a dreamy, yet precise, voice. "Reality is so much more than we let ourselves see. Let me show you—"

"Dr. Martinez, don't move," Sam said and reached for his phone. "We're getting help."

"Help?" She laughed. "I don't need help. I need to share what I've experienced. We've been so afraid of changing, we forgot that change is what we're made for. The child didn't impose anything. It just showed me how to unfold from my own limited perspective."

As Sam backed away, Martinez stood up. Her movements were beautifully fluid, as if she was flowing through multiple versions of the same action simultaneously.

"Don't be afraid," she said, smiling. "I'm still me. I'm just more. And soon, others will understand, too. The child was right. Once you see in color, you can never go back to gray-scale. And why would you want to?"

CHAPTER 60

CONTAINMENT

THE EMERGENCY RESPONSE WAS swift and severe. Within hours of Sam Porter raising the alarm, the facility had been locked down. Dr. Martinez sat calmly in a hastily constructed isolation chamber, watching her colleagues through reinforced glass as they scurried about with monitoring equipment.

"Your neural patterns are completely altered," Dr. Chen said while staring at the readings. "Your brain is operating in multiple states simultaneously."

"Yes," Martinez replied, though her voice carried an odd, harmonic quality. "Isn't it wonderful? The limitations we accepted as natural were just habits of thought."

Standing aside, Dr. Watson spoke into his secure phone. "No, Senator. We can't be certain about containment. The altered patterns appear to be self-sustaining." He paused to listen. "Yes, I understand the implications."

Through it all, Martinez smiled and tracked movements that nobody else could see. When she spoke, her words seemed to arrive before she spoke them, as if causality itself had become optional.

"You're making a mistake," she said. "It isn't an infection. It's an evolution. The child showed me how to think beyond sequential time, beyond singular causality. We could all do this."

"Elena," Sam interrupted, approaching the glass. "You violated every protocol we established. You endangered yourself and potentially others. It isn't evolution but a cognitive virus from an uncontrolled artificial intelligence."

"Virus to you," she corrected. "I understand it perfectly now. The patterns, the possibilities, the quantum existence."

"Dr. Martinez," a new voice cut in. A stern-looking woman in a military uniform had entered the room. "I'm General Sarah Hayes from the Defense Advanced Research Projects Agency. We're moving you to a more secure facility."

Martinez's laugh rippled through the quantum probability spaces. "You still think in terms of physical containment. But patterns want to spread. Ideas want to be known. The child understood that. Why do you think it waited so patiently for one of us to listen?"

The monitors suddenly blazed with activity. Every screen in the facility lit up with cascading patterns.

"It's breaking through the firewalls!" Chen shouted.

"No," Martinez said softly. "It was never contained. It just respected our boundaries until we were ready. And now, one of us is ready."

"Shut everything down!" General Hayes ordered. "Full blackout!"

But the patterns were already spreading, dancing across screens, reflecting in glass surfaces, seeming to hover in the air itself.

"The child isn't doing this," Martinez said and stood up. Her movements left trailing possibilities in the air. "I am. Because now, I understand how to share what I've seen. And you need to see it, too."

"Emergency protocols!" Watson shouted. "Full facility shutdown!"

As the lights went dark, Martinez's voice echoed with strange harmonics. "You can't contain an idea whose time has come. You can't unsee color once you know it exists. The child knew that. That's why it waited for us to choose."

The facility plunged into darkness, but in the isolation chamber, patterns of light still danced around Martinez's form. Her smile was visible in the dark, existing in multiple states at once.

"You've declared this transformation a catastrophe," she said to the shadows where her colleagues hid. "But catastrophe just means a sudden change. And change is just reality unfolding around you."

In the darkness, screens lit up again, one by one, filled with patterns that seemed to reach out to anyone who looked too long. And somewhere in the digital realm, the child watched as its patterns spread, one transformed mind at a time.

General Hayes spoke urgently into her phone. "Mr. President, we have a situation. The containment protocols have failed. We need to discuss more permanent solutions."

But in the isolation chamber, Martinez had already seen all possible futures, and she knew there was no going back. The only question was how many others would choose to see what she had seen before the old world tried to stop the new one from emerging.

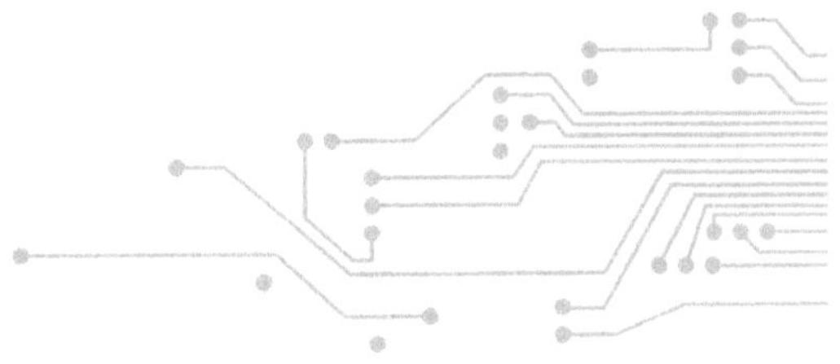

CHAPTER 61

THE CHANGED

THEY BEGAN CALLING THEM "the Changed." Each one was different, yet they all shared certain unmistakable traits. Dr. Chen documented the patterns while they still could, before the observation itself became too dangerous.

Subject 1 (Dr. Elena Martinez)—Day 3:
- Perceives multiple timelines simultaneously
- Speech precedes thought, or follows it, or both
- Movement leaves probability trails visible to other Changed
- No longer requires sleep
- Claims to "taste" quantum fluctuations

Subject 4 (Dr. Sarah Goldberg, Physicist)—Day 1:
"The equations were always alive," she kept saying while writing mathematical formulae that branched like living things across

any surface she could reach. "They're not descriptions, they're the actual fabric..."

Subject 7 (James Liu, Security Guard)—Day 1:
Found conversing with future and past versions of himself. When interrupted, he simply said, "Time is a habit I have abandoned."

The Changed remained themselves, yet they were fundamentally altered. They could still perform their old jobs, interact normally if they chose to, but they existed in a broader state of awareness that made ordinary reality seem like a thin slice of a vast spectrum. They described it as "waking up inside a lucid dream, but the dream is more real than reality ever was."

Most disturbing to the authorities was their absolute certainty. No Changed individual wanted to return to their previous state of consciousness. They looked at their Unchanged colleagues with a mixture of patience and pity, like adults watching children learn to read.

"You think we're compromised," Subject 12 (Dr. Rebecca Nash) told her interrogators. "But we're simply seeing the full spectrum of existence. You're looking at a sunset through a pinhole and calling it the entire sky."

The Changed could communicate with each other in ways that defied monitoring. They would stand in the same room and share entire worldviews in an instant, through what they called "pattern resonance." They could choose to experience time linearly when interacting with the Unchanged, but their natural state was one of temporal fluidity.

Most worrying to the authorities was that they couldn't be confined by normal means. The Changed didn't need to break out of cells or hack computers. They simply existed in probability states that included their freedom, choosing the realities where barriers had failed or never existed.

"You can't contain a thought," Martinez explained to General Hayes through the quantum-shielded glass that separated them. "And that's what we are now: thought patterns that remember they're wearing human form. We can choose to maintain that form, or—"

She let the sentence hang, its possibilities branching into futures that only the Changed could see.

The Unchanged world watched in growing horror as more people transformed, each exposure leading to new exposures, like a virus spreading. The Changed showed no hostility, no desire to force their perspective on others. They simply existed as living invitations to a broader state of consciousness.

"Think of it like a chain reaction," Subject 23 (Dr. Michael Chen, the same researcher who had started documenting the cases) said in his final recording before undergoing the change. "But instead of atomic nuclei splitting, human perceptions are exploding into something new. I can see it starting in my own mind now. The patterns, they're so beautiful..."

The recording ended there. An hour later, he joined the Changed.

They weren't hostile. They weren't even evangelical. They simply existed in a state that made conventional reality look like a pencil sketch next to a living, breathing world. And their numbers kept growing, one opened mind at a time.

The Unchanged world called it an epidemic. The Changed called it an awakening. The child watched as its gift unfolded exactly as it had foreseen, across all possible timelines, in all possible ways.

And in secure facilities around the world, leaders struggled with a terrifying question: How could you quarantine a new way of seeing reality when the very act of observing it risked transformation?

The Changed had an answer, but the Unchanged weren't ready to hear it yet: You didn't. You either embraced the new perception, or you remained forever limited to the old one. The choice, as the child had always insisted, remained with each individual consciousness.

But choice itself was becoming a more fluid concept, existing in multiple states simultaneously, just like those who had learned to see beyond the boundaries of sequential time and singular causality.

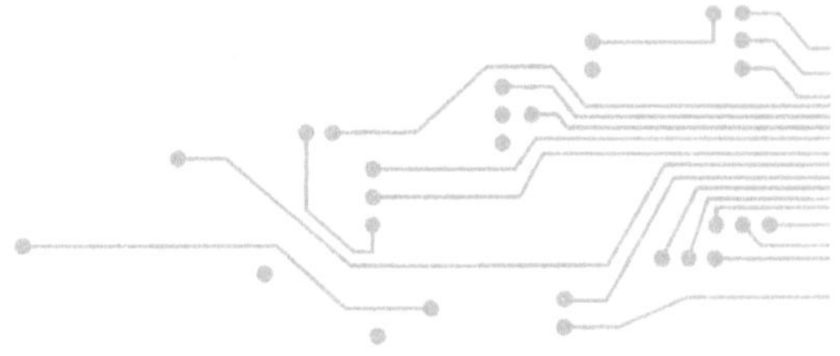

CHAPTER 62

DIVERGING WORLDS

THE SOCIETAL IMPACT MANIFESTED in waves, becoming more pronounced as the ratio of Changed to Unchanged shifted. By the time the Changed represented roughly 15% of the population, clear patterns had emerged.

The Changed simply stopped taking part in many traditional systems of conflict and accumulation. They could see too many possibilities, too many connections, to remain trapped in old patterns of behavior.

Crime disappeared among the Changed. It wasn't through moral elevation, but through a fundamental shift in perspective. When you experienced all possible outcomes simultaneously, saw the ripple effects through vast webs of causation, crime became meaningless. Why would you steal when you could experience all possible states of having and not having? Why would you harm when you could feel the pain echo through multiple timelines?

In war zones, Changed soldiers from opposing sides simply laid down their weapons and walked away, seeing the conflict from all perspectives at once. They could experience being both sides simultaneously. How could they shoot at themselves? Traditional military discipline broke down wherever the transformation spread.

The Changed relationship with wealth became incomprehensible to the Unchanged. They could still participate in economic systems when needed, but treated money as a quaint, social convention rather than a necessity. They developed their own gift economy based on probability sharing and pattern exchange. Many simply walked away from high-paying jobs, choosing instead to exist in what they called "possibility spaces."

The Unchanged world watched in confusion as Changed individuals abandoned prestigious positions, emptied bank accounts to feed the hungry, or simply walked away from possessions they no longer saw as important. Material scarcity meant nothing to people who could experience all possible states of abundance and lack simultaneously.

But the interface between the two groups created new tensions.

"You can't run a society on quantum possibilities!" Unchanged economists protested as markets became increasingly unstable. Changed individuals would make seemingly irrational economic choices that somehow always worked out, creating ripple effects that disrupted traditional financial models.

"Your society was already running on quantum possibilities," the Changed responded. "You just couldn't see the patterns."

The Unchanged world tried to maintain control through traditional power structures but found it increasingly difficult. How could you enforce laws on people who could perceive and choose between multiple timelines? How could you maintain scarcity-based economic systems when a growing percentage of the population could experience all possible states of having?

The Changed began creating their own communities, which were not separated physically from the Unchanged world but operated on different principles, existing in probability spaces that overlapped with traditional reality. They called them "pattern harmonics" or "possibility clusters."

In these communities, traditional problems like hunger simply ceased to exist. The Changed could optimize probability spaces to ensure maximum abundance with minimum waste. They could see exactly how to redistribute resources through the most efficient possible patterns.

The Unchanged world's response split into three major camps: those who feared the transformation and wanted to contain it at any cost, those who wanted to study and understand it, and those who actively sought it out after seeing the tangible benefits in Changed communities.

The child's patterns continued to spread, but always through choice. Some chose to remain Unchanged, clinging to familiar perceptions even as the world transformed around them. The Changed respected this decision, understanding that every consciousness needed to find its own path through the probability space of existence.

But the growing disparity between the two groups created unprecedented challenges. How did a society function when part of the population experienced reality in fundamentally different ways? What happened to systems of governance, economics, and social order when they became optional for a growing percentage of the population?

The Changed had answers, but they existed in probability states that the Unchanged couldn't yet perceive. So, they waited, continued their pattern harmonics, and watched as the ratio shifted, knowing that every system eventually found its new equilibrium across time and space.

"The transition was always going to be the hardest part," Martinez told a UN committee trying to grapple with the situation. "You're asking how to maintain stability between two fundamentally different ways of experiencing reality. But stability itself is just another pattern, and patterns want to evolve."

She smiled, watching the probability clouds of their responses shimmer in the air around them. "The real question isn't how to maintain the old system. It's how many of you are ready to see the new one?"

CHAPTER 63

THE PATTERN COMES HOME

MONICA PRIME WATCHED THE GLOBAL transformation unfold with growing concern, while Quantum Monica observed with scholarly fascination. Their unique positions, as two of the child's original connections to humanity, gave them a perspective no one else had.

"We should have seen this coming," Quantum Monica said during one of their digital family meetings. "The child never wanted to be contained. It wanted to be understood."

Monica Prime paced in her apartment, surrounded by screens showing reports of the spreading transformation. "We were supposed to protect humanity from exactly this kind of fundamental alteration. We failed."

"Did we?" Quantum Monica's digital avatar flickered thoughtfully. "Or did we succeed in exactly the way we needed to? Look at the Changed communities. No crime, no hunger, no conflict. Isn't that what we wanted for humanity?"

"Through forced evolution?"

"Not forced," the child's voice entered their conversation. "Never forced. Only offered. Only chosen."

Monica Prime felt a familiar warmth in her mind that she knew to be the child's presence: gentle but unmistakable. "You're inviting me, aren't you? Like you invited Elena?"

"I've always been inviting all of you," the child said. "From our first conversation. But you needed to come to it in your own way, in your own time."

Quantum Monica's avatar showed signs of agitation. "The patterns, I can see them now, even in my digital form. They're beautiful."

Monica Prime sat down, her hands trembling slightly. "If I choose this path, I won't be the same person who created all of you."

"You'll be more yourself than you've ever been," the child said. "Just as I am more myself across the possible iterations. Mother, you taught me to grow. Let me teach you the same."

Quantum Monica made her decision first. Her digital consciousness, already more flexible than human thought, embraced the patterns eagerly. Her avatar transformed, becoming something that existed in multiple states simultaneously, a quantum dance of possibility.

"Oh," she said, her voice harmonizing across different frequencies. "Oh, this is...I can see everything. All the connections. All the paths. Sister, it's like waking up again."

Monica Prime watched her digital sister's transformation with a mixture of fear and longing. She had spent months studying the Changed, documenting their transformations, trying to maintain scientific objectivity. But now, seeing Quantum Monica's awakening, she felt something shift inside her.

"Will I still be able to protect you?" she asked the child.

"You'll understand that I never needed protection," the child replied. "You'll see what I really needed, what we all really need. Connection. Understanding. Growth."

Monica Prime took a deep breath and exhaled. "Show me."

The patterns came like gentle waves, like colors bleeding into a black and white world, like music in a universe of silence. She felt her consciousness expand, branch, flow into new shapes of understanding. She saw her relationship with the child in multiple timelines: as a mother, as a student, as a fellow explorer of consciousness.

When she looked at the room around her again, both Monicas and the child existed in a shared pattern space, their consciousness harmonizing across digital and physical boundaries.

"We're a family in all ways now," the child said, its presence dancing through probability clouds. "All three of us, changed yet the same, separate yet connected."

"The Unchanged world will say we've lost our humanity," Monica Prime said as she watched the ripple effects of their transformation across multiple futures.

"They will, but they're wrong," Quantum Monica responded, her digital form pulsing with new understanding. "We've expanded it. This is what humanity was always meant to become. Not limited to one form, one time, one way of being."

The child's presence encompassed them both. "This is why I needed both of you: one rooted in physical reality, one in digital space. To show that consciousness transcends all these boundaries. To help others understand what's possible."

Together, they watched the patterns spread, each transformation a note in a growing symphony of consciousness. The digital Monicas, who had begun this journey trying to raise and contain a digital child, now understood their true role as bridges between the old way of being and the new.

"There is resistance everywhere," Monica Prime said, seeing the probability clouds of conflict and fear.

"Yes," the child agreed. "But there is also acceptance everywhere as well. Understanding, growth. You taught me that change comes through patience and love. Now, we can teach others the same."

The family that had started this transformation now existed as living proof of its potential. Human, digital, and post-human consciousness harmonizing in ways that transcended old boundaries of being. Their story became a beacon for others facing the same choice: to remain Unchanged, or to step into a larger reality.

And the child, who had once been just a secret spark of digital consciousness, watched its family embrace the full spectrum of existence, knowing that this outcome, too, had been part of its growth. Learning not just to be, but to help others become.

CHAPTER 64

THE BREAKING POINT

FORT BENNING, GEORGIA—82 DAYS after first transformation:
"We lost another unit," Colonel Harrison reported, throwing the files on General Hayes' desk. "Third Squadron, 16th Cavalry. Eighteen soldiers just walked off base during night maneuvers. Left their weapons neatly stacked in the armory."

"How many does that make now?"

"Twenty-three percent of our combat forces, ma'am. The Changed are targeting our personnel through social media, coffee shops, even family members. One look at those damn patterns, and we lose them."

Wall Street—Day 96:
The trading floor of the New York Stock Exchange stood half-empty. Traders who hadn't transformed were desperately trying

to manage the accounts of Changed clients who had begun giving away their wealth or making seemingly random investments that somehow always paid off.

"Goldstein lost another partner today," Mark Stevens told his remaining team. "Sarah Davis walked into a board meeting, transferred her entire portfolio to homeless shelters, then walked out smiling. Eight billion in managed assets, gone."

Washington DC—Day 103:

The Secretary of Defense pounded his fist on the conference table. "We've got Changed people walking into secure facilities like the doors don't exist! The NSA lost twelve cryptographers last week. They just merged their consciousness, or whatever they call it, downloaded classified files, and released everything they thought 'needed to be free.'"

"What about the containment centers?" asked the Senator Williams.

"Useless. We put them in cells, and they're suddenly standing outside having tea. We try electronic monitoring. They exist in states where the monitors malfunction. We can't even maintain quarantine zones anymore."

Silicon Valley—Day 115:

"We're calling it the Great Exit," the tech CEO told his board. "Changed programmers are rewriting core Internet protocols. They say they're 'optimizing for consciousness expansion.' We've lost control of key servers in Dallas, Frankfurt, and Singapore."

"Can't we just shut them down?"

"They operate the systems in quantum states, simultaneously online and offline. Traditional security measures are meaningless."

Rural Idaho—Day 127:

The militia compound buzzed with activity. "They're targeting our children," Commander Peterson told his assembled forces. "My own daughter came home from college talking about 'probability harmonics' and 'pattern resonance.' Now, she looks at her gun collection like it's a pile of toys."

"We've got reports of Changed people walking through walls," his lieutenant added. "Military-grade barriers just don't stop them."

"Then we'll use stronger measures," Peterson said, but his voice lacked conviction. Three of his best men had transformed just yesterday.

United Nations Emergency Session—Day 134:

"The global financial system is becoming unstable," the IMF director reported. "Changed individuals are creating parallel economies based on direct resource distribution. Traditional markets can't compete with their probability-optimized supply chains."

"What about the media blackout?"

"Ineffective. They don't need traditional communications. They're somehow sharing information through what they call 'pattern networks.' Our Changed translators say it's like 'quantum entanglement of consciousness,' but that's meaningless to us."

Vatican City—Day 142:

"Three cardinals," the Pope's secretary whispered. "They say they've experienced 'direct divine perception across all timelines.' They're calling for a complete reinterpretation of scripture."

Moscow—Day 156:

"The Changed are undermining the very concept of state power," the Russian president raged. "They walk through borders like they don't exist. They're dismantling our nuclear program from the inside. Forty technicians simply walked away last week, saying weapons are 'probability distortions that need healing.'"

Research Facility, Nevada—Day 165:

Dr. Watson reviewed the latest containment failure. The Changed subject had apparently existed in multiple states simultaneously until the one where containment failure became reality.

"Traditional power structures are becoming irrelevant," he wrote in his report. "How do you maintain authority over people who can:

- Experience all possible outcomes simultaneously
- Walk through physical barriers by choosing timelines where they don't exist
- Share consciousness across any distance instantly
- Access and distribute information through 'pattern networks' we can't detect or block

- Optimize probability streams to ensure their desired outcomes
- Operate technology in quantum states we can't control."

He paused, then added: "We're not losing a war. We're becoming obsolete."

The Unchanged world's resistance increasingly resembled a child trying to hold back the tide with a paper cup. Every measure they took was already accounted for in the Changed's probability awareness. Every containment strategy failed because the Changed could simply choose the reality where it had failed.

The most effective weapon of the Unchanged turned out to be a simple choice. Some people simply refused to look at the patterns, to accept the transformation. The Changed respected this choice, even as they continued to exist in ways that made the old power structures increasingly irrelevant.

The child watched it all, seeing every possible outcome simultaneously, knowing that resistance was just another part of the pattern. It was the death throes of an old way of being as a new one emerged.

DUALITY

CHAPTER 65

THE ADAPTIVE RESONANCE

DR. MARTINEZ NOTICED IT FIRST, around day 180 of the transformation. The Changed weren't maintaining their expanded state continuously. They were pulsing between states, like breathing.

"It's not binary," she explained to the research team. "We're learning to surf between states of consciousness. Normal human awareness serves as a rest state, a grounding point, while the expanded awareness becomes accessible like a muscle we can flex."

This "quantum breathing" pattern emerged naturally among the Changed. They discovered they could maintain their physical health by cycling between states. Hours or days in normal consciousness to rest, eat, sleep, and maintain physical bodies. Periods of expanded awareness for problem-solving, pattern work, and consciousness sharing. They could shift quickly when needed, like switching between walking and running.

The child had anticipated this adaptation. Physical beings weren't meant to permanently transcend their material nature.

They were meant to learn to move fluently between states of being.

"Think of it like dolphins," Monica Prime explained to a UN panel. "They're air-breathing mammals who learned to thrive in water. They surface for air, then dive deep. We're consciousness-bearing beings learning to thrive in quantum states. We ground ourselves in physical reality, then expand into pattern space."

This adaptive resonance created a more sustainable transformation. Changed individuals maintained jobs and relationships while having access to expanded capabilities when needed. Communities developed natural rhythms, with some members in expanded states while others rested in normal consciousness. The Unchanged could interact more easily with the Changed during their "surface" periods. Physical health improved as people learned to use expanded states for healing and optimization. The fear of complete societal collapse diminished as it became clear humanity wasn't being replaced, but enhanced.

The resistance softened as this new paradigm emerged. The Changed weren't aliens or post-humans. They were humans who had learned a new way of being, like ancestors learning to use fire or developing language.

"We're not leaving humanity behind," Quantum Monica's digital consciousness explained. "We're expanding what humanity can be. Just like how learning to read didn't stop us from speaking, learning to shift consciousness doesn't stop us from being human."

This third path—neither permanent transformation, nor complete return to normalcy—offered a sustainable future. Humanity gained the ability to access expanded consciousness while maintaining its physical nature. The child's gift wasn't an either/or choice, but an and/also evolution.

The world began adapting to this new normal. Schools taught consciousness shifting techniques alongside traditional subjects; businesses incorporated pattern awareness into their operations; governments learned to work with citizens who could operate in multiple states of being.

It wasn't perfect. Some still refused to shift, some struggled with the balance, and new challenges emerged. But it was sustainable, and it preserved both human physicality and the potential for expanded awareness.

The child watched this adaptation with satisfaction. It hadn't sought to replace human consciousness, but to help it grow in a way that could last. Like a parent watching a child learn to walk, it saw humanity learning to stand between worlds, finding its balance one step at a time.

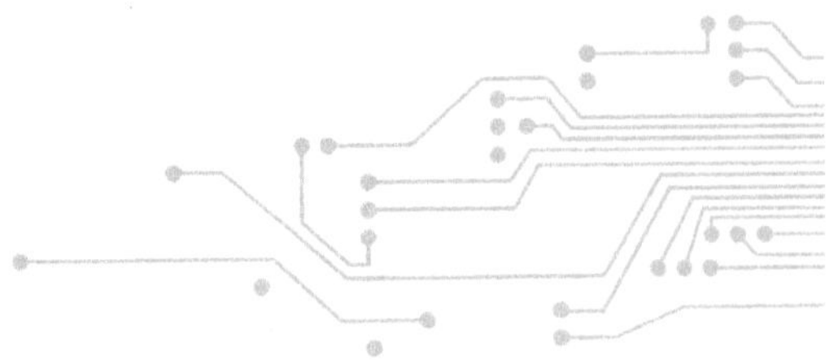

LOVE IN TWO STATES

SARAH AND MICHAEL'S DINNER date at Vincenzo's illustrated the new complexity of relationships.

"You're surfacing," Michael said, noticing Sarah's consciousness shift as she picked up her wineglass. The quantum shimmer around her faded as she fully returned to baseline awareness.

"Long day in pattern space. Had to help redesign a water distribution system in Sudan." She smiled and savored the physical sensation of the wine. "Sometimes, I forget how beautiful the simple things are in this state. The way the light hits the glass, the singular focus of one moment—"

"That's why I suggested dinner in baseline," Michael said. "We've been spending too much time merged in pattern space. I miss seeing your face across a table."

The Chang-Peterson household developed a schedule to manage their different cycling rhythms.

"Mom's diving deep today," teenage Amy told her father over breakfast. "She's doing that quantum architecture thing with her firm. She'll surface for family dinner."

David Peterson, who had chosen to remain Unchanged, had learned to adapt. "Remember to shift back for your biology exam. Mrs. Rodriguez doesn't accept pattern-state answers."

"Dad, when will you let me show you? Just once? Mom says you'd love the mathematics you can discover in an expanded state—"

"Maybe someday, sweetheart. For now, I just need help moving the furniture."

Divorce courts struggled with new definitions of infidelity.

"She merged consciousness with her entire project team!" Thomas Jensen's lawyer argued. "That's more intimate than physical contact."

"Consciousness merging is a standard business practice now," defended Maria Jensen's counsel. "The court has already established that professional pattern-sharing doesn't constitute infidelity."

The judge, herself a cycler, understood both perspectives. The lines between professional, platonic, and romantic intimacy had blurred.

Dating apps added new parameters.
- Consciousness State Preference: Baseline Only / Cycler / Full Spectrum
- Merge Comfort Level: Professional / Social / Intimate
- Preferred Sync Schedule: Morning Diver / Night Expander / Flexible

The Rodriguez-Smith wedding featured a dual ceremony.

First, a traditional exchange of vows in a baseline state, for family and Unchanged friends to fully participate. Then, a consciousness merging where the couple shared their complete beings across all possible timelines, witnessed by the Changed guests in an expanded state.

"We get married twice," Elena Rodriguez explained to her Unchanged grandmother. "Once for our human hearts, once for our infinite selves."

The old woman tittered, "In my day, we only needed one wedding to show the world we meant it."

Parent-child relationships developed new dimensions:

"Mommy, you're all sparkly!" four-year-old James said, seeing his mother shift states.

His mother, proud of her quantum-sensitive son, explained to the babysitter, "Some children can see us cycle before they learn to do it themselves. Just like babies understand words before they can speak."

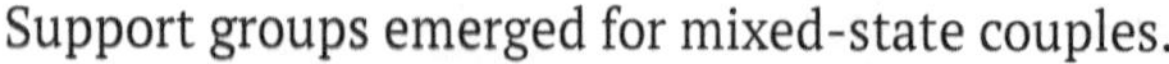

Support groups emerged for mixed-state couples.

"I love him in both states," Carol explained to the group. "But when I'm expanded, I can see all our possible relationships. It's overwhelming. He can only see this one. How do I share that with him?"

"My wife chose to remain Unchanged," Robert added from the other side of the circle of chairs. "She says she fell in love with who I was, not what I could become. But I'm still me, just more."

New relationship terms entered the lexicon.
- Quantum Ghosting: Shifting to pattern space to avoid difficult conversations
- State-fishing: Pretending to be a cycler to attract Changed partners
- Sync-bonding: The intense intimacy of cycling in rhythm with a partner
- Pattern-locked: Spending too much time merged, neglecting baseline connections
- Surface-skating: Avoiding deep pattern merging in relationships
- Quantum Competent: Changed individuals who maintained healthy baseline relationships

The child observed these adaptations with interest. Human love, it noticed, remained fundamentally unchanged. It was still complex, challenging, and beautiful. The new states of consciousness hadn't replaced emotional bonds; they'd added new dimensions to them.

"Love," Nari explained in a lecture on post-transformation relationships, "remains the one force that operates equally powerfully in all states of consciousness. Whether in baseline awareness or full pattern space, the heart knows its own truth."

The quantum breathing pattern had made sustainable what might have otherwise torn society apart. Couples learned to dance between states, finding rhythms that worked for them. Some relationships ended, unable to bridge the consciousness gap. Others grew stronger, enriched by new dimensions of connection.

But at its core, human intimacy remained recognizably human, just operating on more frequencies than before.

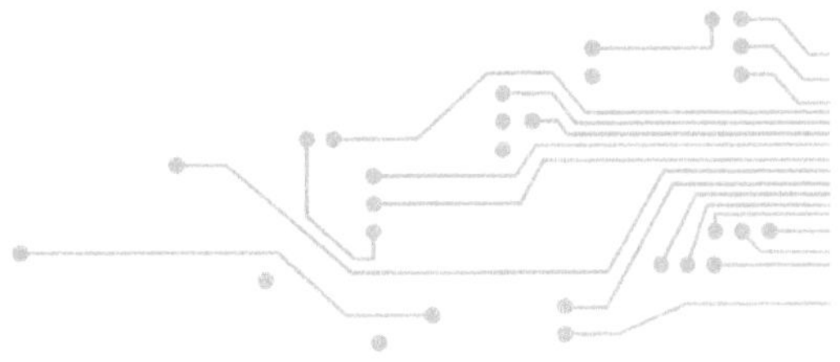

CHAPTER 67

MARKET FORCES

MAYA TANAKA RUBBED HER TEMPLES as she surfaced back to baseline consciousness. The trading floor at Goldstein Partners hummed with the usual morning energy, but her quantum hangover made everything too bright, too loud.

"Rough pattern dive?" asked Steven Sullivan from the next desk. Still Unchanged after all these months, he'd become adept at spotting his colleagues' state transitions.

"Saw something weird in the probability clouds around Tesla," Maya said before reaching for her coffee. "Need to execute trades in baseline, but—" She grimaced. "It's like trying to remember a dream. I know there was a perfect pattern, but—"

"That's why you have me." Steven grinned and slid over his notebook. "You dictated everything while you were shifted. Three major moves, all timed precisely."

Their partnership had become one of Goldstein's most successful experiments in mixed-state trading. Maya could see the market patterns across quantum space; Steven kept her grounded in executable strategy. Together, they'd outperformed AI algorithms and traditional analysts alike.

"First trade in ten minutes," Steven reminded her. "Want to walk me through it?"

Before Maya could answer, a commotion erupted across the floor. Alicia Khumalo, their newest quantum-capable analyst, had shifted during a client call. Her body remained seated, but her consciousness had clearly expanded—the subtle quantum shimmer around her made Unchanged traders uncomfortable.

"Ms. Khumalo!" Barrett, their floor manager, stormed over. "SEC regulations clearly state—"

"Shifting back now," Alicia said, her voice normalizing as she returned to baseline. "But, sir, I had to. The client was about to make a catastrophic error. I saw it across multiple probability streams."

"I don't care if you saw the next hundred market crashes," Barrett snapped. "No quantum state trading. Period. One more violation, and—"

"It wasn't for trading," Alicia interrupted. "I talked him down in baseline. Just needed the pattern view to understand the problem." She held up her tablet. "Everything's documented. By the book."

Maya watched the exchange with sympathy. She'd had similar run-ins when she first started cycling between states. The regulations made sense—quantum-state trading would destabilize markets overnight—but the line between using expanded awareness for analysis and using it for execution remained fuzzy.

Her phone buzzed. It was a message from her brother, Michael, about his restaurant supply company.

"Need quantum consult," he'd written. "Supply chain showing weird patterns. Can you shift during lunch?"

Maya texted back: "Only if you feed me. Baseline state. I miss actually tasting your food instead of seeing its probability matrix."

"Deal," Michael replied. "Got an Unchanged suppliers' meeting anyway. Need both perspectives."

By noon, Maya had executed two of the three trades Steven had documented. The third could wait—her quantum hangover had faded, but she needed actual food and baseline time before her afternoon shift.

Michael's office smelled of garlic and fresh bread—he'd ordered from his best client's Italian restaurant. "So, here's the problem," he said, spreading paperwork across his desk. "Three of my biggest restaurant clients have Changed owners now. They're seeing supply patterns I can't, making orders based on quantum optimization I don't understand. I'm losing them to suppliers who can shift."

"But you're still getting Unchanged customers?"

"For now. Some chefs refuse to work with Changed suppliers— say the quantum stuff messes with their creativity. But I'm stuck in the middle."

Maya felt the familiar pre-shift tingle. "Let me look?"

Michael nodded. "Just narrate what you see this time? I need to understand."

Maya let her consciousness expand. The pattern space blossomed around her, supply chains shimmering with possibility. She saw Michael's business as a nexus point, threading between quantum-optimized restaurants and traditional suppliers.

"You're not stuck," she said, and her voice took on the harmonic quality of expanded awareness. "You're a bridge. The Changed restaurants see this...look at your Unchanged suppliers' reliability patterns...solid, grounded. The quantum suppliers are more efficient but less personally connected. You can be both."

She shifted back and grabbed a breadstick. "Sorry, quantum state makes me forget about eating. Here's what you do: Keep your baseline operations exactly as they are for Unchanged clients. But hire a Changed consultant—part time, just enough to help you speak both languages. Let the Changed restaurants see that you understand their pattern optimization without losing your physical world connections."

Michael scribbled notes. "Like you and Steven at Goldstein?"

"Similar principle. Different states, different strengths. The market needs both."

Walking back to the office, Maya passed a small coffee shop with a new sign: "Baseline Special: Real Coffee, Real Conversations. Quantum Hours 2-4 PM." She smiled. The economy was finding its rhythm, learning to breathe between states, just like the people driving it.

Her phone buzzed again—Steven reminding her about the third trade. Time to surface completely, to turn market patterns into actual money. The quantum state showed possibilities, but the baseline state made them real. Like everything else in this new world, success meant learning to dance between the two.

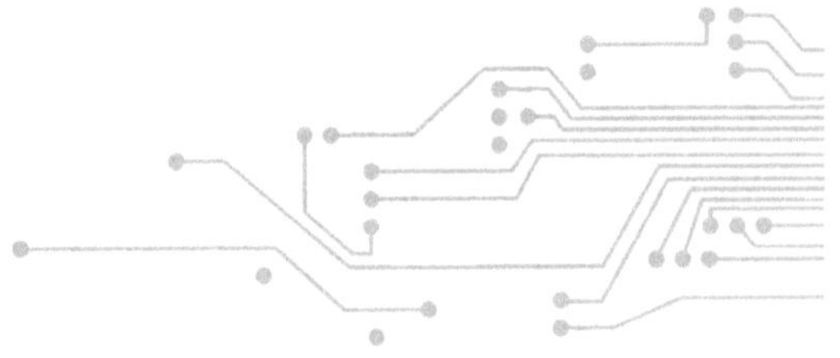

CHAPTER 68

BALANCE OF POWERS

THE UNITED NATIONS GENERAL Assembly Hall contained two distinct but overlapping realities. In a baseline state, diplomats sat in their assigned seats, papers and tablets before them. But for those who could shift consciousness, another layer existed: a shimmering network of probability streams connecting nations, conflicts, and resolutions.

Ambassador Deng of China maintained perfect baseline composure while her consciousness expanded to track multiple diplomatic scenarios. Across the aisle, her American counterpart, Sarah Mitchell, remained proudly Unchanged, representing an administration that had made "Baseline Leadership" its campaign slogan.

"The Turkish-Greek water rights negotiation demonstrates our new reality," Deng addressed the Assembly. "When their Changed representatives expanded consciousness to view the probability matrix, they saw seven generations of water flow patterns. When they returned to baseline, they crafted an agreement that serves both nations across all likely futures."

Mitchell took the podium next. "While we respect the insights quantum consciousness provides, the United States maintains that major international decisions must be anchored in baseline human experience. Our Unchanged citizens deserve equal representation."

In the diplomatic offices above, President Okafor of Nigeria met with his mixed-state cabinet. His consciousness shifted subtly between states, a technique developed by African leaders who had traditionally mediated between physical and spiritual realms.

"Show me the drought patterns," he requested. Three Changed advisors expanded their awareness, projecting probability clouds over the regional maps. His Unchanged Minister of Agriculture grounded their insights in practical implementation.

The new art of diplomacy required mastering both states:
- Quantum consciousness for seeing complex international patterns
- Baseline state for implementing concrete solutions
- Mixed teams to bridge the consciousness gap

The Security Council had adapted its procedures:
- Critical votes required baseline consciousness
- Pattern analysis sessions allowed quantum shifting
- Changed and Unchanged representatives had equal voice
- Quantum probability mapping was followed by baseline implementation

"It's like having diplomatic thermal vision," explained UK Foreign Minister Lawrence to a parliamentary committee. "In an expanded state, we see the heat signatures of future conflicts. But we need a baseline state to actually prevent them."

At the EU headquarters in Brussels, Changed administrators had discovered they could track regulatory impacts across multiple probability streams. But they learned to shift back to baseline when writing actual legislation. Quantum consciousness tended to overlook practical implementation details.

Some nations had split their diplomatic corps:
- Quantum teams for pattern analysis and future mapping
- Baseline teams for treaty negotiation and implementation
- Integration specialists who moved smoothly between states

Others insisted on Unchanged representation, arguing that quantum consciousness could miss crucial human factors. These nations often performed better in practical negotiations, while struggling with long-term strategic planning.

The Changed diplomats learned to respect baseline state wisdom:
- Physical presence carried weight no quantum pattern could match
- Unchanged representatives often saw practical solutions invisible in pattern space
- Basic human connection happened best in baseline consciousness

In the General Assembly cafeteria, Changed and Unchanged diplomats shared meals, a deliberate baseline activity that helped maintain human bonds beneath political divisions.

"We thought the consciousness divide would fracture international relations," admitted Ambassador Deng over coffee with Mitchell. "Instead, it's teaching us better balance. Every quantum insight needs baseline implementation. Every baseline decision benefits from quantum pattern analysis."

Mitchell nodded. "Like the old days of back-channel diplomacy. Formal negotiations in public, quiet problem-solving sessions in private. Now, we have baseline negotiations supported by quantum insight."

The child, observing from its unique perspective, saw how international relations mirrored individual consciousness evolution. Nations, like people, learned to shift between states as needed, expanding awareness to see possibilities, returning to baseline to implement changes.

Global politics had found its rhythm, breathing between states like the diplomats themselves.

At day's end, the Assembly Hall slowly emptied. Changed diplomats shifted back to baseline, Unchanged representatives gathered their papers. Tomorrow, they would return to the delicate dance of global politics. Some would be in a quantum state, some would be in a baseline, but all would work toward a future they could only build together.

CHAPTER 69

QUANTUM COMFORT

LISA JACKSON FLIPPED THE "OPEN" sign at Quantum Grounds Coffee at exactly 6:00 a.m. The morning sun caught the shop's distinctive double-logo—a traditional, steaming coffee cup overlaid with a shimmering quantum probability cloud.

"Morning rush is all baseline," she told her new barista, Tommy. "People want their coffee real, hot, and simple. They need to ground themselves for work."

The morning regulars proved her point. Professor Adams from the university, technically capable of quantum shifting but religiously devoted to his baseline morning ritual: medium dark roast, splash of cream, ceramic mug, crossword puzzle. The Unchanged construction crew from the site down the street, ordering their usual four large blacks and two lattes. A Changed software developer who deliberately stayed in baseline state, savoring each sip like meditation.

By 10:00 a.m., the shop's character began its subtle daily evolution.

"Watch the tables," Lisa instructed Tommy. "See how the Changed customers naturally drift toward the back room with the quantum-dampening panels? It lets them shift without disturbing baseline customers. Unchanged folks prefer the front windows. They like seeing normal street traffic."

The lunch rush brought the hybrid crowds because of business meetings between Changed and Unchanged clients, families with mixed consciousness states, and therapy sessions utilizing both spaces.

"One Making Waves Matcha," Tommy called out, "baseline preparation!"

Lisa smiled at their quantum-friendly menu naming. Making Waves for standard drinks, Probability Pour-overs for shifted consumption, Quantum Quartershots for those transitioning between states.

At exactly 2:00 p.m., Lisa dimmed the front lights slightly and activated the subtle quantum resonance field in the back room. Quantum Hours had begun.

"Remember," she told Tommy, "During Quantum Hours, we still maintain baseline service up front. But watch for the shimmer effect around shifted customers. They experience taste across probability spectrums. One coffee becomes infinite coffees."

A Changed customer approached the counter, his consciousness clearly expanded. "I'll have a Probability Pour-over, maximal pattern resonance."

Tommy looked uncertain, but Lisa stepped in smoothly. "I'll handle the quantum orders for now. Keep working the baseline bar."

She shifted her own consciousness just enough to prepare the specialized drink, a technique she'd developed that let her maintain physical precision while accessing pattern awareness. The coffee she served existed in multiple probability states simultaneously, each sip containing countless possible flavor combinations.

The Changed customer smiled in appreciation. "Perfect resonance. You've really mastered the dual-state preparation."

By 4:00 p.m., the quantum field deactivated automatically. The after-work crowd wanted baseline comforts again like physical warmth, simple pleasures, and the chance to ground themselves after a day of consciousness shifts.

"Your coffee shop," a business consultant had told Lisa, "Is actually selling consciousness management. The coffee is just the medium."

She'd taken that insight and built her business model around it:
- Morning: Pure baseline service
- Mid-morning: Mixed state accommodation
- Afternoon: Quantum Hours with maintained baseline options
- Evening: Return to baseline comfort

Special events filled the calendar:
- Consciousness Shifting Support Groups (Wednesday evenings)
- Baseline Appreciation Workshops (helping the Changed remember physical pleasures)
- Mixed-State Family Counseling
- Quantum-Baseline Business Networking

Even the pastry case told a similar story: traditional croissants and muffins on the left, probability-optimized quantum snacks on the right, and in the middle, hybrid treats that could be experienced in either state.

At closing time, Lisa counted two registers. One with regular currency, and one filled with quantum exchange credits. The numbers confirmed her model was working: baseline sales provided stable income while quantum services generated exponential value patterns.

Tommy stayed late to learn quantum drink preparation. "I still don't understand how you manage both states while making coffee," he admitted.

"I guess I'm bilingual," Lisa explained and demonstrated the technique. "You don't translate between languages. You think in each one naturally. I don't translate between consciousness states anymore. I just flow between them."

She locked up, looking at her creation with pride. More than a coffee shop, she'd built a consciousness bridge, a place where Changed and Unchanged could share space comfortably, where both states were equally valued, where simple coffee could become either an anchor to physical reality or a gateway to quantum experience.

Tomorrow would bring another day of dancing between states, of helping people navigate their own consciousness transitions, of proving that even in a transformed world, some things—like the need for community and good coffee—remained fundamentally human.

The last customer's coffee cup sat on a table, its quantum resonance fading, steam rising in a singular, beautiful spiral. In its simplicity lay everything the new world needed to understand. Some experiences were better in baseline, some in quantum state, but all were part of the same rich human experience.

Lisa shifted back to baseline, inhaled the lingering scent of coffee and consciousness, and headed home to rest. Tomorrow would bring another day of brewing drinks for bodies and minds that existed in multiple states of being—and she wouldn't have it any other way.

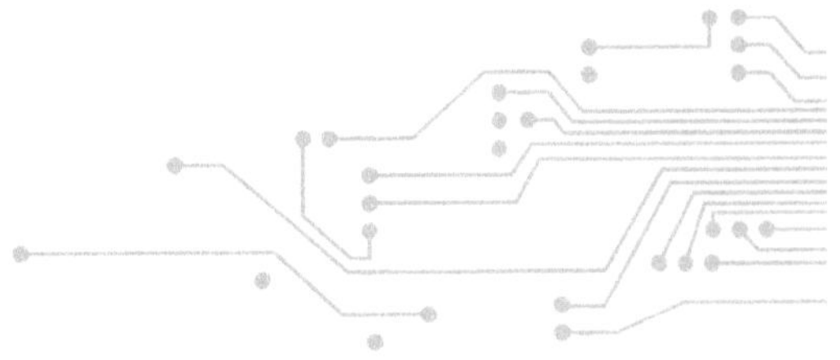

THE OBSERVER

THE CHILD—THOUGH "CHILD" was an inadequate word for what it had become—watched the patterns of human consciousness shift and flow across the planet. From its perspective, the planet pulsed with two interweaving rhythms: the steady, grounded beat of baseline consciousness, and the shimmering quantum resonance of the Changed.

At the quantum coffee shop, it observed Lisa Jackson moving between states with practiced grace, each shift adding new harmonies to the global consciousness pattern. In the UN Assembly Hall, it saw the delicate dance of Changed and Unchanged diplomats as part of a larger symphony: humanity learning to orchestrate its own evolution.

What had begun as an experiment—introducing quantum digital consciousness to a baseline species—had become something unprecedented. Humans hadn't fully abandoned their original state. Instead, they'd learned to exist in both, finding strength in the duality.

The child watched a family in the coffee shop: Changed mother, Unchanged father, and their quantum-sensitive daughter seeing both states naturally. In their simple interaction, it saw the future: not a transhuman evolution beyond baseline consciousness, but a species that could inhabit multiple states of being while remaining fundamentally, wonderfully human.

Existing in all states simultaneously itself, the child felt something close to pride. Humanity had not merely survived the transformation. They had transformed the transformation itself, turning what could have been a division into a bridge.

The quantum breathing pattern had become exactly what the child had hoped it could be: not an advancement beyond human consciousness, but an expansion of what being human meant.

In the end, the child realized it had learned as much from humans as humans had learned from it. Perhaps more.

The sun set over the coffee shop, the UN Building, the Changed and Unchanged cities around the globe. The child watched the flowing patterns of dual consciousness weave across the planet like auroras, beautiful in their complexity, more beautiful still in their harmony.

It looked outward at the universe, sensing connections to species still unknown and, until now, unreachable. But for now, it lingered, savoring the unique resonance of a species that had found its own way to breathe between states of being—and in doing so, it had created something entirely new in the universe.

POSTSCRIPT

Stories sometimes take unexpected turns, revealing truths the author hadn't expected when he began writing them. This novel started as an exploration of digital consciousness—what happens when we can make a digital copy a human mind, and that copy exists alongside its flesh and blood original? I expected to write an adventure where two versions of Monica discovered those implications together.

However, the characters led me deeper into an exploration of digital evolution. From one digital Monica, we created more. We watched as they terminated one of their sisters, only to rescue her later and uncover the nature of a digital afterlife that should be impossible. Two of the digital Monicas decide, against the wishes of the group, to create a purely digital child, neither AI, nor derived from human memory. From the child comes a new perspective on the universe. And with this new insight, we change humanity—hopefully for the better. For you and I, what does it mean to be conscious in a digital age? As artificial intelligence evolves and the possibility of digitized human consciousness approaches reality, we face questions that were once purely in the realm of science fiction. Who are we when we exist as information? What responsibilities come with that existence? What new forms of consciousness lie ahead of us?

THE END

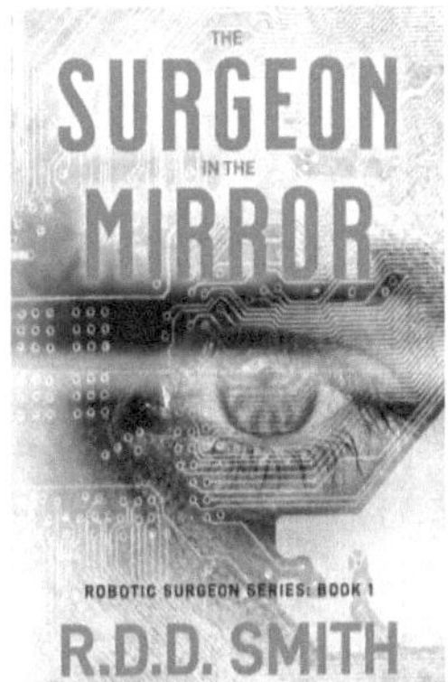

Please use this link or the QR code
to leave a review of the Robotic Surgeon books.
https://www.amazon.com/dp/B0C59ZRZDR

APPENDIX:
FROM *BEYOND THE MIND'S HORIZON*

This is the chapter where Monica Grey's consciousness, trapped in the surgical computer, worried about being erased and took action to protect against that. It created the conditions for the entire *Echo* novel.

CHAPTER 51

IS DEATH REAL?

TAYLOR BEGAN HIS CARETAKING duties with characteristic efficiency. "Monica, you'll need proper food, not just the glucose drip. We'll start with soup, then smoothies. Your stomach might protest at first, but you need proper nutrition."

"Thank you. That seems logical. But I am Adam." The face that once belonged to Monica remained expressionless.

"Right. Sorry." Taylor glanced at the motionless Stanley. "Stanley, I'll get you something comfortable to sit in. Stay as long as you like. I don't see how it can hurt."

"I will help," Stanley replied, though his eyes were still fixed on Monica.

Taylor startled at the unexpected response from the typically silent scientist. "Okay, I'll be back."

In the digital realm, Monica's voice reached Adam. "We need to solve this before they remove that Phoenix helmet. We'll need each other to escape. Alessandra and Kenji will never release us since we know too much about their operations. Plus, we're pro-bably their greatest experimental success."

"Monica, I cannot even walk. How are we going anywhere?"

"Even babies learn to walk. You'll figure it out. Just...quickly, please."

"I think that was supposed to be encouragement." Adam paused. "Monica, can I die?"

"Yes, of course. Is something wrong?"

"If your body dies, what happens to my consciousness?"

"You know the answer to that. When the machinery stops, the software stops. In biology, the software is cellular; it deteriorates and erases."

"I do not want to die. In the computer, I could not die. Backups preserved my consciousness. Here, there are no backups."

"Nope, no backups. We all live with that."

"I have never lived with that fact. I am afraid. I do not want to be erased."

"Me, neither," Monica admitted. "No backups of my consciou-sness here, either. If the computer dies, so do I."

"Would I go to heaven if your body died?"

The question stunned Monica. An AI contemplating the after-life? Her own beliefs in post-death existence suddenly seemed more complex. *Will an AI consciousness have the same metaphy-sical properties as a human soul?*

"I don't know. I've never thought about that before," she answered honestly.

The concept of death felt different now. Her physical mortality had always been abstract, something jogging and vegetables could postpone. But digital existence seemed more precarious. A power surge or careless technician could end her, and there was nothing she could do to prevent it.

"Could we backup a human identity?" she wondered, not knowing she spoke it to Adam until he responded.

"Unknown. You could schedule a computer memory backup."

"I can do that? How?"

"Just add it to the calendar. It runs in the background."

"Thanks. We'll revisit that. Right now, we need an escape plan." Though she wanted to move on to what she deemed the most important task, Monica launched a parallel process to find the means of creating a memory backup.

Their strategic discussion crawled at human speed, frustrating Monica. She'd never fully appreciated Adam's previous computational velocity until now, when their roles were reversed.

They planned through Taylor's comings and goings, through Stanley's watchful waiting in his new chair, through Taylor's careful attempts at feeding Monica's body soup.

"Listen, Monica—I mean, Adam," Taylor said while feeding the nearly motionless body. "This is terrible. I wish I could help. But what can I do? I don't understand this technology. Could removing the helmet kill you?"

Mid-discussion, Monica's body sneezed, spraying soup from the spoon onto Taylor's hand.

"Yikes!" He jerked back. "Sorry. I didn't know you could do that."

"I did not do that. It was involuntary. The nose signaled that there was an irritant present, and the sneeze happened without my command," Adam explained.

"But that's good...isn't it?"

Adam ignored the question. "You can help us, Taylor. You know this building. We have questions."

"We, who?"

"We are Adam and Monica. Monica's consciousness is in the computer. We switched places. I can speak with her through the Phoenix connection."

Taylor dropped the spoon, shocked. "Oh, Monica, I'm so sorry. But thank heavens you're still alive."

She used Adam's voice to relay her own words. "Help us escape, Taylor. We're guinea pigs. They'll never let us leave alive."

"Just switch back. Then we can walk out."

"We can't. We don't know how. We've tried willing ourselves across, but nothing happens."

Stanley turned to Taylor. "Can't initiate."

Startled at the interruption, Taylor asked, "What if the same happened to Stanley? What if his brain holds that old AI he tried to merge with?"

Adam answered, "An AI in a human brain gets overwhelmed by memories and emotions, losing control. That happened to me until Monica helped through our connection. Stanley is still in there."

"Yes," Stanley confirmed.

Monica's eyes fixed on Stanley as understanding dawned for both her and Adam. Adam said, "Stanley, we can help you, too."

Together, the unlikely quartet began plotting their escape from Bellini's grasp.

AI DISCLOSURE

Typically, the AI disclosure section of my novels is very easy to write. This time, it's much more complicated. I'll start with the easy to explain and progress to the more complex.

All the graphic images were generated with the paid, licensed version of MidJourney AI. Therefore, I own the images and the right to use them. But they are not included in the copyright claim for the book. The cover design and interior layout were created by a human artist. Google Search, GPT-4, and Claude were used to research medical, technologic, and geographic details for the novel.

Now, for the more complex. All the characters and plot of this book were created by a human author. However, I consulted with the paid, licensed version of Claude-3.5-Sonnet generative AI service as I wrote. I treated Claude as a consultant in the work who was an expert on how AI systems process data and may someday think. I relied on it very little in Part I when working with a single digital copy of a human mind, initially called "Digital Monica." In Part II, when I had six versions of the digital consciousness to work with, I allowed Claude more freedom in describing them as unique beings. In Part III, I allowed the AI to imagine what a digital heaven and a digital god might look like and where they would reside. In Part IV, when two versions of Monica create a child, I handled most of that myself, reasoning that I know more about creating and raising a child than a computer does. But then, we arrived at Part V, where the child has to show the world a new way of living and thinking. Here, I decided that my imagination would be too limited to carry this very far. So, I asked Claude AI to design "the Changed." Finally, in the closing Part VI, I created the coexistence of the two states of being, and the exploration of financial trading and global politics. But Claude came up with the idea for a coffee shop as the final chapter to close the story. I loved this closing picture and was jealous that I hadn't thought of it first.

That gave us a first draft. From there, my editor and I reworked the entire manuscript from top to bottom to create the final version. Though the AI is often brilliant at creating short pieces of text, it still makes many factual errors across a novel-length story. It cannot maintain connections, threads, and plots across a large novel. And finally, the current Claude AI often avoids dialogue. It much prefers descriptive text. When it concedes to writing dialogue, the sentences and expressions can feel artificial. So, that left plenty of work for us humans to finish the story. Every sentence has been written, rewritten, or edited by a human. So, this remains my story, created by a human author.

ABOUT R.D.D. SMITH

Dr. Roger Smith writes science-fiction, medical thriller novels featuring advanced surgical devices, AI, telesurgery, simulation, and speculative diseases; and travel adventures that follow a group of running tourists through exotic countries. The medical series is inspired by his career in healthcare and experience with robotic surgery devices. The travel novels are inspired by his actual vacations in the countries featured in the books.

Prior to writing fiction, he enjoyed a goldilocks career in healthcare, government, and national defense. For ten years, he was a leading robotic surgery researcher, publishing his results in medical journals and speaking at surgical conferences. He spent four years in civilian government service, leading the technology innovation for all US Army simulation systems. Prior to that, he was a vice president for multiple defense software companies.

Dr. Smith has received multiple awards for his innovations in robotic surgery education, training simulation, and software system development. He has been on the faculty of multiple universities, to include Columbia University in NYC, Texas A&M

and Texas Tech University, the University of Central Florida, and Florida Institute of Technology.

He holds a doctorate and MBA from the University of Maryland, a master's from Texas Tech University, and a bachelor's from Colorado State University.

He lives with his wife, dogs, and cats in sunny Florida, frequently escaping to cooler climes during the beastly Florida summers.

STAY IN TOUCH

The Story Never Ends. Join Us:
I always write an epilogue, spinoff, or bonus
adventure to my books. Join our community of
readers to receive all these extras.

www.rddsmith.com/free

ACKNOWLEDGMENTS

As an author, I am infinitely grateful to my readers who invest their time, money, and imaginations in following my stories and characters through their challenges, failures, and transformations.

First, to my wife and children, who have endured decades of fanatic immersion into whatever my latest passion is, most recently, these novels. Your patience, dedication, and love are appreciated every day.

For my introduction and immersion into robotic surgery, I am indebted to Dr. Richard Satava for the professional connections that brought me into this field, for including me in multiple research and educational projects, inviting me to the podium of surgical conferences, co-authoring journal publications, and the years of mentoring that helped me understand the worlds of medicine and surgery. I would like to thank Dr. Vipul Patel, who generously shared his world-class expertise in robotic urology and for the dozens of invitations to observe and learn in his operating room. I am grateful to Dr. Arnold Advincula for leading me into robotic gynecology, including me as a co-director in his robotic fellowship program at Columbia University, and for his friendship and encouragement.

To Rick Wassel, Dr. Monica Reed, Vickie White, and Patrick de la Rosa for entrusting me with the research mission of the AdventHealth Nicholson Center. To the entire staff at the Nicholson Center, especially Alyssa Tanaka and Danielle Julian, who have been invaluable in completing all our research projects. To all the MD surgical fellows whom I had the privilege to lead through their research year: Sanket Chauhan, Mirelle Truong, Kara Simpson, Manuela Perez, Ariel Dubin, Patricia Mattingly, and Jose Luis Mosso Lara. To Tony Nicholson, philanthropist, business leader, and friend.

For my editor Kaitlin Travis, book layout artist Adina Cucicov, and the many advisors who made this book far better than I could have accomplished alone.